Souvenirs of the Revolution

A M Montes de Oca

The Reworkd Press
Charlotte, 2013

First published by The Reworkd Press, November 2013
Copyright 2013 by Amanda Moody Montes de Oca

All rights reserved under International and Pan-American Copyright Convention. Published in the United States by The Reworkd Press.

Cover design by Lisa Shapiro and Kitty Van Oosten

Moody Montes de Oca, Amanda
Souvenirs of the Revolution/Amanda Moody Montes de Oca – The Reworkd Press, Charlotte, NC, USA.

1 Mexican-Americans – Fiction 2. Mexican-American Diaspora – Fiction 3. Women – Mexico – Fiction 4. History – Mexico- Fiction

ISBN 987-0-9889220-1-3

PUBLISHERS NOTE:
This is a work of fiction. Names, characters, places and incidents are the product of the author's imagination or are used fictitiously. Any likeness to anyone living or dead is purely coincidental.

Without limiting the rights under copyright reserved above, no part of this publication may be reproduced, stored in or introduced into a retrieval system, or transmitted in any form, or by any means (electronic, mechanical, photocopying, recording or otherwise), without the prior written permission of both the copyright owner and the above publisher of this book.

Manufactured in the United States of America

For EW and RS

*Note on the pronunciation of Oaxaca: (Wa-ha-ka)

Table of Contents

Part 1:
The Revolution of 1910					1

Part 2:
Escape to Egypt					104

Part 3:
A Reluctant Saint					112

Epilogue					213

Part I: The Revolution of 1910
Coyoacan, Mexico City

    At the far end of Coyoacan, inside the large stone house on the corner of Benito Juarez and Melchor Ocampo, whose door carried the family crest of a bear with both paws leaning on the base of a tree, Mariabella Montelejos lay dying in the front room. The house stood as she had left it; her dead husband's belongings, discarded where their seventy-three year old master had laid them upon the last day of his own life many years before, were untouched. Mariabella had great respect for things. She believed objects retained an echo of their owner's soul. She also believed herself due for an early grave and impressed this upon her only daughter, Portensia Montelejos, raised by wet nurses, maids, and the portraits of dead generations.
    Knowing her daughter would never possess her charms, Mariabella, afraid for Portensia's fragile health, demanded that she be fed nothing but toast and watery coffee; the occasional slice of smoked ham and, once-and-again, a boiled sweet. Her own mother had died of gourmand excesses, and Mariabella was adamant that neither she nor Portensia would follow in her wake.
    When Mariabella Montelejos thought of her childhood, it was the sprawling home of high windows and timber planked ceilings in Northern Spain she saw in her mind's eye, and humiliation would grip her again as it had when she was very young, watching her mother, Diamantina Cantu del Lombardo, at the bed-side table she used for a buffet. Mariabella's eyes would still fill with tears many years later as she remembered seeing Diamantina stuff cream-filled cakes and anchovy-stuffed olives, petit fours from Paris and thick stew from the mountains into her small cupid bud mouth. The lace and ruffles, whalebone and taffeta of the day were no match for her girth. Though Mariabella pleaded with her to refrain, to curb her mythic appetites, Diamantina, a boisterous woman in possession of large sums of money made by designing high-fashion hats, gloves, and fur-lined

wraps, would only tilt her head at Mariabella and offer her a frosted bun or slice of flan.

Since the day Diamantina had inherited a spinster aunt's small boutique in an unfashionable quarter of Paris, she had drawn the designs for the hats herself, secured the best furs from cousins in the wildernesses of Canada and the finest silks from distant Arabian lands. A natural businesswoman, she grew her aunt's modest boutique into one of the most sought-after gems of Paris by women the world over.

It was in travelling between Paris and the mountains of her home in Spain that Diamantina discovered the satisfyingly intimate relationship that could be had with delicate morsels on the long journey through towns which all boasted their own elaborate palates. Inch by inch she discovered that outside their own La Brecha market with its exotic cheeses and paper-thin slices of cured ham, a route could be plotted from home to Paris and back again by plate. She traveled by course: from the soup course to the fish course, from the meat or seafood entrée to the aromatic foreign fruits and the milieu of desserts made by a hundred ovens in as many different kitchens. Thus, as the fame of her boutique grew, so did her impressive size.

"Eat, eat, my daughter," she would urge. "For tomorrow we may as well be dead." Winking, the rotund woman, secure in her own world of culinary delights would wag her sugar dusted fingers at Mariabella and shrug, for Diamantina Cantu del Lombardo always felt a stirring of pity for her youngest daughter - unimaginative, and much too eager to please.

"Mama, surely you do not need another course," she would say sweetly as Diamantina demanded a fresh plate from the cook.

"It will damage my liver if I do not rest a fish portion upon the cream of hilltop mushroom in my gut." Diamantina believed in the science of gastronomics, and arranged her forks to accommodate the extra place setting the serving girl silently slid beside her.

When they were seated at the table in the grand ballroom, her eleven children were allowed only to join her if they had dressed for the occasion in their finest frocks, their hair combed and faces, hands, and shoes cleaned. Mariabella, spoiled by the attentions of ten elder brothers, was dressed by Diamantina in the glorious cast-off gowns of her youth, which smelt of the cedar chests in which they had been stored unused for so many years. Dressed in neglected silken ribbons and hard hoops of crinoline, Mariabella watched in silence as the brothers before her wed and separated themselves from their mother, and started lives in far-off cities with dark, doe-eyed women with strange accents. Occasionally, they would bring their wives to dine in the grand ballroom, babies in arms or toddlers on shoulders, but even they could not compete with Diamantina's ravenous hunger and only came enough to satisfy the gods of propriety.

Thus, Mariabella was the only one besides her mother who never missed a meal. Mesmerized, she would sit at Diamantina's right hand, guardedly condemning each bite.

"Mariabella," Diamantina would exclaim, "You are curdling my innards with your stares."

"No, Mama," she would reply, "That must be the *Paella Negra*."

Diamantina, greatly distressed by what she saw as a denial of life, tried all manners of fattening up her daughter, but Mariabella, disgusted by the corporal rotundity of maternal love, refused completely. She had no head for business, and could not be made to understand the value of money, nor the genius required to move it from here to there – from beaver traps to fancy mannequins, from the ledger to the display window. She detested the long road and many hours spent in the carriage from Paris to their mountainous home.

When Diamantina finally accepted that her youngest daughter could not learn the love of food or the art of making money, she rechanneled her efforts from teaching her about the delicate nature of a woman in business to funding a dowry that would tempt a duke. The elder sons had not required dowries, and the good woman's efforts to teach them, at least, had been rewarded with a natural ability to multiply the contents of their wallets. She did not worry for her sons: it was her daughter who kept her awake in the night and near the ice-box during the day.

The many bounteous chests grew and dwindled in size and splendidness, for as Penelope wove and unwove her shroud, so did Diamantina add and subtract from Mariabella's dowry, both eager and afraid to lose her only daughter.

"This silk is not fit for a beggar," she would lament to the servants, within Mariabella's hearing. "And this dye has run and ruined the lace," she would continue, rifling through the chests: silks, taffetas, lace, hats, gloves, shoes, stationery, silver place settings, dusting powders, perfumes, and all the secret ingredients that every woman needs, scattered to and fro. "We must order these all again from a better merchant – no respectable woman marries without good quality lace!"

The servants would nod and agree, no, no, certainly not a respectable woman would not think of doing such a thing, and Mariabella would huff and fume in her private quarters in the midst of the one hundred strokes her hair required with an ivory comb. Ready to leave the ministrations of such a mother, who could not be induced to retain the beauty of her youth, or see the errors of her gourmand ways, Mariabella, as ripe as could be, waited impatiently for life to begin.

Thus, while Diamantina searched for a dowry to set even the bitterest tongues to wagging, the problem of an adequate match concerned her enough to upset the iron-clad stomach long used to matters of the nervous system. The era and locale being what they were, men came with Reales in their eyes and homemade wine on their breaths, dirty boots and tight belts. The mountain squires who dined in the great ballroom in place of their sons were too rough for the heiress of a high-class Paris boutique, and when they learned Mariabella could neither cook, nor sew, nor knew the care of horses or goats, they retreated after splendid meals poisoned by Mariabella's coquettish flounces. Diamantina considered taking Mariabella to Paris herself, but had learned through long experience that the men in that city were very good at masking the realities of their purses.

But then the morning came in their home of high timber ceilings, in the northern mountains of Spain, near the Spanish/French border, when Diamantina received a letter from a titled land-owner in Mexico, having heard himself of Mariabella's beauty from a distant nephew and common relation to both the Lombardos and the Montelejos. He was not only titled, but included newspaper clippings and tales of the social doings of the large circle of his family: high teas, meetings with foreign dignitaries, polo on the lawns of great mansions, feats of military valor, and more balls than an English lord. Depositing the letter amid the papers of her secretary, Diamantina counted her prayers answered with a hand on her breast and began gathering Marabella's chests in earnest.

It was Cristoval's father who advised his new daughter-in-law to ask for a fortune in jewels. "A man will take away his wife's dowry and all her lands, but it is a cold husband who will take the adornments from her hair, Mariabella." Osvaldo Montelejos, his voice made raspy by the tar of a lifetime of small brown cigarillos, would daub at his watery eyes with a starched monogramed handkerchief. Still strong in his declining years, he had been the first to give Mariabella the kind of jewel he meant – a bird's nest brooch set in silver, holding a large heart-shaped egg made of ruby.

It was also he who had secured Mariabella from San Sebastian, the town from which the Montelejos had left two generations previously, and arranged for her passage across the ocean, then from Cancun overland to Merida, by small cruiser to Veracruz, by steam rail to Mexico City.

"Marry a girl from our own people, my son," Osvaldo had dictated to Cristoval since he was a boy, "A woman from our village in Spain, who knows the land from which we come."

The son would bow respectfully to his father but was privately determined to remain a bachelor. His world was one of horse shows and European tours, of candle-lit nights at the *Theatro* and a manservant who had never in all his life left his side. To aquire a wife, even one chosen by his father for the gentility of her upbringing, might be unavoidable, but was certainly unnecessary. His circle had accepted without comment his chosen state of bachelorhood, although in the eyes of many ladies of standing, it was certainly a shame that such a good name should go to waste.

In this way, the years unrolled themselves leisurely for Cristoval like an old scroll. Rumors of his father's gambling and bastard children were merely inconsequential gnats at his ears, and now at fifty-six, he no longer paid the old man any heed.

"I am writing a letter to distant relations in Spain," Osvaldo told him one day. "A wife is what you will have before I am in the grave."

Cristoval had not believed him, thinking that nothing would come of it. But when Mariabella arrived at their home on the corner of Benito Juarez and Melchor Ocampo, nursemaid, handmaid, cook, and eight trunks in tow, he realized he had been duped, resigned himself to the marital state of husbandry, and let himself be led by his father to the altar.

"She will make you a fine wife, Cristoval," his father told him on his wedding day, "Your life need not change because of her."

"She is a girl, father, and a flirtatious one at that."

His father sucked at his ever-present cigarillo and chuckled. "That may be true, my son. But where a man might find his pleasure in many women, a wife may only find it in the whims of Society. Let her dazzle our circle; her light manner will find many friends, and you yourself will be lifted up again in their good graces." Osvaldo inspected the dark tip, mashed by his tobacco stained teeth. "A man in Mexico is not a man until he is a husband, my son. Remember that."

Cristoval, surprised that his father was so well versed in the unspoken rules of Society, did not comment further. He allowed his newly acquired wife to lavish upon his father the attention he so craved and modified their old home to her specifications. Cristoval accommodated himself stiffly to her ministrations, and by and large, nothing changed until his father died. It was then that instead of marital bliss, he found himself hounded by matters of which, until recently, he had been so ignorant. It seemed he had not only a few illegitimate siblings, but seven in total born of four different women. After his father's death there were reparations to be made, houses to secure, and yearly stipends to be decided upon. The sons were keen to go into trade, and the girls were barefoot and knew nothing of life outside the market and the Church. Cristoval did what he could to secure his bastard brothers indenture to gentlemen trades of various sorts, but the girls he could do nothing for – three of even the most modest dowries were simply out of the question.

Mariabella had a very good idea of her father-in-law's secret doings, as well as those of her own husband, but did not concern Cristoval with the knowledge at her disposal. She herself was committed to providing her own offspring the tools she would need to secure its future, and did not worry for the squalling babes of loose women. It was within a husband's nature, she knew, to go beyond his marital vows and seek a willing concubine – such was a woman's lot. But in public, hand in hand at the Opera, or hosting balls in their grand home, she silently read each of her husband's glances, each slight pressing of perfumed gloves, each uplifting of his lips, astutely guessing his intentions and the likeliness of a match.

"The Señorita del Valle has certainly become a beautiful young maiden," she said one night to her husband as they dressed in their bedclothes.

"I had not noticed," was his reply.

Mariabella climbed into the canopied bed with its intricate rosewood inlay and sighed melodramatically. "Last year she was but a child. How time slips away."

Cristoval turned onto his side, shielding his face from her, having already known the charms of the young Señorita del Valle quite intimately. "What is it they say? 'Time is the oldest thief.'"

Neither Mariabella nor Cristoval actually believed that their marriage would produce children, as advanced was Cristoval's age and as indifferent as Mariabella was in the marriage bed. When Portensia had come, wet and angry from her mother's womb, and stayed angry throughout her infancy, neither Cristoval nor Mariabella knew what to make of her. They employed the best wet nurse available, arranged her nursery with all the toys, books, games, and dolls they could find, but nothing seemed to please their little girl. A permanent scowl etched across her face, she did not speak until she was nearly four years old – and by then her parents had become accustomed to addressing her as though she were an adult mute in child's clothing. Cristoval only saw her at meal times, when she would quietly munch upon the scant portions her mother allowed her. He regarded his wife stingy in her proclamations upon the child's diet, but did not protest in Portensia's defense. Children, after all, were within a wife's domain. Mariabella quietly went about the business of teaching her daughter to command servants, the proper way to set a table, and to dress herself in the manner of their class. She made enquiries about the boys who would become eligible suitors in time, and began to gather Portensia's dowry as her mother had done not so long ago.

Thus the years limped by in the old stone house at the far end of Coyoacan. Unrest grew in the countryside, Marxist rebellion rumbled in the Universities, wars bubbled to the surface of far-away places, but the small circle of *Portfiriatos* sat each Sunday in each other's drawing rooms, unaware that anything would ever change.

"Your father's family is distant relations to both *El Presidente*, Portfirio Diaz, and Benito Juarez before him, Sita," Mariabella would tell the little girl when the visits reached their suffocating end. "The era of Señor Diaz has been kind to us, but so was that of the Juarez brothers," she mused. "What will follow in their wake only the Christ-child can know."

Each day Portensia Montelejos awoke at her usual hour and ate the dry piece of toast Mariabella had prescribed for her.

"Do these things," Mariabella had said all her life, "And you will live to be the matron of a long line of children, *mi hija.*"

Portensia, a thin frail girl, knew not to speak when her mother delivered her many witticisms; she would listen stone-faced as Mariabella cheerfully related moribund tales of her deceased husband's squandered fortune, the great stone house and greater family line that had died with him, the many lands and Royal title from Spain that would not be passed down to Portensia – the last child, sadly, a female, who could not inherit any of the family's past grandeur.

"This beautiful place - ruled by only a handful of families," Mariabella would tell her only daughter, "Ours was once one of these, but," she would sigh and caress Portensia's light silken locks, unbuttoning the back of her tiny dress - a velvet miniature version of her own grand designs, "You weren't a boy and your father's father had many children. The lands have all been sold to pay the many debts your grandfather left us, although with only you to continue our name they would have been given to your husband anyway to do with as he pleased, and so, what does any of that matter, *mi amor?*"

Her eyes became misty as she looked about them at the old stone house. "Cristoval Montelejos left you only his name with which to make a good match." Mariabella tugged the thick woolen stockings down her daughter's smooth white legs. "Your Mama is a silly woman, Sita. She loved your Papa, but he was too old for your Mama. He was too old for your Mama but he paid a good price for her. And your Mama paid a high price for you. Though you don't know what this means, to pay for people," she began rolling the stockings. "Why don't you answer your Mama?"

"Because Mama hasn't asked a question."

"Does my Sita love her Mama?"

The child searched her mother's eyes for the correct response. She was too often fooled when no meant yes, pleasure meant pain, and love meant hate. "Sita's

Mama is a beautiful bird," she said and Mariabella laughed, delighted.

"She is, Sita!" Her laughter substituted her grief and ended when the nurse came to relieve Mariabella of her only child — a child who did not cry when her Mama died. Mariabella stood to adjust her emerald earrings and matching choker. The nurse silently led Portensia away from her mother's dressing table. "I go to the Ballet with the Valencias," she called to her daughter.

Portensia knew she did not go alone; there were men who waited for her, always waiting.

The few years of Mariabella Montelejos' own life were not filled with dry toast — there were dinner parties, galas, and nights at the Opera. There were extravagant, weeklong festivals for the Baby Jesus and the Pope, glittering costumes perfumed by candlelight and food. Food heaped upon food, and guests stuffing themselves until they vomited into the shrubbery in the courtyard. In the last years of Mariabella's life, while Mexico City and her daughter starved, gnawing upon their own bones during the Revolution, as the old families crumbled into the same dust with which their great houses had been built, she dressed like exotic birds and entertained faceless legions of worshipers.

"Look Sita! I am a macaw!" But even as a child, kept hungry by her mother and afraid of the impending doom of death, shrouded by the opulence of old wealth in its final decline, Portensia clung to the austerity that would mark her life.

"You are not a macaw," the little girl would coldly tell Mariabella when, filled with bubbly drink, she would lie on a brocade divan like the heroine from an Opera. "You are my silly mama who only wishes she was a macaw so that old men might feed her berries out of their hands — I've seen them."

Her mother, gay and bright until the day death took her, would smile into her daughter's pinched face and leaning down she would whisper admonitions. "Never let them make of you a spectacle, Portensia. Let your suitors eat maggots before you entertain their whims. You are beautiful, Sita. Your mama was beautiful too, but she was a spectacle." She would take hold of the little girl's face and cup it tightly in her hand. "Keep your heart cold, Sita, and you will live to see us all buried and usher in God's kingdom with your own time-worn hands." And laughing still louder, so that her guests might hear the gaiety and mask their own sorrows with it, her mother danced away in Portensia's memories, surrounded by a thousand revelers.

When the time came for men to wait for her, Portensia Montelejos hid herself beneath the great stones of the ancient house. That morning, the shade of her father would not leave her in peace, adamant that she should heed his messages. Portensia was in no mood that morning (nor any other) to humour her dead father; his messages were never important or timely. He came bearing stories of the Indian's bloody rebellions in the Haciendas, of the students who read Marx with tears in their eyes and devotion in their hearts, of families who sent their beloved sons to Paris rather than see them wasted in fighting for the government. Portensia did not care for any of it. The President's struggle to continue his many years in power had secured the life to which her class had been accustomed, but one which Portensia herself did not know very much about. The ghost of her father, saddened by the short future sight all dead possess, fearful of the Mexico that would emerge from the ashes of so many years of foreign rule, imperial designs, and the dwindling numbers of the last of the old families, sought to inform the only one who could hear him. For his daughter's part, she was angered to realize that this father who had paid her very little attention in life, only in death wished to redress such inattention. This enraged Portensia enough to throw dishes at him when he appeared with his concerns for her safety.

"Go warn the children of your other wives, my father," she would haughtily say to the murky form of his thin earthly self, "For I have no need of you."

Mariabella's presence kept such annoyingly spirited ghosts at bay, for since the death of her husband, Mariabella only cared to amuse herself and was thus blind to the world beyond. She kept Portensia at her side during all the waking hours of the day, but when Omar Codo del Valencia y Garcia, the fourth suitable suitor who had called upon them was announced, she left Portensia in the full care of her aged nurse. Omar Codo, who would not be put off as easily as the three suitors before him, simply refused to leave when the girl could not be found (to her mother's delight, for so it was that Portensia's sternness frightened her mother as much as it won her admiration) arguing that he had only this day to see the little girl, for next week he was to enrol at the Officer's candidate school in Chapultepec.

"My husband had a cousin who was one of the Boy Heroes of Chapultepec," she told him. "Not the one who threw himself off the highest tower of the Castle when the Americans invaded Mexico City; one of the other five." The sound traveled faintly down to Portensia hidden beneath the stone and floor boards.

"What an illustrious family history, Señora Montelejos," responded Omar distantly, secretly envious of such deeds.

Mariabella smiled sweetly and demurred that history was of the utmost importance and should be remembered, don't you agree? He mumbled his agreement and his own determination to aspire to such bravery himself and politely enquired if he, as a suitor, would be acceptable for her daughter's hand.

Beneath the stone, hidden from ghosts and sticky, sweet-smelling boys who thought war was fought with miniature statues on grand tables with maps and stratagems, Portensia listened as her mother tried to sell her for the price of a new carriage.

"Now, Señor Codo, you know what it is to own fine horse flesh. It is the same with a woman," her mother began upon the business to which he had alluded. "To be broken is what she needs. Surely you are man enough to tame a little girl?"

"How little a little girl?"

"A mere seventeen years. Still much to be undone but not so much as one who has reached her twenties, after all."

"She looks frail, Señora, if you don't mind my saying so."

"Ah, but Señor Codo, though small, she is wire and bone with a good name and good health. Ask anyone of our circle."

"What is the dowry price for this bone-wire girl?"

"Sadly, hardly anything at all. She has no lands, but such a good name, and a good history as you well know – you will find many doors will open for the name Montelejos. Her dowry is scant but her potential is quite high. She knows how to handle servants, run a household, and has never stepped foot outside our home unchaperoned. Thus, she is above reproach and will make a fine wife. I ask merely a few hundred pesos for her widowed mother and she is yours."

There was silence above while below Portensia burned in equal parts fear and rage.

"The price is not so much, it is true."

"And you know, Señor," her mother's voice became hesitant and sly, "she doesn't know better, as life in this house is not so fine and will not cost you much in upkeep."

There was a shifting of chairs and then the young man said, "But can you promise me she will one day grow into as marvelous a beauty as her mother - inherit the same repertoire of charms?"

"I cannot guarantee that Señor, no. But I do agree that any such mother would show gratitude towards the man who cares for her only daughter. Perhaps, should he avail himself of worth to the girl's social standing, provide the girl with children - yes, that mother may be inclined to show him favor of her own invention, perhaps?"

There was another scraping of chairs and silence there after.

Portensia eased herself out of her hiding space and marched, each step laced with righteous indignation, to her mother's sitting room. "So you want to sell me away to this man-child?" she whispered vehemently as she

13

slipped into the room. "How wonderful, how sickly adorable we will be: the pathetic suckling and her Prince."

"This does not concern you, Sita. Go and play with your nurse." Mariabella did not bother removing her hand from the young man's thigh.

"This is the fore-mentioned little girl, no?" the young man stood from his gilded chair, smirking and ready to command her. She was truly very little, hardly there at all.

"Nurse?" Portensia snorted contemptuously, ignoring the boy's proffered hand. "Who will carry our auspicious offspring, Mama? Who will nurse them? Tell this feminized fop the truth — that his offspring will kill me and his money wasted!"

The young man's eyes widened with surprise. "Señorita Montelejos, I assure you I am an honorable man, whatever you might think of my fashion sense."

"She wants to sell you damaged goods, doe-eyed Princeling," Portensia hissed. "This heart will not withstand the fruit of your loins." Her eyes became dark furnaces, a skill she had perfected on the sink mirror. "Take her into your bed and give me your name, but know your line will end there — with an old woman and an invalid."

"Señorita!" exclaimed the scandalized young man, "I certainly do not know, have no idea what you may think...what is meant by..." the young man stroked his hat as his brain worked to rebuff her meaning, but his thoughts became flaccid and disturbed by the sight of the little girl's hateful, thin face.

"*Dios mio*! This one looks ready to drop with fever," her nurse rushed in behind her errant charge. "She does not fall ill often; it is so rare we must keep her confined lest she forgets she was ever ill at all," and the nurse went to take hold of the frail child who turned and hissed cat-like at her. The nurse, a superstitious woman, halted and crossed herself as the room's occupants stilled uncertainly. Portensia shook off her opposition and stepped toward the young man, still beside her mother.

"It was a pleasure to entertain the notion of your proposal," she said, "But I would rather marry the butcher than a man who quails before the sight of a wayward little girl. You are a weakling besides a fool," and turning on her heel she stomped out as she had come — leaving a strange sense of relief in her wake.

Her mother's bright gay songs, Portensia soon learned, were the death rattles of an entire class. The French and whoever could leave had left by the time Mariabella danced her last bird dance, and thus it was only by charity that her daughter survived the decade.

Portensia's personal secret to survival was no secret at all. It was her mother's advice, simple lack of movement. "A lady does not do labor," Portensia contended when poverty demanded she find a genteel trade to sustain herself and a rapidly deteriorating Mariabella.

"But Señorita," the servants pleaded," We haven't anything at all to eat — our clothes are in tatters."

"Then pretend you are also ladies," Portensia grumbled. She long knew the sting of hunger — fear of it had left her many years before. The servants, distrustful of Socialist rhetoric and reluctant to let their ancestral home fall to disrepair and neglect, appealed to a distant relative.

"We are starving and she does nothing!" they bemoaned. "That child's mother is sick and bedridden. Without kindness of some sort we are dead."

"They miss the parties and roasted pigs," Portensia reported when the relative called upon her. "They fear the retribution of the dead."

"It is not parties they miss nor retribution they fear. They fear you," he replied.

But Portensia only raised her hand feebly and banished the relative and what was left of the servants. When the fighting intensified, the government's troops falling faster than reinforcements could be summoned; Portensia shut the great door of the house on Benito Juarez and Melchor Ocampo and awaited the end of the world.

The erratic beating of her heart finally silenced Mariabella's gaiety. As she choked on her blood and slowly suffocated, Portensia sat in silence in the upper atrium of the stone house. She listened as the Doctor came and left with the news and a lock of her famous mother's hair but shut herself away from the neighbor's eyes and prayers and did not stir. As used to immobility as she was to hunger, Portensia's mind worked feverishly. There, on the verge of becoming an orphan at the age of nineteen, alone in a stone garrison large enough to quarter an army, Portensia looked at the years' accumulation of things without purpose: gold-leaf gilded serving carts, lacquered wardrobes that stood nine feet high, miniature diamond hair clips for once-cherished dolls, furniture brought from Spanish port cities on long perilous journeys, three generations of silver wedding cutlery, place settings for a standard five course meal for twenty-eight guests, golden goblets plundered from ship-wrecked vessels, and sixteen chests of clothing that no one had opened for at least fifty years.

Portensia looked at the acquired wealth of her family from her perch at the top of the old stone house and decided never to marry. No man would ever hold the reigns of her yolk – Portensia would be free. Suitors came, but as they had come for a younger version of Mariabella, left with painful jabs to their delicate macho pride. But neither would Portensia learn a trade, for fear of her own demise. A yolk she would not have, nor a man in authority over her, but neither would she work – at least not with her hands. For while she did not fear death, as she had long learned to live with the dead - it was failure she could not accept. If she could not excel at the chosen trade, Portensia would be humiliated. To be respected among her mother's peers, to be so far above them as to not even need that respect, was Portensia's goal. It had never entered her imagination that her mother would live so long, but neither had Portensia imagined her life without her mother's childish predilection for silk and sweets, heart-shaped rubies the size of robin's eggs, and song. Mariabella had kept the dead in closets, in portraits on walls. Portensia learned to live behind her mother's noise for a shield against them and by making herself as unobtrusive as possible and now, as her mother herself lay all but dead downstairs Portensia had no idea what she would do: how she would keep the ghosts at bay.

    The house was in ruins, but intact. Mariabella's habit of speaking to her possessions to imbue them with her spirit had so frightened her servants that they dared not steal from her; especially now as the Lady lay ready to cross that final sea into that most foreign of lands. Without servants, the nearly dead in a downstairs room, the house lay silent. So Portensia sat in her stone garrison large enough to shelter several families and decided to gather the silver doorknobs and wedding cutlery, the golden goblets, golden furniture hinges and picture frame name plates, and the masses of her mother's jewelry and seek a man who knew the art of smelting. She would make coins from the junk — for hidden coins could be tucked into secret vaults and under clothes. With the hidden fortune, she would leave Coyoacan and buy a small but respectable house using the only thing her father had given her: his name. With it, she would become a quiet spinster and do as she pleased.

    On the last day of her life, drowning in her own fluids and defeated by a useless heart, mute Mariabella pleaded for a kiss from her daughter. Her cheeks, sagging but unblemished, quivered in their final supplication and her eyes, mournful and accepting, beseeched Portensia: Please forgive me.

    Portensia wanted to turn away, to show that her heart was the ice-cold jewel her mother had spent so many years polishing, but she could not. "They say it is going very badly for the government," she told Mariabella as she sat rigidly beside her deathbed, the makeshift divan Portensia had pulled into the front room by its iron-clad claws. "The rebels will soon take the city. They will divide all the old haciendas into small tracts so that everyone can have his own acre and the great houses in the city will be used for the new government."

    Mariabella did not speak; unable to breathe, she closed her eyes in horror of Portensia's predictions.

    "I don't mind very much," Portensia continued, "What does it have to do with me? What am I? A female, the last of our kind, the daughter of a man's plaything – isn't that right, Mama?"

A gurgling sound emanated from Mariabella's throat as bile, blood, and sadness welled up from inside her. Her eyes remained closed. Her hands, clasped in the attitude of prayer, locked in place around the bare knuckles that once bore so many elaborate rings. Her neck, the sagging skin of a chicken, turned pale and still and ceased trembling. The eyes beneath the pale lids also stilled, and although she could not see them, Portensia imagined they clouded like the end of a storm, and became empty.

When Mariabella's body was cold, Portensia walked out of the front room and did not look back.

Having decided to remain free forever, at midday the same day her mother died, Portensia stepped into the street already forgotten by the world. Outshone by her mother and obscured by her father, she was a stranger. Portensia took a deep breath and began counting time. Flipping her fine shawl around her bird-thin shoulders she stopped the first man she saw. "I wish a taxi," she said, hiding her ignorance behind an icy tone.

"They do not pass along this street," the man said, averting his eyes politely, "But they frequently pass the next. It is more public than this one."

Portensia continued on her way without thanking him, terrified, and angry with her mother for not preparing her for such simple tasks. "A lady does not venture into the street unescorted," Mariabella had told her. The packed dirt of the small street grew dusty and did not settle when she passed, still counting time. The midday heat was white and hard as Portensia straightened her veiled hat and glanced into empty courtyards and saw maid's household tools, lying carelessly beside shrubbery and potted gardenias.

"Taxi, Miss?" The man's voice came as a relief — she had not meant to walk so far.

"Yes."

The man clicked the carriage door behind her as softly as possible as she arraigned her skirts and shawl around herself.

"Where might I take you?"

Portensia did not look at the man; she was secretly examining a frayed edge of her glove. "Do you know of one who smelts ores?" she asked quietly.

"I do, Miss."

"Then it is there I wish to go."

The taxi bumped along the cobblestones of Coyoacan. The Cathedral loomed ahead as Portensia made the sign of the cross. It was only a four-minute walk to the Cathedral, she guessed. Eight minutes of walking per day was small enough to go unnoticed, she reasoned. "Do you know Independencia?" She called to the driver.

"Yes, Miss."

"If I pay you a weekly advance would you be waiting at the far end of it both Wednesdays and Saturdays?"

"Yes, Miss."

Portensia nodded to herself, watching the brightly colored shops glide by her window. Before she dismissed the maids, they had complained of the empty shelves because of the Revolution — they whispered that only the Indians who still grew their own food and the Marxists would not starve. And, of course they added, Evil Portensia. She had heard it whispered in the big stone house that surely someone who could survive on toast, the occasional egg and a bit of hard cheese would find herself in some strange place in hell when *she* died. Portensia knew what they had said of her in her mother's house - that she was so dry she could only defecate stones, so humorless she made flowers wilt. She looked at the street vendors selling small *huilotas* carcasses, their wings spread wide for the pleasure of passerby's, as if any stomach could survive on birds smaller than pigeons.

Yes, Portensia knew her own servants despised her. She knew she could not keep them, could not tolerate their gossiping or bear their laziness. Mariabella had accepted servants the way others accept that wine is good for thirst and sun bad for the constitution. To keep them from joining the Communists, she provided them food and warm beds when her neighbors could not. Portensia did not have this luxury – she did not have her mother's charm to buy credit from the butcher. She only had the stone house with its open atrium and back stairwells, and nothing else. The servants, now that Mariabella was gone, would have gone hungry and eventually left Portensia in the house alone regardless of their fear of ancestory or the promise of a warm bed.

"This is the place that smelts ore, Miss." The carriage driver leaned back to announce.

"Your name?" Portensia asked, jutting out her chin.

"Generaldo," he replied.

"Fine, Señor Generaldo. I await your taxi this Saturday." She got out of the carriage carefully taking precaution to behave as properly as possible — as surely this crowded street was no place for a lady of any standing. Past her rushed servant girls and men smacking mules, ragged children and stern soldiers. Recoiling, she shaded her eyes to view the shop across the street from her. It was empty and darkened by large leafy trees. Portensia crossed the street and pulled the bell at the open gate.

When a young man came to the door, wiping crumbs from his moustache, Portensia Montelejos for the first time in her life knew what would really kill her. It would not be the delicate fluttering inside her bird chest: it would be this young mustached boy with his frank, honest face.

"Are you the man who melts gold into coins?"

"Among other metals – I am he," the young man answered.

"Do you possess discretion?"

"That," Hernando had answered, "I possess in great amount."

With her mother dead in a downstairs room, Portensia, nineteen and now free to convert the remaining goods of her household to those small convenient coins, was told that man who had come to call upon her once - the man her mother would have been happy to oblige with her own "inventiveness" – was bayoneted in the Revolution.

"Omar Codo suffered, they say. He got it in the *panza. Ay, pobresito*! The guts are the worst place to get it, they tell me. Your Mama knew this boy, yes?"

Portensia sniffed at the myopic neighbor-woman who stopped to call on her each Saturday before she went to meet the ore-smelter. These visits were customary between neighbors, as only women of a certain age and rank could move about their small circles freely – Portensia would have to wait many years until she would be one of these. The elder Señora Flores, having privately decided to chaperone the young Señorita Montelejos in lieu of that scandalous Mariabella's absence, enjoyed their weekly visits so much that she never realized she repeated the same news each week. "Remember my son is fighting for the President?" she asked Portensia.

"Is he winning?"

"He is very brave."

"I hope for your sake he is under the ground. I knew your son. He was no great asset to you, Señora." Portensia's sharp tongue did not bother the Señora, who knew the girl was fatherless, and with that lazy *fadonga* of a mother, what kind of chance did the girl have to marry well? It was a wonder she could string a sentence together in good order, the woman considered and said, "I have not seen your Mama lately," to which Portensia answered, "She died, Señora."

This was the extent of their conversation each Saturday, as the old woman in addition to being myopic was also senile. She had no son fighting; he died in the first skirmish, with soiled pants and an unused gun. Both he and Omar Codo del Valencia y Garcia were in the same regiment, both officers and horsemen. Dressed in their finest Caballero jackets, tight pants and sombreros, they had charged the enemy together, fallen only meters apart -

their fine clothes, shoes, and coins taken after the battle by the same masked scavenger, a small eight year old boy.

Señora Flores, the only witness to Portensia's secret asset conversion, cared for her pregnant widowed daughter-in-law with cold compresses and the generosity of her senility. She did not know the price of a pig now equaled a small fortune and thus managed to wheedle whole chickens out of the butcher, whom she regarded as stingy when he did not sell them to her. The poor man gave Señora Flores the chickens when he had them and pigeons when he could not. She never complained.

Portensia delivered the fuel for the ore-smelter's furnace in bundles of rags and used laundry in the taxi that met her at the end of *Calle Independencia.* Hernando returned her booty wrapped in newspapers and potted plants. No one knew in either household the fortunes the young people traded between themselves. The sacks, heavy with dusty silver candelabras and golden fleur-de-lies paperweights, took Portensia some time to convert to those small convenient coins. Her mother's massive amount of French jewelry took just as long.

When the taxi usually stopped in front of the ore-smelter's home, Hernando would open the door and take the sack from her. Often she did not look at him as he sat the potted plant or folded laundry stuffed with newly minted coinage at her feet and closed the taxi door. "*Ja,*" he would signal and she would be gone.

But one Saturday as the taxi stopped, Portensia pushed Hernando out of the way. "I must speak with you," she said, dismissing the taxi. The street, normally loud with servants, water sellers and carriages, today only rustled leaves and unsettled dust — solitary and strange. He took the sack from her and ushered her into the office.

"There are but few things left."

"You know I will keep my word of discretion."

"Yes, that is so," Portensia placed a hand on her heart to feel its beating wings. "I have," a pause, "need of..." hand on heart Portensia stood silent and Hernando, nervous because of her, fiddled with the contents of the sack — and being nervous, forgot himself. Inside the sack he found a child's chamber pot, a golden one, and he remarked, "I finally understand the Revolution!"

And Portensia, grateful for the respite in her difficult subject, answered, "Imagine a child using such a valuable prop for the dirtiest of all deeds."

He held it up and inspected the object. "And how bitingly cold!" he added. "Why, even extreme coddling and cajoling cannot often induce a child to seat herself upon even a cloth-covered pot at all." He laughed at its ridiculousness.

"You have dealt with children?"

"Ah," Hernando's laughter ceased abruptly. "I am well versed in but a few of life's roles." He resumed unloading her goods for the smelting fire, turned his back on her and carefully sidestepped the truth. It would have been improper for Portensia to ask further and for that Hernando was glad: he did not speak of Gloria willingly. People pretended she was Hernando's sister, out of respect for his feelings (for still after two years, Hernando would vent his grief in loud messy sobs should anyone mention the girl's mother, Evelyn Cuthbert, dead from childbirth.

The whispers were not as kind. It was said the big Mexican stud had been too much for the delicate Englishwoman — reported to have been frail, as everyone knows how delicate are the *Ingleses*. Portensia did not know any of these facts. Hidden herself since a child, regarded now as cold enough to shatter glass, no one but the senile Señora Flores bothered her with news of any sort — and that particular old woman saw the *Ingleses* as uncouth children and did not bother with their news at all, even if it did involve one of the oldest families in Mexico City.

Hernando's daughter Gloria had inherited her father's clear brown eyes, but they had retained her mother's round English shape. The little girl's coloring was becoming more Vasquez than Cuthbert, and but for her long straight nose and those fat, round dimples she was more like Hernando than he ever would have conceded. An ill-tempered and peevish child, having perfected a look of blameless innocence, Gloria demanded the servants lie for her when vases were broken mysteriously, and take spankings in her place. The servants, afraid of the hold she had on her father, obeyed the four-year-old as though she were already their mistress.

Hernando, unaware of his daughter's dictatorial tendencies, let her play in his workroom as he fired metals and worked on his geological maps. His mother had given the girl a set of old picture books, and with these alone the toddler had learned to sound out the words, to link them together, and most fascinatingly, to ask her father what they meant. But when the doorbell clanged on Saturdays, signaling Señorita Montelejos' grim arrival, no one could ever find the wayward Gloria Vasquez. The strange, thin, Señorita Montelejos and her severe countenance had filled the little girl with such a heavy foreboding that she usually disappeared into thin air during her visits.

"I want to give you thanks," Portensia began again, ignoring Hernando's remarks and half-truths, "and to ask for one last obligation." Her voice retained its characteristic coldnesss, but the slight tremble betrayed her. "I am in need of a priest."

Hernando stopped sorting her junk for the furnace, calculating her motivations for such a request. "A priest?"

"Not for me."

"No."

"It's for my mother."

Hernando's brow furrowed.

"She is dead," Portensia said.

"Yes, I have heard this is so."

"And she is still in the parlor."

"Ah," Hernando gathered the chamber pot, a bracelet and twelve table knives and expertly threw them into the fire. "I understand."

"It's the smell," Portensia regained her breathing, again counting how many beats her heart could withstand per mortifying sentence. "I am afraid someone will notice that she putrefies."

"She was no saint, your mother?"

"Apparently not, for she rots and sinks deeper into her deathbed each day." Portensia placed a finger on her thin lip. "Some day soon she will need scraping from the sheets."

"I will find you a priest," he said and closed the furnace door.

When the priest called on her, Portensia sat in the great stone hall once full of junk and listened to the Latin Mass. The priest had come alone to perform the ritual and consecrate the body. She heard him bless it, wash it in holy water and rosemary, and pray for her mother's journey to God. Portensia examined the wooden chair's scrolled arms and wondered if the priest cut a lock of Mariabella's hair as the doctor had done. She imagined he brushed her hair aside, marveling at its waxen light brown ringlets. Were they intact? Did the provocative purple slip seep with her blood, acquire a deep rusty stain? Had the sheets saturated themselves with her last mucus, bile, skin slough? Portensia did not know who removed the stained sheets, closed the open window or even covered the woman's face for Portensia would never enter that room again.

At last, Portensia did not fear the future suitors who would or would not come as they had for Mariabella. She listened as the priest chanted his meaningless words, secure in her chair in the high stone room because she had stored away exactly six hundred and thirty two bright gold coins, three hundred and fifty-nine shiny silver ones and the rubies, diamonds, sapphires and jade of her mother's favorite shape: a heart. Her personal carriage at the ore-smelter's house waited for the journey further south and having counted and recounted, Portensia knew: no one would ever ask her for the right answer ever again. No one would ask, "Do you love me?" and slap her when she would not lie: no, I do not love you.

A heavy hand fell on the door as the priest abruptly stopped his chanting. Boots scuffled together and stabbed the tiled floors as careful hands searched the cupboards and furniture and men shouted to each other below Portensia's damascene chair: Where is all the gold? Where have they hidden it? She allowed herself a small smirk before rising to her full height and descending the staircase wrapped in icy righteousness.

"What do you want?" she asked the tallest man. She had learned to identify the Marxists with heavy beards and hungry gazes.

"Señorita, you must leave this house. It belongs to the people."

"Very well."
"Where are the rest?"
"They have all died."
The men shifted their booted weight uncomfortably: they acquired the Socialist sneer much later and as yet possessed not the bravado to beat a little girl.

"Why is this house vacant?" The leader of these men knew the wiles of the wealthy. Like rats, they found escape routes and bore upon their backs the ills of their own makings.

"I am not speaking into a darkened room." Portensia pushed her face up towards his, nonplussed by his four guns, two boots, sharp voice and charming smile. "I tell you, they are dead."

"But where are all your things?"
"We never had any things. We lost them while you were still at school learning about injustice, repression of the Indians, and brotherhood. We have only these stones. The rest turned tail long before you against your own." She lifted her thin coat from the closet rack and pulled her arms into its sleeves. "And now you may have even those." The men watched her walk toward the door and leave quietly, in awe.

"She would've made one *quavaso* of a revolutionary, no?" one said as another sniffed the air. "*Ay, caray.* What is that smell?"

Portensia did not look back as she settled herself into the awaiting taxi. "Señor Generaldo, drive quickly," she closed the taxi door before even settling her skirts. "They have taken my house, and I pray have not taken the ore-smelter's also." Portensia's heart beat so fast she thought it would take flight.

"No, Señorita, it is not so. Do not worry yourself."
"What do you mean?" Frozen fear stilled the beating.

"They need the ore-smelter. They took his mines instead."

The taxi bumped along until they came to the ore-smelter's shop. She did not wait for the taxi driver or ring the bell. As hurried as she dared, she slipped into the shop and searched for Hernando. He was at his desk, crouched, with a small nugget of ore in his hand. Gloria sat at his feet caressing a much-loved picture-book, and looked up in alarm when Portensia entered.

"Hello, Señorita Montelejos. A fine day for the world to end, no?" Hernando wiped his tools with an old rag, his bifocals at the very tip of his nose.

"My carriage was not taken for the Revolution by those damned Socialists?"

"No, Señorita Montelejos," he glanced up at her. "But they have taken everything else."

"What is this word, Papa?" Gloria's voice pierced through Portensia's fraught mind with her petulant tone. Having forgotten the child was there, hidden beneath Hernando's heavy oak desk, Portensia's heart gave a tiny jump. Gloria's voice, having perfected the pitch which most gained an adult's attention, was irritating to everyone but her father.

"'Tormented,'" Hernando replied.

"And this?"

"'Handsome.'"

"Why would the 'Handsome' Prince be so 'tormented'?" she asked him.

"I don't know, *mi amor*, perhaps he didn't get the beautiful Princess?"

The little girl turned the page guardedly, having known beforehand the answer to her questions, a most cumbersome trait. When Hernando looked at her it was not himself he saw in her features, though that was what everyone else saw – a spoiled brat the spitting image of her father – he saw Evelyn: Evelyn frowning, Evelyn examining the edge of her shoe, Evelyn's round, bright eyes in clear brown like his own.

"Papa, can I have a kiss?"

"Of course, *mi amor*." He lifted her into his arms and blew kisses through his moustache against her creamy skin while Gloria giggled and pushed his face away from hers with hot, sticky hands.

"They need my skills and so they have left my shop without even entering." He told Portensia through his daughter's hair. "But the mines outside the city are owned, what did they call it? Commanded by the people. Yes. The people now own my mines. I then, am no longer even a person."

Portensia did not care for dusty silver mines like anthills or that Hernando was already a father. She perched herself on one of his cane-backed chairs. "Have they taken my carriage? Are my sacks of coins hidden still within the seats?"

Hernando nodded and pushed Gloria off his lap. "Except the stones in your pocket."

"And it is ready to leave for Oaxaca?"

"It is."

"Who is to accompany me?"

"Gloria and my father." Hernando pulled papers from drawers and gave them to her. "Gloria is not safe here, and being old and ill my father cannot remember much, but he can still shoot and quarrel."

"Will you not come?"

"I cannot leave my shop. They do not want old-fashioned carriages." He reassured her softly, to keep her from panic. "Especially with the broken ugly mare I am hitching to the front of this one."

Portensia arraigned herself back into the chair and listened to the open window. Somewhere nearby, loud voices raised an objection and a single shot broke the springtime breeze. "There is a pregnant girl next door to me," she said. "What do they do with pregnant widows?"

"They kick them out like everyone else,"

"But this one's mother...she isn't right, touched in the head they say."

"Is she a friend?"

"I have no friends," another shot and two more in rapid conversation.

Herando stood. "Stay with Gloria, *por favor*, and I will go see about the fat neighbor woman." He pulled on his jacket. "What is her name?"

"Señora Flores. The both of them."

Hernando sauntered through Coyoacan in long strides, careful not to seem as though he were on important business. The Socialists had taken Mexico City completely, even the tiny village of Coyoacan could not resist. Revolutionaries milled about on street corners and fed the Indian servants platitudes and promises. There would be equality now, they said as he passed, those light-skinned *rateros* would never again run things around here, *ay caray,* no! The breeze lifted the scent of distant burnt fields. That old man stood there and waved his gun around, they laughed. They spat and rubbed scrubby beards. "We took his animals and his house without a fight but he stood on that land and waved around that gun. And when we shot him, he lay there and bled." They scratched the hair beneath their caps.

The neighbor's house was quiet when he arrived; the gate yawned open, a lazy testament to bloodless theft. Men sat outside and quietly talked of what they would do now. The men inside handled the home with care — it housed a new master. Hernando glanced around before passing on farther down the street, listening. After a few minutes, he saw the women walking slowly, the large-bellied widow struggling to hold senile Señora Flores upright. He came up behind them and took one of the old woman's arms, a weightless branch.

"Come with me," he said. "I hope you like the South."

To Milly Flores, Portensia Montelejos Vasquez was the only woman ever worth admiring. She was cold, strangely dashing, and she told people whatever she felt like saying. Milly, sequestered from birth to three rooms of the family home and unaware that Portensia came from similar circumstances, was unprepared to face life after the Revolution husbandless. Big as a pumpkin, she shouldered the Old Señora as long as she was physically able. When Hernando Vasquez came to take them to his home it was the first time Milly Flores had left their side of Coyoacan.

And so Señora Mildred Flores, daughter of a middle-ranking government official and an actress, arraigned her hairdo and imagined someone noticed. She was no great beauty but her mother had taught her from a young age to dress well and in doing so, she gained many friends and suitors. Her parents, living extravagantly until the future stood in bold contrast to the present and highlighted the need to begin hording, pampered their only daughter – the last child born to a family of three boys. She tended exotic flowers and tropical birds, read Ovid and Plato (understanding none of it), wrote nature poems in the style of Lord Byron (in English!) and indulged in painting. Her father planned on teaching Milly to drive the new Mercedes roadster when he was killed and her mother never recovered enough to care for anyone else, so Milly married. Her husband was neither clever nor kind and Milly was not sad when he died as well.

But it was when her older brothers joined her husband and father that Milly grew a grave for her heart and tried to keep it buried. She admired Portensia chiefly because she had no heart at all.

"Is this the girl and the old woman?" Hernando whispered to her frightening neighbor.

"It is so, yes," came the coldest, iron voice Milly had ever heard. A long, thin hand gestured to her. "Will you be a bother on this trip?"

She shook her head, trembling. What would this ramrod do if she became 'a bother'?

"I hope that is the case," Portensia continued. "You will wait to have your lie-in until we can purchase a house in Oaxaca City." Portensia took Milly's elbow and looked fully into her face, forcefully. "Do you understand me?" she asked quietly.

"But how can she help it if it starts before then?" the Old Señora asked from behind them.

Portensia kept her gaze on Milly but frowned slightly. "Has she no will? If she cannot make the child obey now, how does she expect it to do so in future?"

"It will love me!" Milly blurted out, spluttering frightened tears at the same time.

"Don't be stupid," Portensia sniffed and motioned for them to mount the carriage.

When the baby insisted on coming at dawn the next day, the Flores women knew nothing about it. The senile old woman began to cry out for water, bandages, a blanket, her nursemaid until Portensia slapped her face and silenced her.

Milly suffered with each bump of the road with glistening sweat on her forehead but when she could keep her screams muffled no further, Portensia banged on the carriage roof for Hernando's father to stop. "Señor," she called out, "What do you know about birthing?"

"*Ay, nina*, I know only that the men smoke cigars and wait for the midwife, or if they pay for it and the mother approves, a doctor."

"What," the young Señora Flores gasped as she pulled Portensia's skirt, "happens now?"

"You birth that silly baby of yours, who doesn't even know enough to wait until we have purchased a house."

"I can't," she heaved, "do it here!"

Portensia glanced around her at the miles of empty scrub. She saw a farm house surrounded by tall palms a mile away. "Señor Vasquez," she called, "Can you get us to that house?"

"I will try," he answered as Portensia did her best to placate the girl, who was mooing in cow-like pain. They bumped further along the dirt road until the Señor jumped down to bang on the door of the small shack. A woman answered, wiping her hands on an apron, frayed but clean. "There is an emergency here, Señora, I am sorry to disturb you," Barely had the Señor begun than the woman pressed her hand against Milly Flores' stomach.

"It comes soon. Take her arms — she must come inside — I have medicine there."

The woman changed her apron and sprinkled holy water on the ground before Milly Flores lay down. She lit candles to the saints and chanted to the Virgin as she blew into the girl's face. The scent of burnt rosemary and wax calmed her. Her eyes focused inward. Milly Flores prepared to birth her daughter.

Night descended on the deserted plain, the crude animal-fat candles flickering dull, smoky light, as shadows played against the rough wooden walls of the woman's hut. From the safe distance of the cold carriage, Gloria cowered against her grandfather and whimpered as each savage bellow erupted from Milly's mouth. Portensia attended to the elder Señora Flores, still babbling about boiled water and christening dresses, telling her dead sons and husband about the baby who would soon be born. The woman who assisted Milly, her chapped hands steady and sure, pressed on Milly's abdomen and massaged the birth canal – as she had done so many times with mares and goats.

When the baby's head crowned and Milly gave her final push, the woman wrapped the wiggling child in her mother's oldest dress and proclaimed her healthy. Milly kissed the child and named her Juanita, after her father, before falling into a profound sleep.

In the morning, as cocks crowed and light flooded the solidary Hacienda, the woman gave Portensia a basket of hard boiled eggs and a loaf of pit-fired bread.

"Go with God," she said, and backed away to watch the carriage continue along the dirt path to Oaxaca City.

The road continued for another twenty-five miles and there, in the distance, the deep peels of the bells of Santo Domingo chimed their Sunday proclamation. In a hotel just inside the ancient city walls, Portensia sat watching as Milly and her newborn child, a fatigued and resentful Gloria, and the old man dozed on cots and narrow beds. When she knew them all to be asleep and snoring, she took out one of her mother's jewels and examined it in the light. Glittering and perfect, she knew it would open at least a few doors.

"I will buy this house," Portensia said the next day as she and Milly stood beneath frilly parasols and newly-bought dresses of Parisian watered silk and tooled lace. The cathedral's bells rang out resoundingly behind them as the man listening shielded his face from the noon-time sun and laughed a dark guffaw.

"It belongs to the people," he said and crossed his arms.

"For thirty thousand pesos in gold and jewels it belongs to me."

The man reconsidered this slip of a woman. The house was not large and it faced the street — a very public domicile. Within sight of Santa Domingo he knew he would never get away with anything if he lived within its solid walls.

"You will sell it to me," Portensia concluded defiantly. "And you will draw up a document to that effect." She took out one of her mother's jewels — a bright green emerald the size of Milly's baby's fist. "Surely you know a girl who will appreciate your generosity to an old woman, two widows and a foal." In this time of many widows, certainly no one would bother to check.

"I am sorry to hear of your husbands, Señora," the man replied, taking the jewel and her explanations, "but let me personally welcome you to Oaxaca City."

When Hernando followed unexpectedly four months later, unsurprised and flustered Milly could only keep darning the baby's socks with downcast eyes, but Portensia had said, "And so," stuffing her sock into the sitting chair. "We did not see the last of your face then?"

He held his hat in hand and shrugged as Gloria wrapped herself around his legs. "They took my shop in the end as well. But," he drew in a breath and let out a grimace, "I am reborn here as my cousin, Ernesto, the cousin with the Southern mines."

"And how will you explain your miraculous conversion? Is your cousin a bull as well that no one should notice?" Portensia raised a ridged brow. "Certainly this convenient cousin will want the wealth of his mines."

"Fortunately, he has no use for them. He dwells in far richer an abode. Apparently, the streets are gold and the gates pearly."

"And if it is actually a few degrees warmer?"

Hernando let out a full-bellied laugh. "Then no amount of gold or silver will help him — the Devil cannot be bought at so cheap a price!"

Portensia arose and pulled on her kid gloves. "Come," she motioned to Hernando as her narrow silk skirts slapped her stalk-like legs. "There is a private matter to discuss."

Hernando bent down to reassure his daughter, when she screamed with frenzied fear that her beloved Papa would leave her again. "*Mi amor*," he cajoled, "I will return in one moment's time, when we will sit and read your books, and perhaps we will have tea with your dolly? Hmm? Only permit me a moment's conversation with the Señorita Montelejos."

Gloria, filled with hatred of Señorita Montelejos, narrowed her eyes but accepted his proposition. Left with the mewling baby and still-fat Señora Flores she plucked brocade fibers from the sitting room sofa until a small hole had been made and her sense of injustice was slightly appeased.

"They think you are a widow," Hernando had said that afternoon when they were alone in the garden.

"And they will think you are Ernesto Vasquez," Portensia answered.

"Yes, we have equal concerns. What if someone from our Coyoacan circle joins us?"

"That is simple. No one knew me — I was a ghost and am only now born."

"But they all know me."

"Did anyone in Coyoacan know your Oaxacan cousin?"

He thought to himself, unrolling the short years of his life. "No," he concluded.

"So, tell people that now that the Revolution has ended you prefer the name Hernando as it is more the people's name. 'Ernesto' seemed so very out of touch after the killing violence. You are a new man reborn, as it were."

"That is a lot to explain in passing," he pointed out.

"Yes, but you know Marxists — either they use too many words or the point of a gun. Be one of the long-winded ones."

"Certainly."

"Well, then. Congratulations. You are an imperialist in Marxist clothing."

He smiled. "I think of myself as a capitalist."

"I've seen your shop's inefficiencies: it hemorrhages pesos to be bandaged by more pesos. You are not a capitalist."

"Well," Hernando stopped to shake her hand as men did. "Then I thank you for your objective viewpoint. I go now to tend my mines."

She let him go because she was afraid of him. He was dangerous to her; his warmth threatened to see the end of her; she feared his charming smiles, his easy-going manner, and the simple love he had for his daughter. When next Hernando came back from his Southern mines, he bore a dead lamb across his back. It was Easter, and as such they remembered it in those days as Jesus himself remembered the feast - as it was explained in Exodus. Portensia moved to accommodate the fleece-less gift into her kitchen, the young servant girl who trailed in Hernando's wake disrupting her calculated speed with fumbling nervousness.

"Get out of my way, pebbles for brains! Why is this here?" She motioned to the girl.

"She is your Easter gift," Hernando replied.

"Are you being stupid or cruel?"

"Neither."

Portensia called the girl from the corner to which she had managed to squeeze into and pinched her arms. Neither finding rot nor laziness she sniffed, "This will do."

When next Hernando came it was a proposal he bore on his back, and they married the following Sunday.

"I do not love him," she told Milly Flores as they dressed for the Cathedral, "but he is a kind man and does not love me either. We must be resourceful; the Revolution gave us new lives and that newness we can communicate not to another living thing." Milly Flores bowed her head and arranged Portensia's veil. "Our marriage is an export," Portensia continued, "and because he is still in love with the shade of his daughter's mother, will not be a yolk about my neck. Instead, Hernando will facilitate our lives here in Oaxaca City, Milly. His gender will allow us the ease of movement and respectability we sorely need."

Head bowed further, Milly Flores let fall a very small tear: for the broken heart of Hernando, for the coldness of Portensia's rationale, for her own loneliness in the deep hours of night.

When he was not at his mines in the dry countryside of Oaxaca, Hernando Vasquez would sit in the parlor of his wife's regal but modest home, listen to the gramophone Portensia had newly acquired, watch Milly Vasquez tend to her baby and his daughter read at his feet, and think about typewriters.

It was during the third year of the Revolution that Hernando Vasquez had sat in his front courtyard and tried to kill himself over a woman. It had not rained for 84 days and the flies had become offensive. The old people died easily in those hot days, sighing wistfully of past times as they sat in groups and played dominos together, their feet in basins of standing water. Hernando could not believe how difficult it was to die. Just the month before, his neighbor had dropped dead in his garden and had set into motion his own attempt. Hernando clutched his chest at the open neckline and groaned. It should be easier than this, he thought. Perhaps if he exposed more of himself to the heat of the sun: but no. He was, unfortunately, an ox — an unloved, clumsy, brown ox.

"Ay! Hijo! What are you doing out here, and with your shirt undone? Disgraceful," the cook leaned over the prostrate boy and gave him a poke with the kitchen broom. "Whatever is wrong with you should wait until later."

Hernando sighed from deep within his tortured breast and moved his bulk aside for the cook's broom.

"Who is the woman?"

Hernando sat up at the question. "How did you know it was a woman?" he asked suspiciously.

The cook shrugged and continued his sweeping. "It is obviously a woman, all this sighing and lying on the ground."

"And?"

"And you are trying to give yourself heat-stroke over this woman?" the cook tisked his old tongue.

"And?"

"And it is stupid, young Señor," and he punctuated his observation with a jab of the broom.

"I will mangle that if you touch me again," Hernando pushed the cook away angrily.

"And?" The cook shrugged, "I go down to the market and the old woman there makes me another, and your mother's dinner is late." Hernando yawned. "Cold and late," the cook finished quietly, leaning on his broom.

"It is the English woman," Hernando said, inspecting the beginning of his first full beard. The bristly edges were scattered. It was the fourth time he had shaved it in the hopes of some regularity of growth. The cook took again to his sweeping as Hernando contemplated the only Englishwoman in Oaxaca.

She was called Evelyn, and as the only Englishwoman she operated the only typewriter the people had ever seen. It was a beautiful typewriter: slick, black and functional. Hernando had met the Englishwoman at the neighbor's funeral one month prior: the one who had dropped dead in his garden. She had heard the story and was distraught over it — that anyone could die so peacefully surrounded by his roses. Her white flour cheeks flushed and her light blue eyes filled with tears of sorrow for a man she did not know. They had been standing not two feet apart during the Mass. Hernando had watched her take out a delicate handkerchief and blow her long thin nose in front of him. It was a simple gesture, complete in itself, and graceful. She had tucked the handkerchief into her sleeve to continue with her ill-spent grief — and he had loved her from that moment.

Hernando had tried all methods of introduction. The Vasquez knew many people in the Gold industry, themselves also mine owners, but somehow the people she knew sought at all costs to shield her. An introduction was impossible. He had left various calling cards at her front door, paid her maid to let slip his name in casual conversation, and once, he had almost touched her shoulder on the street before shirking back to duck into a dark alleyway. Hernando found himself dreaming of her, of swimming in a pool of her tears and flowing down her milky white breasts on a raft of her wheat-colored lashes. He saw her in his mind's eye upon waking, and he ached for her before sleep overcame him. His studies in the metal sciences were at an impasse, for when he looked into the Earth, he felt her presence elsewhere and went to seek it. His uncle worried over his nephew's state and his mother secretly purged his room of evil spirits with rosemary sprigs. Hernando could feel the tremor of an earth-shift five kilometers away but he could not feel his heart beating without her. It was Evelyn he needed.

And so it was that as he was trying to kill himself over a woman he was being pestered by a nosy cook.

"And what is so wonderful of this silly English woman?" the cook asked him.

Hernando sat up and began to button his shirt. "I do not expect a man who boils the heads of chickens to understand frustrated love."

"Because I boil chicken heads I do not understand the art of wooing a woman?" the cook put his broom aside and leaned over the boy. "I do not know the mating rituals of the English, this is so. But I do know how to make a woman forget her native tongue."

"How dare you!"

The cook looked over his shoulder furtively and pushed Hernando back to the bench. "Sit down, you silly boy." The cook looked deep into Hernando's eyes and said, "Do her a favor," and leaned back expectantly.

"Excuse me?"

"A favor. Be there at the right time to provide assistance. Gain her gratitude."

"To what purpose?"

"A woman is not a helpless beast. She is a hard worker, and often we men ignore the labors of our women. As is correct, boy, they labor as they should."

"Women of our class do not labor."

"Stupid boy! All women labor, and all women bear their responsibilities silently, as good Christians. But it is admiration that drives a woman. Notice her labors and unburden her of them for a moment, only without intruding, and you will not only gain her attention, but her respect. A woman remembers a man who can see her worthiness." The wise cook sat back and rubbed his eyes. "And also: go to church."

"You are telling me this will require an Act of God?"

"I'm only saying it can do no harm."

And so Hernando Vasquez went to Mass each morning for a year. As he walked along the cobbled streets he followed the vibrations of Evelyn. She is at the tobacco shop, he would imagine. They have what she is looking for, but it is under the counter. They have saved it for her specifically. Then she went to the Post. Perhaps she has letters from England. Now she is at the butcher's. They are telling her they haven't any beef and she needs someone to wrap the three chicken thighs she must buy instead. They are telling her all the beef went to the Revolution, Hernando Vasquez would daydream.

Evelyn Cuthbert did not care for the Revolution - there was war in her home also. She did not cry for the lack of meat nor dead soldiers. She did not flinch at the sight of rifles in the square or the burnt shells of buildings. She had come to Mexico City seeking to escape war in Europe only to find a fresh one, and then found it could not touch her. No, Evelyn Cuthbert did not care for the Revolution. She only cried for the death of innocents;

the old man in his garden, overworked donkeys, and when the occasional bird accidentally ate the poison set out for the rats.

It was her mother who suggested she come to Mexico. She had feared for Evelyn's future in that home without men for protection, guidance or funds. The days then stretched before her into weeks. She went without a car to drive her when there was no petrol, without work when there was no paper, and one day the butcher had no meat because of the Revolution, and Evelyn Cuthbert realized she had been away from England for two years.

Amusingly, her mother's plans had not been ill spent. Men now sought her hand - rich, young, old, and dusted with scented powder. In their best attire, they flattered her and preened; they brought lilies and hard-won chocolate and copied love poetry in their best hands from books. In England, Evelyn was the daughter of a shop owner and had learned the skill of typing by helping her father with his accounts and letters. No man in England would don a ridiculously outdated frock coat and threadbare top hat to call upon her! But here, at least once a week the Señora Ramos would come bearing a calling card and proclaim the unworthiness of yet another suitor. How nervous they always became that first day! How they sweat through wool and hair grease to present their intentions of marriage — which was the most amusing thing of all. Evelyn regarded herself no one in society; she was the daughter of a shopkeeper, after all. And yet, in this colonial Mexican city of fountains and monasteries she was the most sought after young woman of the day. Evelyn knew she could have her choice, but she was also a particular girl about life's choices. She would have a man who didn't shine himself up like a prized cock, a man who knew the value of a hard-working wife. Such a man would win the heart of Evelyn Cuthbert.

And so it was that the English daughter of a shopkeeper was waiting to buy meat at the butcher's simply to be told there would be no fresh meat at all for the unforeseeable future and would she like some salted ham?

And also, it would be that after a year of fervent prayer Hernando Vasquez passed that same butcher shop to hear Evelyn say in her sonorous and grammatically incorrect Spanish lisp, "Salted meat for the past month? I suppose we shall starve for the Revolution as well?"

"I cannot apologize enough, Señorita Cuthbert. It is beyond my control." The butcher gestured helplessly behind him to the rows of empty cases. Cured meat hung from the hooks in the ceiling, and crates held pickled pigs' toes and fried chicken feet but there was certainly nothing fresh.

"Well, then there is nothing to be done," Evelyn sighed, and then she noticed Hernando. "Oh, my excuses, sir. Please," she gestured to the butcher.

"I as well am looking for something fresh," Hernando told the butcher.

"And to you I say the same. We all looking for something fresh," the butcher replied.

Hernando laughed and bowed to Evelyn. "There truly is nothing to be done. Please," he gestured to the door. "After you." As she turned, Hernando quickly wiped the sweat from the back of his neck. There, in that moment, he felt the presence of God. This was the answer to his prayer — this and that wily cook.

"We have not been introduced," Hernando began, "my name is Hernando Vasquez. I believe we are in the same industry."

Evelyn cocked her head quizzically. "You operate a typewriter as well?"

Hernando laughed again at his leisure, marveling at the lack of tension. "Ah, no. We work for people who drill for ore."

"Oh, that. Yes." Evelyn glanced around her for the nearest carriage, her shopping trip now finished.

Hernando sensed that the fair young woman would soon slip away and so he played the only hand he had. "You know," he said to her conspiratorially as they walked along the cobblestones, "We have fresh meat."

She leaned forward, playing his game. "You do?"

"Yes, we do. It is a secret of the Vasquez' that we share only with dinner guests."

"And this secret — does it bray, squawk, oink or moo?"

"Bray? Certainly not! It both squawks and burbles. It is a talented secret. Perhaps you would be willing to visit with it?"

Evelyn smiled, amused at this young man who eschewed convention with his frank but playful manner. She was taken with this — for it was a camaraderie she missed, one that made her feel as though she was a shop girl again, a refreshingly normal thing to be. "I would be delighted to visit with it. May I bring my escort?"

"Of course," Hernando replied as the world shifted beneath his feet. He was someone else entirely: someone suave and resourceful and completely unlike himself the previous day. He watched himself call her a carriage and help her into it. He listened as he gave her the Vasquez address and cringed as she called out, "Adio!" from the moving carriage, leaving off the "s". And then, completely himself again, turned and ran toward his home, the leather soles of his father's fine, handed-down shoes slapping the pavement frantically.

After leaving Portensia Montelejo's fine home in Oaxaca City, having kissed the tear-stained cheeks of his daughter and the hard hand of his wife, Hernando boarded his train to the southern mines inherited from a briefly-known cousin. He would look into the reflection of his window and think of Evelyn Cuthbert, many years past, sitting in her office in Coyoacan at work on her Smith-Corona portable typewriter.

Oaxaca City, Mexico, 1925

On school days, Gloria Vasquez and her half-sister Teresa Montelejos walked the one-half block to the Convent school together, bellies full of castor oil, fried egg, and a cup of black coffee, their arms full of overnight assignments and a tin lunch pail each. Portensia had made it very clear that Gloria's position as elder sister made her accountable for Teresa's scholastic success and had her beaten when invariably Teresa failed in her lessons. It was not that Teresa was stupid – it was that when the Irish nun began explaining the multiplication tables, the view from outside the window was so much more inviting.

Gloria took the beatings, lashings by their Grandfather Vasquez with his old leather belt, and resolved in her tiny breast to see that ox of an unwanted half-sister somehow suffer. She toyed with various means while recuperating on the porch with no dinner and a growling belly, but a sort of impotency would fill her mind as schemes were tested and abandoned one after the other.

She had taken to stealing Teresa's completed pages of homework – laboriously recopied by the light of the kitchen stove – and ripping the pages into a fine pulp which she used to stuff Teresa's childish dolls. This, of course, only caused more beatings for Gloria when the nuns sent home notices of failing grades for missing homework, but the momentary relief she felt when her sister's bovine features register the loss of all her hard work in front of the severe Sister almost made them worthwhile.

Still, she would muse as the chambermaid applied salve to her swollen legs afterwards, there must be a way to torment Teresa which would be secret, and which left her blameless.

It was by these mechanizations that Gloria met their new cook, Concepcion.

It had been a drowsy summer night, a hot damp air sat over the town, stifling even the rowdiest children, and Portensia had gone to see Juana Flores, sick with the measles. Her father was still at his mines in the South and while Gloria expected to see Portensia later in the evening, Hernando only came to their home in Oaxaca City on Sundays.

Dolores, who had cooked for the family for many years, had been in the kitchen until early evening, when she had gone to see the chemist's son, an Indian boy who had recently been accepted into the University. Gloria hated Dolores, who doted on her sickly half-sister, and liked to bake tarts and sugared sweets, *capirotadas* and *charamuscas,* for Teresa alone. Like two mice in a cupboard they would whisper about the neighbors and lick the sticky dough off their fat fingers, foreheads glistening with sweat as the stove issued forth its continual heat in all seasons.

"Why are you always in there?" Gloria complained to Teresa, "Dolores smells of onions."

Teresa shrugged. "I like onions," she said.

On the fateful day Gloria went looking for Teresa and found the kitchen empty, the stove slowly cooling, she sat down on a hard wooden chair to consider her revenge. Ever mindful of Portensia's strict regulations, Gloria tried to imagine what offense would provoke Dolores' outright dismissal – for if anyone could discover Portensia's inner workings, it would be her step-daughter. No one knew Portensia Montelejos as well as Gloria did. No one spent as much time from so early in life guardedly watching her movements, analyzing their meanings, and storing the information to be used at a later time. In short, no one reviled Portensia Montelejos more than Gloria Vasquez.

For example, Gloria recalled the dismissive way Portensia had spoken of various powerful men in the city, openly complaining of their graft, corruption, and embezzling. When her father had asked what should be done about it, Portensia responded, "That is not for me to decide; I can live my life without concern for theirs."

Hernando had laughed at his wife, who did not care that men abused their power. But once Teresa had forgotten to leave an easel in the classroom and was found absentmindedly carrying it home – an infraction for which Portensia had her severely punished.

"But Mama, I just forgot!" she wailed.

"Forgetfulness lies in the belly of Satan, Teresa," Portensia had said.

It had been satisfying to see her step-mother punish Teresa, Gloria reflected. And it was then that Gloria's gaze moved up from her clasped hands to Dolores' apron. There, in a side drawer, half-opened, was a packet of yeast. The apron on the peg, the yeast in the drawer, and the lateness of the day conspired together in Gloria's heart.

Tearful denials of theft notwithstanding, Portensia turned the cook out then and there when the packet was discovered in Dolores' apron.

"But Señora ," Dolores wailed fruitlessly, "I did not know that yeast was in my pocket!"

"A liar and a thief," Portensia fumed, "Next you will tell me a tricky wind has landed it there."

"By the Virgin I did not take that yeast!"

"Ay, Dolores – theft, lying and blasphemy?" Portensia remarked coldly, "The Saints are weeping."

Teresa too pleaded against Dolores' dismissal, but Portensia shut her ears and hired Concepcion, a small-wristed Indian woman.

"An older woman is who we need," Portensia decreed, "One who knows how to hold her tongue and keep her fingers out of the family stores."

Concepcion came to them from the same camp Hernando ran for his miners, summoned by Portensia the night Dolores was dismissed. Concepcion's bundled bed-roll and a mysterious red satchel sat in the servant's quarters so recently vacated by Dolores, both suspicious and tempting.

It was Gloria who spoke to her first, the last week's lashings still rankling in her breast, Teresa having slipped away to the house of that old woman, Maria Eugenia.

"Do you have anything useful in that old rag bag of yours?" she asked from the safe distance of the kitchen door.

"Usefulness depends upon need, little girl," Concepcion replied without turning.

"Can you get rid of my sister?"

"Why would I do that?"

"I've heard you are a witch."

Concepcion turned, holding the heads of eight young broccolis. "I've heard you are a spoiled *sabre-todo*."

"So we meet upon a platform of understanding," Gloria chirped.

Concepcion smiled, the wrinkled masses in her face lifting in amusement. "Your sister is a docile house pet. Why get rid of someone like that?"

Gloria folded her arms and perched on the edge of the cool stove. "Can you bring my Papa home?"

Concepcion went back to her piles of vegetables for the *sopa caldada*. "Yes, and more, but you want to learn for yourself to do these things, no?"

Gloria's eyes narrowed. "So you are a witch."

Concepcion shrugged her ancient shoulders and said, "Are you the Inquisition?" When Gloria sullenly refused to say more the old woman took a matchstick and lit the stove, faster than Gloria could jump away.

"You're a quick old *vejita*, aren't you?"

The old woman, now standing eye to eye with Gloria, laughed full in her face. "Come by each night as I cook the dinner, and I will see that you learn what you want to know."

"Good girls don't learn to cook from the cook," Gloria parroted one of Portensia's many opinions. "They get sent to Paris."

Concepcion sighed and wiped her eyes. Then the old woman bent over to scrub the potatoes in the sink. With her back turned, she spoke with emphasis.

"Who said you will learn to cook?"

"I have heard you are spending time with Maria Eugenia." Portensia's stern voice rattled with displeasure.

Teresa shrugged her shoulders compliantly. "She's so lonely over at the Inn," she pleaded, "What harm is there in spreading God's cheer?"

"She has no business befriending a young girl of only twelve years," Portensia said flatly as she moved her hair aside for her daughter's nimble fingers. "She is my age after all. It is disgraceful to retain this friendship."

Teresa finished buttoning her mother's suit-dress and smiled at her in the mirror. "It does no harm, Mama," her voice soft and pliant. "I am not far from the house and will always be ready when you return."

"Why does this woman herself not go to Mass?"

"I believe that is between Maria Eugenia and God."

"Nonsense — it is between her and the Church!" The Señora pulled her suit front straight. "It is a matter of good upbringing and class. If one has the capacity," Portensia flustered guiltily, covering her embarrassment at having alluded to her daughter's frailty.

"And if one does not have the capacity, one must do God's work in other ways, Mama. I will keep this woman company as you walk to Mass." Teresa kissed her mother as the quarter bell of the Cathedral chimed. "Pray for me," she said with a kiss to the cheek.

"Every day," came Portensia's automatic reply.

Teresa huffed her way down the walk of the great house to see her Mama off to Mass, waved and disappeared over the low concrete wall to Maria Eugenia's Inn. It was a house like all the rest, enclosed by a high brick wall, with a hanging bell and wrought iron windows. Inside the enclosure, the rooms surrounded a courtyard with a small garden and fountain. Within the water of the fountain lived four real Japanese Koi fish. It was seen as a great coup to possess these fish, and Maria Eugenia and her husband took great pains to build them a lavish home, complete with orchids, moss and a small wooden bridge which guests might walk over to view them. The guests were allowed to feed them bread bits, but only on Sundays had they first gone to the noon Mass.

Some people thought the fish possessed restorative qualities and some even claimed to see them bubble out messages between the lily pads, but Maria Eugenia did not believe these things. She believed the Koi brought order and tranquility only because she watched the guests so closely when they admired them. Maria Eugenia was not in the habit of looking for miracles. She simply explained what she saw below the surface and simplified. Most things became obvious when one accepted all possibilities but remembered the difference between probable and possible and the interconnected nature of things. She first encountered the child from next door when, unhappy and gasping for breath, the girl passed one of her street-side windows. Head downcast and chest heaving, Teresa had tried to go as far as the corner general store, only one street away. Returning clutching her prize, a silver medallion of St. Sebastian, she leaned against Maria Eugenia's window. They began talking and Maria Eugenia, seeing the child's illness and isolation plainly, invited her in for *un café*.

"Mama is at Mass for another fifteen minutes," the child acquiesced. "Maybe just one cup."

Maria Eugenia saw the child's blue lips and heard her shallow breath. "Why do you go so far from home, niña?"

"I have nothing to do," Teresa complained.

"Then why not come see me? I am a bored old lady. My children have all gone away." Maria Eugenia poured another cup. "I miss children's games."

"I am sorry, Señora," Teresa had replied. "I know no games."

"I will teach you some," Maria Eugenia promised.

Portensia, by then middle-aged and entrenched in the rigid morality and lack of sentimentality which she took from natural inclination and nourished in escaping the war, allowed her young daughter the acquaintance with the old neighbor woman not from any kindness but because she was tired of resisting. Teresa's plodding but sincere good-will exhausted Portensia's sense of justice. She watched from behind thinly veiled scorn her daughter's laborious movements to dress herself and her mother. Curling her mother's hair and setting her makeup, Teresa would tell stories she imagined or the going-ons of the neighbors. Portensia only half-listened to these trivialities — marveling instead at the chirping cheerfulness of Teresa's disposition in direct contrast to their gloomy home.

"Mama," Teresa suddenly interrupted Portensia's disinterest. "Why have I no brothers or sisters?"

"Because your father and I had no more children."

Teresa cocked her head inquisitively. "Yes, but why?"

"It is a rude question, Teresa."

"I did not mean rudeness, Mama. I only wanted to know. Mari says it is because you are sick too like me."

Portensia calmly pushed her daughter's hand aside, hovering above her fringe. "You speak of familial things with strangers?"

Teresa shifted uncomfortably. "Was it a secret I have no brothers or sisters?"

Portensia released her daughter's hand but held her gaze. "Yes. I am ill as you are. You, however, are the worse." She stood to walk to the dresser bought that first month of freedom, the true beginning of her power and control. "I will tell you a story, Teresa. Once upon a time your Mama and Papa came to Oaxaca—"

"After the Revolution?"

"Yes. Don't speak when I am speaking." She paused to make her point known and continued. "We had very little but a few jewels and our good names. With only this and our hard work we now have the mines, the shop, and our lovely home."

"And me."

"You came later and when you did you came too soon. The Montelejos are an impatient people—most of our women come too soon. But because we are impatient our lives are spent like sugar in cake — sweet but filling — until we leave this world impatiently for the next."

"So we leave before our time because we are sick?"

Portensia gazed sadly at the lemon trees in the courtyard, their branches heavy with fruit. "Teresa, do you see that tree?"

"The lemon one, Mama?"

"Yes."

"Yes, Mama."

"Now, sometimes the fruit gets big and fat and ripe and Lupe goes and plucks it, no?"

"Yes, Mama. Her lemon water is better than the carnival."

"When have you been to the carnival?"

"Papa took me."

"Ay, Dios mio, that man. Regardless — sometimes Lupe doesn't pluck the fruit because it falls to the ground before it is ripe, yes?"

"Yes, Mama."

"And what happens to it then?"

"It stays on the ground."

"Yes, Teresa. And no one wants it because it is unripe and bruised besides from the fall. Do you see?"

"See what, Mama?"

"That we are those lemons, Teresa."

The little girl did not answer. Her cushioned pink lips pursed in thought and remained so as Portensia finished dressing in silence. Teresa pondered her mother's assertion that they were lemons, wandered to the front room with the heavy bay window and the balcony overlooking the street. It was a balmy day, dry air heavy with looming thunder hanging uncertainly over distant mountains.

"Blue mountains," the child mused as she leaned her elbows on the cast iron railings and watched the passersby on Independencia Avenue.

There was Lupe, hailing a taxi for Portensia. There was Portensia, leaving for *café con cacao* and cake with that silly prig of a woman — the Señora Milly Flores. Her daughter, Juana, pinched Teresa so hard once it left a mark, all for innocently remarking on her father's absence. It wasn't her fault after all, if it was said her father never fired his gun during the Revolution! Who cared anyway? She certainly didn't. There was Mama gone now and only maids in the street. They weren't interesting to watch. Teresa's favorites were the fashionable ladies of Oaxaca City who dressed in frilly hats and silken spring dresses and clicked from shop to shop on tall slender shoes, or the families returning from Mass or Pavilion in the square in their Sunday best - matching dresses for the girls and new toys from the balloon sellers in hand.

As Teresa mused on the life below a man passed beneath the window and heard a deep and theatrical melancholy sigh from above. Teresa, unaware she had made such a sigh, was startled when suddenly a face turned upwards toward hers — a face who smiled and tipped its hat. She immediately withdrew, but peeked briefly back between the rails. The man still smiled so the little girl smiled back and waved. The man stuck his hands into his pockets and continued on his way to the square. Teresa watched him from between the rails. His suit, newly made and exquisitely tailored as fine as any woman's dress, hung attractively on the man's lean frame. Teresa knew enough of watching people that the man's attention to his clothing made him what they called "vain" and yet he seemed to wear this vanity nicely, as though he and his vanity were on friendly terms. As the man's form vanished, Teresa prayed to God. "Please God," she begged, "some day give me someone like that, and make me an elegant lady. Just give me that, and I won't care that I'm a lemon. Amen," she whispered, and crossed herself with childish sincerity.

Gloria, eavesdropping on her sister, was not unaware of Teresa's insecurities. She had done her very best in making sure they were implanted far inside Teresa's tiny little head.

"Teresa," she would innocently remark, "have you ever noticed how much you look like your mother?"

And Teresa, who loved Portensia blindly as only a young girl could, thought of Portensia in her strict skirts and austere mannerisms and was disappointed; for her mother, though respectable, was not the fashionable lady Teresa hoped she herself might one day become.

"I," continued Gloria at such moments, "look just like my Mama, Evelyn. And I'm sure that one day I will command men to fall at my feet as she did, possessed as she was of such great beauty."

Teresa, having ferreted out Gloria's stash of old photographs, knew in her heart that Gloria was right: that while she and Portensia were lemons, Gloria was destined to become a beautiful lady, just as her mother had been. It did not matter that the truth of the situation was that Gloria much more closely resembled their father Hernando, or that Teresa was the image incarnate of a young Diamante Cantu – the notion placed in Teresa's mind was that she was to one day become as humorless and respectable as her mother, which of course made her weep openly with great passion.

"Here," Gloria would comfort her sister. "Drink this tea. It has special herbs in it that will promote glowing skin and shining hair."

The tea, bitter and thick, was made from a bark Gloria found in a nearby swamp, and used by the local Indians as a purgative. "Go on," Gloria would chide when Teresa gagged, "Don't you want to be beautiful?"

Portensia did not allow the girls to join her for Mass except on Sundays when all the family rode to the Cathedral in the carriage. She was committed to Teresa, that she would live to become a woman - although she was so ill that Portensia's own heart squeezed each time she looked at the little girl. When Teresa had been born, Portensia turned her this way and that, looking for defects, searching out the small baby's hidden weaknesses. She gave her over to a wet nurse to suckle and made a pact with God. If he spared her only daughter, Portensia would go to Mass each day, an unceasing prayer of thanks upon her lips. Teresa, in her twelfth year, was clearly not healthy, but God had kept his part – she was alive and growing.

At Mass on Sunday, the Saints whispered to Teresa in unknown tongues, impossible to separate from one another, mysterious messages lost on the girl. Forbidden by Portensia to speak of such preposterous things, Teresa simply allowed the strange voices to wash over her amid the Latin prayers; the kneeling, crossing, chanting, singing mixed with the echoed whispered of the stony saints. Gloria, convinced her sister was not only stupid, but disillusioned, rolled her eyes when Teresa's attention darted from statue to statue, like a cat chasing a piece of string.

"Stop it," Gloria would say, pinching Teresa, "Or I'll tell Papa you wet your bed."

"I never did!" came Teresa's whispered protest.

"Then I'll pour a cup of water in it to make it look as though you did – now sit still!"

Hernando, wedged between his frigid wife and ever-doting daughters, would sigh and mentally return to the ore samples on his desk so many miles away.

"I can't help it Gloria – they're talking to me."

"Christ alone, Teresa, shut up! I'm not taking a beating for you over made-up voices."

At this vehement hiss, Portensia would crane her head around the girth of her husband's middle and point her eagle-eyed gaze in their direction. No sound from Portensia was needed to hush the children, who both immediately clutched their hands together and bored holes into the priest's back with the intensity of their attention.

Teresa would fiddle with Saints' medallions, having collected hundreds of them from general stores, corner shops, and small church stores, which she kept tied together on a string in her pocket. She knew the Saints' stories from the moldy books kept by the nuns at the Convent school, and would ask to read them during the meal time.

The stories told of the wounds suffered for the Faith; girls who had resisted temptation at the hands of oppressors and attackers, men beheaded, children burnt, women with breasts cut off and tongues ripped out - a multitude of horrors which, if withstood with eyes fixed firmly upon Jesus' merciful heart, would lead to benediction and one day, sainthood. Teresa, enthralled by such a depth of depravity (on the part of the world, of course, not the Saint), read open mouthed and only begrudgingly gave back the old books when it was time again to take up her schoolwork.

Gloria racked her imagination for some kind of trick to play upon her sister to show her the idiocy of such devotion, but could find none worth the effort. If Teresa wanted to rub medallions like talismans, it did not matter to Gloria, so long as such displays of piety were confined to the silence of Teresa's pockets during Mass.

"What is this Saint good for?" she would sometimes ask her sister, picking at one of the medallions on the string.

"Orphans."
"And this one?"
"Travelling by sea."
"And this one?"
"Impurities of the flesh, I think."

But Gloria knew such stories were worthless, for each malady a Saint could cure, a secret herbal potion could cause.

And thus the years went steadily by in the house on *Independencia*, until the girls were ready to leave the safety of the Convent school and become ladies.

The ball, organized by Portensia to the highest standards of social protocol and to be attended by only those from families of which she approved, was to arrive in time for Teresa's fifteenth birthday. Gloria, now nearly twenty, considered herself cheated – how can an old maid come out to a society to which she was already familiar?

The young ladies' dresses, white organza with seed pearl detailing, were pressed and cleaned by Guadalupe that very morning, and their stomachs were only filled with an orange each with weak tea. As they made their entrance, Hernando looked up and smiled sadly, for this would be the ball in which possible suitors would come for the first time, seeking his daughters' hands in marriage.

When Hernando thought of the possibility of his daughter's unions, his mind returned again to his late wife, Evelyn.

"When will you tell your family of our nuptials?" he had asked her when she accepted his proposal.

"The war has made it very difficult to get letters back and forth over so great a distance," Evelyn had said. "And besides, there is only my mother left, and she is unwell. I would hate to create a commotion." Evelyn stroked his rough hand against her soft cheek. "She bid me farewell when I came to this land, my love. She must have been aware it would be the last she would see of me."

Her words saddened Hernando, for as desperately as he needed Evelyn, his own mother's blessing had been an integral part of his decision to ask for her hand in marriage. "If it makes you happy, my son," his mother had sighed, "Go ahead and ask her. And may you be blessed with many children."

His father had no definite opinion on the matter, but that his son would finally go back to his studies and the family business. "If this will put to end the wretched condition of your weakened constitution," he told his son, "then ask the girl." But the Señor Vasques was said to have muttered to his wife, "But should the woman refuse, so help us merciful Lord in heaven, I don't know what he will do."

Happily, Evelyn had agreed, and happily she had occupied the grand Vasquez home, charming his parents and the neighbors until no one could complain of the Señora Evelyn Cuthbert Vasquez's erroneous Spanish or strange accent. When the child she bore killed her amidst her labor pains, Hernando had been inconsolable. It was not until he conceded to look upon the infant four months after her birth that he came back to himself. Gloria's childhood was a shadow of the love her parents bore each other, and though Hernando gave her what he could, a mother he was not.

To have such happiness as Evelyn and he possessed, as brief as it had been, was Hernando's hope for each of his daughters. For Gloria he was not concerned, as he had convinced himself she could flourish whatever her position. But as time went by, and as Teresa grew sick, the light of Hernando's hope for his younger daughter dimmed until he feared his daughter would die untouched by a man.

Ten years before becoming a Montelejos, Ebner "Ed" Collins finished serving the last of his five year sentence for several counts of theft, forging documents and impersonating a judge. The theft and document forging were for money, of course, and the impersonation charge was spite; the judge in question was his father.

When he met Hernando Vasquez, he had been newly freed from jail and looking for another profession using the only two skills he possessed: the ability to speak Spanish and an innate business sense. When he won not one of Hernando's daughters, but two, he thought he had struck gold. But it was not until he met his wife's daughter, Paulina, that he learned he wasn't in love with the Montelejos-Vasquez – he was in love with what they could produce.

In the sweltering heat of the Oaxacan countryside, Hernando watched the young man beside him blow up the side of a mountain. He himself was fairly good at knowing which angle would produce optimal results, having moved effortlessly from ore-smelter to miner many years ago, but this man had a familiarity with heavy explosives that also came from long experience – of a slightly different nature, perhaps.

Hernando had met him one day, when newly arrived on the last train (their small village being the last stop on the line from Mexico City) this nameless man had stood in a wrinkled and faded but curiously elegant brown suit. The man held his hat, and scratching the back of his hand, waited.

The office had been deserted, his men looking for a new vein based on a hunch. The men trusted Hernando's instinct to produce enough food for their large families, to shod themselves and their children with the silver brought up from the depths of the darkness, the crawlspaces, the dank and freshly dug earth. Hernando's men knew their *jefe* had the nose of a rat for silver.

"Are you Hernando Vasquez?" the man had asked in thickly accented Spanish.

"I am he," Hernando answered, lumbering out of his chair to lean across the desk. "And who are you?"

"A worker," the man replied.

"Have you a name, worker?"

"I do not."

Hernando grunted and nodded toward the scars on the man's hands. "Break rocks for fun, friend?" He fully expected this American stranger to cram his hat back upon his head and be gone. Instead, he was treated to the lonely smile of a solitary celestial being. This man could become beautiful when he chose, Hernando learned (as did both his daughters two years later).

"Not for fun, no, Señor. But I broke them honestly and I will use the same force these hands possess for you." The stranger's eyes were earnest and Hernando realized that he liked this man.

"No, name, eh?"

The man shook his head.

"I have always liked the name Jorge. God did not give me the opportunity to ever use it." Hernando eased his large frame back into his chair. "I have a Jorge Ruiz coming for the truck tomorrow morning at dawn. Be sure you are him."

The stranger nodded and placed his hat carefully upon his head.

"We will see this force of your hands," Hernando said quietly as the man had turned to leave.

Early the next morning, when Hernando's truck rumbled up to the office, there was the man now known as Jorge Ruiz. He stood waiting, having slept there the night before. Ruiz was taken along with the other men to the depths of the new mine, still dressed in his curiously elegant brown suit. Until the midday meal he hauled and hacked at the walls of the tunnel, periodically checking the flecks of his fingernails for silver dust or other ores.

When the men came up for their portion of tortillas and black beans Ruiz ate sparingly and crumbled the loose rock at the entrance of the shaft, examining it closely, his nose against the lines of the wall.

"What do you see?" Hernando asked the convict.

"Your explosives have gone against the fissures of this rock line, *Jefe*," Ruiz answered.

"Sometimes it can't be helped," Hernando responded.

"It can always be helped." Ruiz ran a hand along the rock wall. "Here, see this blast patter? Your detonation point was not in the correct position. It has weakened the passage." He handed Hernando some of the crumbled rock from his hand.

"Because of the weakening your miners will only be able to go so far before the shaft collapses."

Hernando peered along the shale fissures Ruiz pointed out. "*Ja, ja*, I see." He chewed his soggy cigar. "What would you have done differently?"

Ruiz chuckled good-naturedly. "Well, first off, I wouldn't have just blown away at some hunk of rock. I would have looked at the strata to see where the natural fault lines were. That's where I would have set my charges." Ruiz took off his Panama hat to wipe the sweat from his fair hair. "And I wouldn't have used so much."

"A soft touch?"

"Like to a scared mare."

Hernando chomped his cigar thoughtfully. "We'll work this shaft until the vein is tapped or the walls come down, but you can set the next one where I tell you – *ja*?"

"*Ja.*"

Jorge Ruiz, once Ed Collins, set the charges from then on, selecting the amount of dynamite and the angle of the explosions. Hernando, duly impressed, paid him for his services and bought him a new suit.

It was only a few months later when Ed turned to Hernando, this man who did not yet know he would give Ed both his daughters, and smiled a beautiful smile.

"Have you decided about our lost cause?" he asked. He had learned the Dominicans were arming to march on Santiago, and he was sure there was money to be made blockading, hording, and expediting guns, materials, and women. This man called Jorge Ruiz had kept his ear to the ground, and in the camp he had listened to some of the other workers, the men who discussed the politics of the North American continent, the Dominicans, and the rising wealth of the Cubans. He had learned that both the government and the rebels of the Dominican were in need of guns, money, and rations.

Ruiz saw the unlimited potential of war – he knew he could arm both sides, line his pockets, and make Hernando Vasquez' money multiply overnight when the open conflict began.

Hernando brought the wet cigar to his teeth, stained the same color as his moustache and grunted eloquently. "I worry for my family," he said.

The man Hernando had named Jorge Ruiz shrugged. "There is money to be made, *Jefe.*"

"*Ja, ja*, I know."

"In these uncertain times, let us play upon our advantages."

Hernando chomped on the cigar thoughtfully. "It is exactly those uncertain times which worry me."

Jorge knew Hernando would not trust merely an employee with this ambitious plan – to convert a part of Hernando's vast holdings into an even more lucrative field than the Dominicans – but he would, Jorge was certain, trust his son-in-law. However, he could not ask outright. These Mexicans were in many ways as blunt as their Northern neighbors – but when it came to their daughters Jorge knew he could not intrude.

"*Jefe*," he said one day as Hernando chomped on a new cigar, "*Jefe*, I have come up with a plan to multiply your holdings with our Southern neighbors while keeping your hands clean."

"How stained will yours become?"

Ruiz looked down at his scarred, work-worn hands and laughed, "Stains wash out eventually," he said. "It will be these scars that linger."

"Let me hear your schemes," Hernando consented.

Ruiz squatted down to the fine red dirt at his feet and drew a map of Texas with a stick. "Here is Texas, *Jefe*. I know it well. When the century was but a babe, I began my life as a man by working as a meat packer in one of the factories in Ft. Worth which supplies the North with their share of beef." Ruiz drew a line with his finger in a Northerly direction. "The cattle used to come up the Shawnee Trail, here, but once the railroads came in, the cattle drives were done away with. Now, the railcars bring up the cattle and deposit them at the stockyards. Then they are packed in the plant and taken again north to Chicago and New York."

Hernando chomped thoughtfully.

"It can be said, however, that as a point of transit, Cowtown has many goods to offer." Ruiz stood up and rubbed out the map with his toe. "From the Midwest comes grain, from the West comes minerals, from the North comes textiles and manufactured goods, and from Texas itself comes meat, oil," Ruiz paused before adding quietly, "and guns."

Hernando's eyes, having glazed over for much of the history lesson, widened. "Which guns?"

"Guns, unused and unwanted, from the war with Spain; Gatlings, captured Mausers, Trapdoor rifles (though they are not much desired, *Jefe*), Hotchkiss rifles." Ruiz paused again and added, "Even a few Colts if the price is right."

Hernando pursed his lips in thought. "These sound like very old guns, my son."

"They are, *Jefe*, and that's what makes them the right arms for the Dominicans. No one would miss these guns. The Great War left us, in terms of weaponry, much more advanced instruments and thus, these old machine guns and rifles are simply sitting in a store room rusting in their crates."

"And how do you plan to liberate them to Southern causes?"

Ruiz shrugged. "I broke rocks with these hands, *Jefe*, but I did not break my mouth in the process. There are people with whom I can discuss such matters."

Hernando, intrigued by the simplicity of Ruiz's plan, shrugged and said, "Do you not have an ill mother to attend to in Texas?" Hernando had never heard Ruiz speak of such a mother, but he assumed Ruiz had not simply come into existence alone. Ruiz, sniffing the game in an instant, nodded. "Perhaps you should go and see her before she is in the ground, *hijo*. Take three train cars and buy grain, textiles, and the famous goods of the North of your country. Bring them back with you once you see to your mother."

Ruiz, complicit in his understanding, made preparations to leave the next morning.

The sack containing the silver and gold Hernando had given him lay heavy on Ed Collins' mind. But neither the cattle he planned to buy in Laredo en route to Cowtown for pennies on the dollar nor the silver in his satchel weighed upon him as much as the worry that

Franklin Larington would not be where he had seen him last. Before prison, Ed and Franklin had worked together in the Stockyards, doing odd jobs as boys before becoming strong young men. They knew every inch of every building, depository, and factory floor. Sent on errands as children and apprenticed as teenagers, as young men both Ed and Franklin could do any job on the premises. If Franklin was not where Ed had last seen him, he feared he would only be remembered for his notoriety - for being sent to prison by his father.

The old railcar rumbled along, the passenger car empty save Ed Collins, the cargo car full of braying cattle bought on the dusty ranches of Loredo. Ed watched the country-side slide by his window and rehearsed in his mind the plan he had conceived to exchange the cattle at the stockyards for grain and textiles, and the bag of silver in his satchel to old guns, with Franklin's help. The old storehouse where he had once worked was grimy with inattention, so much so that the men often laughed together and took the old guns from their rusty crates, wiping straw and sawdust from their chambers, unsure that they would even shoot straight.

He and Franklin marveled at the complexity in the old weapons and agreed – it was a pity they were so neglected. Such guns as these had always captured the imaginations of boys, riding imaginary horses over rough terrain in search of Injuns or Mexicans.

Ed had brought the scope of a Mauser up to his eye and commented to his friend - they should be liberated. Franklin couldn't think who would want them but Ed was adamant; guns that could still shoot a man down would find a likely buyer. His friend was not convinced – after all, what with the guns now made, such relics would surely not hold their own against them. Who would want one of these old guns when the Army had such superior weaponry?

Ed Collins had the answer, and having it, Ed's inner demons took again the shape and tenor of his father's voice. "You'll never amount to nothing if you don't know what's right in front of you, Ebner. Remember that a man is only as good as his word, and his word is only as good as the last time he used it."

The old judge did not speak often, and was thoughtful in his pronouncements. He shook his head at his son's curiosity of the world and preached diligence, piety, and honesty in the face of all things. "A good man is one who puts his head down and works toward his goals, Ebner. A soft man with woman's ways asks 'Why?' but a good man is too busy engaged in his work to wonder."

Ed had always wondered, and it was this precise character flaw that irritated the old judge so much.

"Why? Why? Who cares why, son! Let things be as they stand and get on with your schooling!" Judge Collins had shouted when his son was still in short pants. The judge had taken to going over the boy's arithmetic when the teachers had complained that his son was guessing at the answers.

"Why do two and five make seven? Because they just do," Judge Collins had said, irritated. He rapped the boy firmly on the head. "Learn the facts, son, and leave the why to those of them that need not work for their bread." Ed had not forgotten that lesson, though many years had passed.

His father, still an acting judge in the county that bore his family name, was not a patient man, nor a forgiving one. When Ed had been brought before him for stealing legal documents and falsifying them, his father had given him the harshest penalty the law allowed.

"Selling land claims, Ebner?" Judge Collins huffed after the hearing. Behind the iron bars of the county cell, Ed hung his head in misery. "Let's see here – I bet you were offering some New York dandy lakefront property in Beaumont." Ed said nothing. "No? Alright, oil land above pipe lines?" Judge Collins shook his head in disgust. "You didn't even copy the seal in its entirety, Ebner. Shoddy, hasty, illegal. What son is this I have produced?" The judge turned his back. "I hope five years of hard time will teach you a thing or two, son. A thing or two."

It had, but perhaps not the lessons his father was hoping he would ingest. Ed Collins learned to speak Spanish from a few of the other inmates, having themselves learned scouting during the war and having lived among the Mexicans of Texas. He learned how to falsify documents correctly, the proper handling of explosives and when to shut his mouth and open his ears.

When the train finally rumbled into the stockyards, Ed was calm, alert, and fixed on his plan. He was resolute that he would transact his business and find Franklin in the span of two days, not more, and successful, be on his way before anyone had anything else to say on the matter.

"Well look what the Conductor dragged by my door. Lordy, it's Ebner Collins."

Ed gripped Franklin's hand firmly and pulled him close. "I have something I think you're going to want to hear."

They went to Franklin's office above the main gate as Ed's head turned in admiration.

"Head spiker," Franklin explained. "After the war they needed men who knew what the place was on about, so despite my many reservations and dismal failings, they placed me in the position."

Ed laughed and thumped the hard-bound leather chair in front of Franklin's massive oak desk. "Like letting the fox run the henhouse, ain't it?"

Franklin pulled out a bottle of Kentucky Bourbon. "That's the joke round these parts, Ed. So, what's the deal?" he asked. "Where you been; what you got for me to hear?"

"I've come into some money," Ed replied. "A lot of money. And I need those old crates of guns in the secondary store room below the main depository."

Franklin drank from his glass. "How much money?"

"Pure silver in fresh mint, untraceable, and gold still in nugget form."

"Nuggets? Haven't heard that in twenty years!"

Ed gulped down his drink and pushed his chair back. "But this nefarious ordeal needs to be concluded before the sun goes down, Franklin, and I need to be on that train unloaded of my cattle."

Franklin pursed his lips and poured himself another whiskey. "Then we best be telling those monkey workers down the stairs there that you need a hand with your cattle," he said and drained his glass. Franklin replaced the bottle in the desk drawer. He turned the key and stretched. "What a fine surprise you are to me, Ebner," he said, "Just when I thought you were off with the mermaids you come back here and offer me a fortune."

The cattle were unloaded and exchanged for gingham bolts, New York buttons, Wisconsin cheese wheels, and north pine lumber; the crates of guns nestled amid the disarray. Silk could not be procured, but a shipment of Kentucky Bourbon had been located and the men had come to the understanding that the sack containing Hernando's minerals was sufficient to liberate both the Bourbon and the old crates of guns.

Franklin Larington and Ebner Collins struck a quick handshake and parted ways.

"When we be seeing you in these old parts again, Ed?"

"Oh, I'm sure we'll find some ways or others to come up this way from Old Mexico."

Franklin guffawed into his fist and thumped Ed's back. "Doozy of a story, Ed. You break rocks and learn to speak that Spanish; you go down South and what do you know? You run into a man with a gold mine. As I live and breathe - an actual gold mine."

"And trains."

"And he's got trains." Franklin wiped his eyes with his handkerchief. "Well, you let me know if I can help you with anything else, you old con."

Ed clambered aboard the passenger car, "Always a pleasure, Franklin," he called and raised his hand in a final gesture.

When the train rumbled into Mexico City two days later, a team of three men came to meet him at the station. They did not speak, but handed Ed Collins a small, heavy suitcase and loaded the crates onto a wagon teamed by a pair of broken mules. He peeked inside before the men had finished their work and saw what he had given Franklin Larrington had miraculously multiplied like some kind of biblical parable. He silently thanked his father for sending him to prison and re-boarded Hernando's train.

When he arrived in the miner's camp two hours south of Oaxaca City, Jorge Ruiz jumped from the train and threw the heavy bundle to his employer.

"Have you brought me rocks, *hijo*?" Hernando asked.

"No, *Jefe*, I bring you the future."

Ruiz supervised the unloading of his American wares and went to his room to sleep a sound slumber, now assured of Hernando's trust in his abilities.

Thus, having proved his skill and usefulness (and the economy of his pocket by saving his wages and indulging on neither women nor drink as did some of the other men), Ruiz set himself the task of being introduced to Hernando's family.

"*Jefe*," he said casually the day after he arrived back at the camp, "Is there some way to wire a portion of my earnings to my beloved mother? As you remember, she is ill and the money I have made will help her pay her doctor." Ruiz's mother had died many years before, but he knew the only way to wire money was from a main bank – the closest being in Oaxaca City.

Hernando was inclined to say, "Yes, *hijo*. But you must go to Oaxaca City for such a transaction."

"Well, *Jefe*, it is alright then. I will go myself when it is convenient."

"Let us not stand on ceremony, Jorge! You will come with me on Saturday to the bank and church with my family on Sunday." Hernando, perhaps thinking of his first wife fondly then added, "I know Mexico can be difficult, socially, for outsiders. You will dine with us on Sunday. I extend to you the invitation."

Ruiz, relieved his plans were finally coming to fruition, smiled beautifully.

When Portensia Montelejos was told (by cable, no less) of her husband's intention to bring a man from the mines home for dinner, her natural inclinations toward caution were instantly summoned. Having never entertained a solitary man from her husband's company, the social protocols in the situation were unknown to her. Even if she had had friends, she would not have asked their opinions, but simply acted from her own repertoire of experience and natural judgment. After two days of pondering, she decided that yes, the Sunday dinner would be held as was their custom, but it would be a formal meal, and Gloria and Teresa - having come out to Society the previous year - would be heavily veiled. After all, this man might mistake himself for a worthy suitor, a state of being only Portensia herself could bestow.

The wearing of veils by unmarried maidens, she reflected, was not an unusual custom, having come to Mexico from Spain with their ancestors and the whims of fashion – veiled hats, after all, had always been a woman's comfort. Her own Mama had even used a veil during her mourning period – though on Mariabella it looked more like one of Salome's veils than a widow's weeds.

Jorge Ruiz then arrived at the house in Oaxaca City in his new suit, which had been washed and pressed early that same morning by the staff at the Grand Hotel in the Zocalo. His business the day before in the foyer of the First National Bank of Mexico had gone smoothly.

"Give me the account details, *hijo*, and I will see to your money," Hernando had said.

Jorge gave him the details, a ghost account he had set up in Kansas many years before.

"*Ja*," Hernando said when he returned from the bank manager's office, "I hope you send your beloved mother a telegram to inform her of her good son's munificence."

Ruiz assured him that he would.

Now, as he sat in the Vasquez parlor, hat in hand, he awaited the good family's journey in the carriage to the Cathedral.

Down the short staircase, two women appeared, floating and serene. The first, straight as a pin and about as thin, went directly to the chase lounge opposite him and settled there. The second, shorter, plumper and struggling to place her feet where she would not stumble, being blinded by the heavy veil, sat beside the other and took her hand. Ruiz got to his feet and bowed as Portensia entered the room.

"May I present my daughters, Teresa and Gloria."

"The pleasure is mine, good ladies."

The girls nodded gracefully.

Portensia checked her small wristwatch and puckered her lips sourly. "We will be late for Mass. Where is Hernando?"

"I am here, my love," he called from the hallway. "My boots needed polishing." His daughters twittered nervously. Portensia raised her eyes to the crown molding. Ruiz stifled a smile, but caught one of the girls' attention and winked. Beneath her veil, and therefore invisibly, Gloria's eyes narrowed. This man her father had brought home, whose presence necessitated the ridiculous veil and hat combination, was light as sand, spry and curiously rough. Her eyes drifted to the long, tapered fingers holding his hat steadily, neither quivering with nervousness or damp with sweat. Gloria somehow knew that he was also looking at her, naked beneath her clothes, and it was in that moment she decided that one day she would have this man.

The Mass was uneventful, as had been the carriage ride both to and fro. No one spoke – pleasantries were not well received in the Vasquez-Montelejos household. Upon the family's return, lunch was served in the main dining room. Portensia directed her husband to his place at the head, hers at the foot, the man her husband had brought to her left hand and her daughters to her right.

Lamb with *mole poblano* was served silently, and water goblets were filled with *agua fresca con limon*, the bitter lemons sweetened with heaps of sugar. Ruiz, the only one who did not look uncomfortable, ate delicately, watching the girls lift their black veils demurely to place tiny morsels in their hidden mouths.

"You must tell me, Señora Vasquez, of the history of your fine home." Ruiz wiped his mouth and drank a mouthful of the acrid drink.

"There is none," she answered.

"Surely, there is a history, Portensia," exclaimed Hernando. "It is simply that we do not know it."

"Thus there is none," his wife concluded.

"We came here after the Revolution," said Gloria into the silence that followed. "From Mexico City."

"A fine city, Mexico City," Ruiz offered.

"So they say," Gloria responded.

"From where do you come, Señor Ruiz?" Portensia dismissed the servants with a wave of her hand.

"Texas," he lied.

"Strange," Portensia said, "there isn't anything in Texas."

"There are many things in Texas, Señora . Cities, cattle, open land, ranches, trading posts…"

"Prisons," she said, pointedly staring at Ruiz's hands.

Ruiz's mouth, having opened to continue naming the bounties of Texas, did not close. Hernando guffawed and coughed loudly. "Now, Portensia, let us be polite to our guest."

"He is your guest, though he sits at my table."

Ruiz, now recovered, smiled at the taller sister. "Have you been to Texas, Señorita Gloria?"

"Gloria is to be wed," Portensia said coldly, stating facts as only matrons were inclined to do. "Guiermo Fuentes de Solis," she added. "And therefore has no time to view the rustic charm of cattle land."

Gloria, her tongue held by social convention, could not dispute her step-mother – at least not in public.

"Thus congratulations are due, Señorita Gloria."

"I accept them soberly, Señor Ruiz," she answered with a smirk.

"Guiermo Fuentes de Solis is a very lucky man."

Portensia rose suddenly from her seat and declared lunch concluded. "I would offer you coffee in the parlor,

Señor Ruiz, but I feel you and my husband have much business to which you will attend."

The men rose as the ladies withdrew, and Hernando excused himself to the lavatory, half-finished with his lamb *mole poblano*, to wash his hands. Gloria, the last to leave the room, turned swiftly as her father disappeared into the adjoining washroom and lifted her veil from her face. "I might one day be a rich man's wife," she whispered to Jorge, "but that doesn't mean I'll become a nun."

He smiled. "I will remember that, Señorita."

Gloria stalked out as Hernando reappeared, wiping his hands on the linen napkin to continue on his portion of lamb.

"Your daughters are charming, *Jefe*."

"Ay," Hernando sighed. "They can be, *hijo*. But that Gloria – ay. She is the daughter of my *carinada* first wife, Evelyn, who sadly passed when Gloria was but a babe." He wiped his mustached mouth with the linen napkin on his lap. "She is a good girl, but a difficult one."

Ruiz, treading lightly, let a moment pass and then asked, "Will she marry this Guiermo Fuentes de Solis?"

"If Portensia Montelejos has decided she shall, she shall."

"If you don't mind my saying so, *Jefe*, perhaps that is best."

"Why would you say such a thing, *hijo*? The Fuentes de Solis are all stuck up so high in the air one day they will become swallows."

"Yes, but *Jefe* - clearly, Señor Fuentes de Solis is a man of good repute. With an illustrious name such as his, he will be able to provide your daughter with the most comfortable life."

"That might be true," Hernando replied sadly, "but what is a comfortable life without love?"

"Surely love will grow. From beauty to devotion to love, such is the ladder upon which man might climb."

Hernando guffawed and blew his nose on the napkin. "This is all very well. If Portensia has decided Gloria will marry Guiermo, it is done. But it is not Gloria for whom I worry. It is Teresa."

"Yes, certainly she is the sweeter blossom, and must be more guardedly cared for."

"It is not the ridged dictates of Society that so concern me with Teresa, nor guarding her blossom, *hijo*." They shared a hearty laugh and settled back upon the creaky gilded chairs. "It is that a man must be found for her while she is still young. For, though you may not have noticed, Teresa is sickly."

Ruiz, having very well noticed, expressed his surprise and concern.

"Yes, yes," Hernando continued, "She is ill and Portensia is convinced she will forever remain but a child." His voice quivered, "How sad a fate for a woman – to remain all her days in her mother's house, a child, without her own family to care for."

"But why must she remain in her mother's house?"

"Ay," sighed Hernando melodramatically, "What man will have a wife who is sickly? In our circle, Teresa is not even considered amongst the best families, and although she came out to Society, she will remain here with us for lack of suitors. That is my belief."

"If a man were found who was a good man, a hard-working man, but perhaps not the man your wife would have chosen for her – would you accept his proposal?"

"It remains to be seen, my son."

It was in these melancholy states that Ruiz consoled his employer, elevating Teresa's natural sweetness and youth to such a pedestal of desirability, that where once Hernando had only seen timidity and childishness, he began to admire her lack of conceit.

"I always thought her a little empty-headed," Hernando said to Ruiz on one such occasion.

They watched the smoke from a distant blast. "Empty-headed?" Ruiz had said, with a show of disbelief. "That is only her demure good-breeding, *Jefe*."

"But she never has an opinion."

"All the better to learn a matron's ways, as a valuable extension of her husband's household. As the good book says, "And the LORD God said, 'It is not good that the man should be alone; I will make him a helper suitable for him.'"

Hernando, his eyes opened to the once-invisible charms of his youngest daughter, asked Gloria to take Teresa to the dressmakers, for Ruiz had made it very clear - a child she was certainly no longer.

When Ruiz came courting for their youngest daughter, Portensia had laughed in his face.

"You are mad," she had said, "if you think this girl will make you a decent wife."

"I am not mad, Señora," the man replied. "I am certain she is exactly what I need."

Portensia snorted in derision. "Does a man not want children, a clean house, a healthy wife?"

"Excuse my impertinence, Señora, but sometimes all a man wants is a companion to care for."

This woman who would never declare herself his mother-in-law leaned closer to him that anyone had yet dared in that genteel country, "I don't believe you," she said quietly. "I think you are a liar."

"Will you let your husband decide?" he asked with equal composure and deadly calm.

"Do not speak to me of my husband – this is a woman's realm. I will not allow it," Portensia had said sternly, repulsed by his tone of voice – so alike in tenacity to her own.

That night Hernando had argued more strenuously than he ever had with Portensia Montelejos.

"What could that man want with our daughter?" she had spat when he came to convince her of Teresa's happiness, that she be allowed to become a woman.

"He wants to be a part of this family, to care for our daughter."

"This is folly – stupidity. Even a monkey could see through that pretentious ass of a man."

"He is an ass because he is a handsome man?"

"Ay, Hernando, he is an ass because no one but a womanizer cares to have the sick wife of a prominent family."

Hernando pleaded with her to reconsider the man's motives, but Portensia Montelejos knew the truth more than anyone else would admit. She looked at Jorge Ruiz and saw a cheat, a charlatan, and worse – the death of her precious child. For though she treated Teresa to a cold distance, Portensia loved her only daughter. Advised never to conceive, she had thought this child would shorten her life – but she bore her without complaint. And now this man, this American in fancy dress, wanted to take that child away.

"Let yourself be duped," she told her husband, "but I shall never be deceived by the devil in a silk suit."

They sat side by side in the parlor on Sundays, Jorge Ruiz and Teresa Montelejos, on the ancient brocade divan bought by Portensia many years ago.

"How are you feeling today, Señorita Montelejos?" Jorge would ask.

"I am well, thank you, Señor Ruiz," she would answer.

They spoke only in these generic pleasantries until Gloria, who had been appointed by her father as their chaperone, would embark upon a change of topic.

"I find it dull in Oaxaca City," she said one Sunday.

"How can you say that, sister? It is full of loveliness."

"Loveliness is dull."

Jorge, having accepted his fate to watch Gloria wed another man, assured Teresa that Oaxaca City was indeed lovely, but winked at Gloria agreeably while the words still lingered in his mouth. "Have your families set a date for your wedding, Señorita Gloria?"

"Yes, the month after this one."

"That is not so far away. You must be very excited."

Gloria crossed her arms and incanted a spell in her mind before saying, "I am to be the second wife of an old man, Señor Ruiz. Did you not know?"

"I had been told Señor Fuentes de Solis is a widower, this is certain."

"Had you been told I am a full twenty years his junior?"

"I believe I had that knowledge at hand."

"Then you must also be aware it is my sacred duty to carry his offspring."

"I assumed that was the case."

Disgusted, she spat out, "I don't even like babies. They smell of vomit and shit."

Teresa, wide-eyed and certain this was no way to entertain a suitor, softly chided her.

"Don't tell me to hush," Gloria continued, "We'll all be family soon anyway, so why hide the facts of the matter?"

Teresa blushed, her dream of marriage to the elegant Jorge Ruiz still a mirage in the desert.

"That is true, Teresa," Ruiz took the opportunity to hold her hand, "One day you will have sacred duties of your own."

Blushing still harder, Teresa hid her face and fled the room. Gloria watched her go and then took a cigarette out of the pocket of her summer dress. "She'll go straight to Maria Eugenia," she told him, "and cry, but be glad at the same time." Her golden lighter clicked loudly, and she inhaled the sweet fumes. "She loves all that *mierda*. Babies, Church, socials, public dances - any chance to wear a costume or cuddle something." Gloria snorted, "Teresa thinks she is a woman when, really, she is nothing more than a baby herself."

"She will learn, don't you think?"

Gloria leaned forward and blew smoke at Jorge. "I think her reins must be tightly held."

"Meaning?"

"My meaning is simply that the little girl doesn't know one thing about men - pleasing one or keeping one."

"Do you?"

"How dare you ask me such a thing?" Gloria stood to stub out her cigarette in a crystal ashtray on the table beside Ruiz. She turned to him and laid a hand on his lapel to smooth its fine fabric. "Either you are an idiot, or you are baiting me." She grabbed the lapel more forcefully than he anticipated. "And while I abhor idiots, I could certainly do with a little baiting."

He grabbed her wrist from his lapel and yanked her down upon his lap. "There would be nothing more pleasing to me than baiting you," he said, "But let us be frank. You will be wed in one month's time, and your sister and I will follow in six." She grimaced, squirming delightfully upon his lap. "Thus, let us make arrangements now so as to not lose time in the tumult such ceremonies can create. I own an apartment in Volcanes, do you know it?" Gloria nodded vigorously. "I will await you there later tonight. Will you come?"

"In my best corset," she said, freeing herself from his hard embrace. "So we are decided? You will marry my sister and live your best moments in my bed alone?"

Jorge Ruiz smiled and shrugged. "I have sacred duties, sister-in-law. I must give her children. Is that not what the Church commands?"

Gloria returned his smile with a poisonous smirk. "Copulation need not be pleasant," she said. "And with Teresa, it will be like lovemaking to a fish. I've taught her the proper way myself."

Ruiz bit his lip so as not to laugh loudly enough to startle the maids in the next room. "I'm sure you taught your sister her wifely duties well – will she simply lie still and gaze at the ceiling demurely?"

"You can count on it."

"If you marry this man, *hija*, you are not my daughter." Portensia Montelejos raised her finger in the air signaling an oath to God. "He will make your life a hell, and if you do this I will not lift one finger to save you — though you go in rags begging in the streets."

Teresa rolled her eyes. "How you exaggerate, Mama."

Portensia breathed through her nose, willing herself calm. Her daughter's suitor, some American dandy in an expensive suit, waited on the other side of the door: waited to take her only child away.

"He is a good man, Mama."

"Are you blind, girl? That man has philandering written all over his ingratiating face. This I expect from your father's daughter, but from you? *Dios mio*, can you not see the truth?"

Teresa took her mother's hand in hers. "Gloria's husband is also a good man, Mama. Jorge loves me and will care for me."

Portensia shook herself from her daughter's grip. "*Ay, Teresita*. Don't you see that no man will care for an ill wife? He only cares for you for his social standing, to be able to say: I am a Montelejos. With your name he will prosper and you will be alone with only your tears each night. You have been listening to your sister's lies."

"You are wrong, Mama. He will be a good husband to me."

"He isn't even a Catholic!"

"He converted."

Portensia clenched her teeth, and felt her heart flutter within her breast. "Will you not be convinced of the folly of your dreams, Teresa? To live this long as a child in your mother's house without the corruption of man – will you not heed my warnings?"

"Papa has agreed to the match, Mama," Teresa said firmly. "And while you have always said marriage was a woman's domain, the law disagrees with you. I will wed Jorge, and he will take care of me." Teresa's voice softened, "Just as well as you took care of me," she said.

Portensia, retreated to the window, saddened by her daughter's eyes so full of hopes, dreams, fantasies and blindness, turned to raise her finger into the air once again. "Teresa, I am a woman of my word. I saved your sister, two women, a newborn and myself from the Revolution. I bought this house with my mother's jewels and made it our home. I gave you life although it took some of my own. I made a pact with God that should he allow you to live that life I would praise his Name each day of mine." Her hand fell to her side, and her face aged ten years in a moment. "But *hija*, if you marry this man, you do so alone. You will be as though a motherless orphan who must rely on the charity of strangers and distant family relations. You will be set adrift in the sea of the Unknown, and I will not be there to help you, for if you set yourself upon this course – I will leave you to your fate."

Emboldened by the words of her sister, the yearning for a man's touch, and the recklessness of youth, Teresa stepped toward her mother, kissed her cheek, and walked out of that house forever.

Within the month, Gloria Vasquez and Guiermo Fuentes de Solis were married. On the wedding day, twelve-year-old girls were crowned with fruit to dance in the courtyard of Santo Domingo behind huge paper mache puppets - always the same, from the only puppet shop in town. The massive round heads of a man and woman were balanced by sweating men, skipping and panting beneath the native ritual of strenuous dance. There was a globe, covered in the newlyweds' names, which spun beside the huge, indigenously dressed heads. It swirled, and the men beneath the heads sweat. The globe spun, the girls shuffled their feet and the crowd of mingled friends and family sang and posed for photos in the hot sun.

The wedding Mass was the usual length, and only rivaled by the time it took the bride's impossibly long train to arrive at the altar. The Mass was open to all who would come, to those dressed in their best finery to witness a miracle – the union of two families older than the Republic itself. Candles shone from the Mass into the staring faces that framed the two-story wooden doors. Invitations, having arrived at the most exclusive homes in the city two months before, written in gold lettering, contained the coveted ticket of entry to the reception, perfumed by the latest scent from Paris. A small fortune was spent on the celebration; the champagne flowed until someone's Tio had been picked up off the floor for the fourth time.

When Teresa followed her sister to the altar six months later, the puppets were not hired – no one danced or panted beneath neither giant heads nor globes. Portensia would not release the funds necessary for such a celebration – one she denied until the hour it occurred. Hernando paid for a small dinner at a nearby hall, but no one coveted the invitation, and merely came out of pity and social obligation. To be married in the Catholic Church was free to all its children; Ruiz only had to convert to its doctrine to attend as the groom.

The bride wore a simple white gown, unknowingly the height of fashion further to the North, but shockingly plain from the perspective of high Oaxacan society. There were no lace or beads upon Teresa's dress, no overflowing train or ruched bodice. But her face, alight with pride, fear, joy, and determination was more fitting decor than pearls and diamonds. Hernando wept with relief when Teresa entered the Church alone, to meet Jorge Ruiz and stand with him before the priest. Her sister had taken ill the night before unexpectedly, discovering she lacked the stomach to see her lover wed her sister.

Having taken Jorge as her lover, Gloria knew it was only time that prevented Teresa from finding out the true nature of her husband. It was Gloria's hope that Teresa would be dead and cut through by worms before she knew — Jorge was the dirtiest, most clever lover Gloria had ever possessed. He could do things with his hands alone that made her squeal with wet delight. They made love frantically, with sweet cruelty, tit for tat - for while she would pinch his nipple tightly or bite him with sharp teeth, he would pull out small tufts of her dark nest of hair, or lightly slap her face.

Jorge liked her to dress in the furs and diamonds her husband gave her and would throw her to the ground in mock disgust at her infantile ways only for the game to begin anew. In Gloria's eyes, Guiermo was only equal to that ox of a half-sister of hers and could not even ask to be allowed into her bedroom. She mixed roots and poison into his soup to keep his docility fixed, but never realized that Guiermo did not trust his wife enough to eat the food prepared by her hands alone. Always the Spanish gentleman, Guiermo grew more silent with each passing day – Gloria did not suspect that he had his own ways of retaining his youth.

Ruiz would come, laughing and demanding Gloria's sardonic comments and cocktails but stayed for the rough coddling and spanking, which she awaited in trembling anticipation. They behaved as their fantasies dictated, for neither had married for love but money and admiration. They could never have married each other.

"Our sins die with us — no thief will take us in the night," Jorge once told her. "We will outlive them all."

Gloria laid her head upon her outstretched arm, dressed in the meticulous style befitting a Vasquez: fox furs, diamonds, and pearls by the handful, and asked, "Don't you ever feel sorry for her?"

"Never," he replied. "I hope she rots in hell's bile."

"What did she ever do to you?" Gloria asked as Ruiz lit her cigarette, the golden holder glittering reflective fire. He did not answer readily.

"They are a hateful people, your Mexicans," he said at length.

She gave a throaty laugh. "And you are the balloon seller."

"He is the worst — and a charlatan besides." He pinched her cheek and she blew smoke in his face.

"I tire of you, old man."

Jorge sat against the pillows and contemplated his sister-in-law. Then he smirked and stroked a bare nipple, the tender pink belying the mettle of the mistress.

"I was nothing before I came here," he began to say and stopped, expecting a barbarous retort. Gloria's eyes were closed, however, intent on his stroking finger upon her breast. "Nothing," he continued, "Until I met your father." Jorge's eyes glazed over as he envisioned himself not ten years before, penniless, hungry, an American convict newly freed — despised and unable to find even menial work. "He gave me a new name. I carry it still."

"You are a fool to take anything but money from my father." Her eyes opened to a slit, "Especially his daughter."

"But he has many good stories, you must admit." She shrugged. "One particularly. That your father's name is not Hernando as you thought but Ernesto. Hernando is a long dead cousin who died for the Glorious Revolution."

Gloria sat up and slapped his hand away.

"Or something convoluted like that – I couldn't keep it straight," Jorge continued, "No one is who they say they are. The players changed before you were old enough to milk a cat." He brought his lips down upon her breast and bit down lightly. "We are all liars in the end," he said.

Standing before the priest, taking his wedding vows, Ruiz remembered having said these things to his lover, who was now his sister-in-law – his admission of hatred for Teresa's dough-faced stupidity, her desperation to please him without any knowledge of what a man needs to be pleased, her yearning for him to give her a child without knowing what such an act required, the emptiness of her eyes and thoughts – and he echoed the meaningless words the priest asked of him.

It was nine months from the week of their wedding night when Gloria birthed her first child - a son, the spitting image of his father, Guiermo. It had been a difficult pregnancy for everyone but the mother. Gloria's rages found themselves excused, allowed to erupt in both public and private. Banished from her bed when found with child, Guiermo, having prayed for the son he had always wanted, afraid childbirth would kill his second wife as it had his first, withstood Gloria's treacherous moods and ravenous appetite, the insults and mockery as though her behavior was natural to a woman in such a position. He thought perhaps the child within her would be a fire-eater, a sports man of Spartan proportion, a warrior. When the child was born, docile and blond like his father, his mother wept with disappointment and handed him to the wet nurse beside her.

Guiermo was overjoyed with his son. He denied him nothing and was only again invited to his wife's bedroom when she was chastised by her mother-in-law. "Surely, you are healed sufficiently from your labors," the good matron said, "to be fruitful once again, and provide this family with another heir."

Gloria, disgusted at the suggestion that she should ripen like fruit, waited until she knew she was fertile, and became pregnant by Guiermo again – and swore it would be the last time. When the babe was born, again fair and docile like his father, Guiermo was never again invited into the bed of his wife. The children were raised by their father and several nannies, Gloria was busy with her own public life in the city and her affair with Jorge Ruiz.

Teresa watched her sister birth her children, turn from them in disgust when they came from her womb, and was greatly saddened – but also hot with jealousy. She would cajole Jorge to stay with her in the evenings, and lay very still as she had been taught while he grunted above her, spilling his seed within her body. Three times she had been with child, merely to miscarry in the first few weeks; three times she had sent her maid to Portensia's door. Three times had Portensia refused her. "Your mother sent Guadalupe with a message for you," the maid had reported. "She says, 'An oath before God is binding.'" Eyes red with weeping, Teresa went to Gloria to beg for her help.

"I can't carry them!" she whined through snot and tears. "What can I do?" she implored Gloria.

"Be thankful," came her sister's reply. "Children are such a bother."

Two steps away, having crept there at the sound of Teresa's sweet voice, the Señor Fuentes de Solis stood eavesdropping behind the heavy wood patio doors, wringing his hands. Several weeks before the family had gone to Mass together as was their custom, and he noticed his sister-in-law's eyes shining with an ethereal quality.

"Sister," he had whispered to her, "You look saintly in your devotion this morning."

"I am with a child!" Teresa had whispered to him excitedly.

"Felicitations!" he had said, having heard the gossip that Teresa had already lost two other children. Worried for the poor girl, so hopeful, so radiant in her happiness he asked the maid about her later – for Gloria did not bother to speak with him about such matters.

"No, Señor , the Señora is no longer with child," the maid told him, peeking over her shoulder should the mistress see her speaking with her husband. "It has come out of her like water from a fountain."

The Señor frowned and nodded that he understood; no more conversation was necessary.

Now, seeing Teresa lost in abject misery, his heart was stirred with pity for her. It was only natural that the girl would want a child. As far as he knew, children were the jewels of their mothers' crowns. He had always believed that his own wife would one day see their sons as rubies - that surely his wife's madness would pass. And now, seeing Teresa's distress, he marveled at the force of it – the sheer insistence through such failure that she should be a mother. Guiermo realized how he admired the tenacity of his sister-in-law, how tender she was to feel so deeply, how brave to persist against such odds.

"What must I do?" Teresa wailed weakly, holding her aching chest with both hands. Gloria saw how blue were her sister's lips, and hoped Teresa would make herself sick enough now for bed rest and leave her to go to Jorge's secret apartment off a side street from the Zocalo. She patted her sister's back, feigning concern.

"Perhaps you should try to carry one last child," Gloria offered.

Teresa hiccupped and wiped her face. "Dr. Sanchez says it will kill me."

"I thought you wanted one," Gloria said coldly.

"I do, sister," Teresa answered. "Do you know another doctor who might help me?"

Gloria did but instead offered, "Have you tried Yoruba root?"

Teresa miserably shook her head.

"Don't you want to try to carry once more?"

Teresa nodded and dried her eyes.

"Drink Yoruba root in your tea at home and then see." Gloria called for a maid. "Go bring me the Yoruba in the pantry," she said. It was brought to her and she took another withered root out of her pocket. She handed them both to Teresa in a sachet, herbs meant to induce romance and fertility. She knew bringing a child to term would kill her sister, but merely smiled as she handed them to Teresa. "If you're sure," Gloria said as her husband, knowing what his wife knew and more, tiptoed away with whatever dignity he could retain.

Guiermo Fuentes de Solis went into his dressing room and shut the door behind him as quietly as possible. He yearned for that sweet girl, so reminiscent of his dead wife. Had Portensia even mentioned her, had he met Teresa first, had she not been ill...Guiermo knew how his advanced age might seem to such a young girl, Gloria had not been so young when he married her, but Teresa, fresh, sad, desirable, soft, was youthful in face, body and mind. His hands trembled just to think of her. His first wife had died in childbirth, along with their son, and listening to Portesia Montelejos yammer at length of her stepdaughter, had agreed to meet the girl. At once, he recognized a caged intelligence and a sharp wit, but it was her beauty that lingered the longest for Guiermo Fuentes de Solis, lonely since the death of his wife. Gloria was not eager to please him, which pleased him, and knew all the social graces he had come to expect from the women of his world. In the beginning, he tried conversing with her only to meet stonewalls. Born wealthy, he naturally assumed this was a woman's way of demanding fine gifts — that she was too finely bred to simply ask for them. He continued making impeccably proper small talk to himself, presenting Gloria with furs and jewels, and yet still he was met with silence.

Would Teresa find him repulsive as Gloria did? Was he repulsive? He studied himself and pulled at his hair, felt his chest, puffed out his cheeks. He felt an old man at fifty-five, but perhaps Teresa would not think so.

Guiermo found her the next day crying in the kitchen. "What is the matter, Tere?" he asked.

"It's Jorge," she wailed. "He has no time for me and my plans are ruined." She sobbed louder and gripped the coffee cup which had only that morning held the root needed for ease in conception. "Where is Gloria? I need more of this root."

The Senior Fuentes de Solis came to her side and embraced her, trying to convey his love for her though the simple touch. Guiermo felt her stiffen slightly and then relax as she nestled her fair, soft hair into his shoulder.

Her tears, hot and plentiful, fell upon his familiar shoulder as she mourned.

"What shall I do, Guiermo?" Teresa whispered, her soft breath upon his ear, a shiver upon his spine.

"I do not know, Tere," he answered.

She pulled away from his embrace and Guiermo could resist no longer. He brought his mouth to hers and when she returned the tenderness, he took her into the bedroom, gingerly laying her upon the bed. Teresa, unused to such ministrations, responded as a flower blooms in spring, and moaned with sheer needfulness. Neither hearing nor seeing, the pair consummated their frustrated desires until each looked into the other's eyes and saw the realities of their situation.

Teresa was the first to jump up and cover herself once the fire in her loins had extinguished itself; her face hot with shame, she escaped her brother-in-law's bed, terrified of what she had done, of what punishment such an action would bring. Unsure of what to do, she hid in the closet of her marital bedroom as a child who steals forbidden sweets and cried tears of remorse.

Guiermo, more ashamed that he could mistake his sister-in-law for his first wife's incarnate form (she having never been as clumsy as Teresa in fulfilling a man's desires) than for the single act of adultery, confessed to the priest the next day.

"I have copulated with the half-sister of my wife," he told the Priest.

"In your heart or with your body?"

"With my body."

"Do you ask the Lord for his forgiveness and foreswear never to again commit the sin of adultery?"

"I do."

The priest assigned his task of penance, which Guiermo completed easily, and then he thought no more about it.

When Teresa was found to be with child one month later, Guiermo thanked the Savior that Jorge Ruiz had finally accomplished his husbandly task, and never questioned the paternity of her child. The child, as far as Guiermo was concerned, was that of Jorge Ruiz. But it was when his own wife was also found again with child that Guiermo knew his task as husband was finished, for he had not been in her bed since Gloria was found to be carrying their second son.

The sisters grew fat together; Teresa radiant with joy, Gloria morose but bearing the child no ill, thinking both she and her sister carried children from the same father.

"What will you name your child?" Teresa mused one day as they sat in the courtyard.

"Jaime," Gloria answered, trying to reconstruct a recipe from memory which Conception (now nearly seventy) had taught her.

Teresa caressed her full belly and said with misty eyes, "Jorge likes the name Paulina." Gloria, preoccupied with the recipe, did not respond. "It seems like the kind of name you don't hear very much, a name you can say sweetly. Paulina. And of course, if it is a boy, we will name him Jorge."

Gloria remembered the recipe (one which brought about the early delivery of babies from their mother's loins) and brought her attention to her sister, mooning about like a cow with calf. "How nice," she said. "I chose Jaime because that was Guiermo's grandfather's name."

"Oh! A family name," Teresa smiled, "how sweet of you to honor your husband so, sister."

Gloria gripped the table and lumbered to her feet. "Yes. Now, if you'll excuse me," she said, "I want to make something in the kitchen."

"But sister," Teresa sat up in her chair, suddenly, "What if you have a girl?"

Gloria only paused for a moment. "I don't have girls, Teresa," she said. "I only birth men."

Jaime Vasques Fuentes de Solis was born three weeks early, small and wizened like a summer apple, and was brought to his father while his mother slept. Guiermo looked at his son and knew it was no son of his, but felt love for him nonetheless. When Gloria, having only labored for an hour, awoke and called for the babe, to the surprise of the entire household, she lovingly caressed his face. "May you be like your father," she whispered to him and kissed the black hair of his head.

Ruiz, overjoyed that his seed had finally manifested itself in living spawn, could hardly keep himself from Gloria's bedside. He came only when the mandates of Society allowed, with his own wife at his side, nearly ready for her labor as well. Teresa held the child upon the table her belly created and innocently remarked, "He looks so much like you, Gloria. Why, I don't see Guiermo in him at all!" Those assembled laughed good-naturedly, for nothing can spoil the peace that is a mother who is pleased with her newborn babe, but Gloria's eyes narrowed imperceptibly. "You can see Guiermo in his mouth," she protested. "See, they have the same mouth."

Yes, yes, it was agreed by all assembled; the child had his father's mouth – although in reality he did not.

"Your time will come, Teresa," Ruiz said to his wife. "Soon we will have another birth to celebrate, yes?"

Teresa, never having felt so singled out, so special, so beloved, smiled contentedly and handed the child back to his mother. "Soon," she said, and rubbed her belly.

Her labor began two days later, when no one was home. As it progressed, Teresa unable to go for help alone – already stressed by her illness, she was barely able to stand for more than five minutes. The pains grew in duration and intensity as she waited for someone to come to her aid – having not the strength to even call out for help. Teresa lay herself down upon the cool tiles of the courtyard, reserving her energy for what was to come, and wondered where her husband was. She breathed deeply, and was completely without fear. It was then in that moment that Teresa suddenly understood the murky details of her cloistered life. Her sister and her husband were adulterers. Jaime was the offspring of her husband as much as her own child was the offspring of Guiermo. She was an adulterer. Teresa was stained with sin and her husband, her sister, and her brother-in-law were damned.

Her mother had been right. She had been duped. The pains subsided, and Teresa managed to get to her feet.

"Maria Eugenia!" she called to her neighbor, panting with the effort, "I need your help!"

This child, Teresa reflected while it slept in her arms, was yet perfect – and, though the world had now become blemished in Teresa's newly opened eyes, this perfect thing, now hers, must be saved from the mire of her family.

She smoothed the newborn's hair, like strands of the finest cobweb and wondered – how long she would live. Who would protect her from Gloria and Jorge when she had quit this world? She had no one without her mother, that lioness had long sworn never to see her, and Maria Eugenia, who had always been an old woman – eternally so she would remain.

"Who will care for my daughter?" she asked herself aloud. The child seemed strong and intelligent – and yet an aura of sadness and depth surrounded the girl. But certainly, no child could be so knowing. Her eyes had not been the blue others had predicted, even for the youngest of children. Never had this child been blind or deaf. Her eyes were open at birth – staring, unblinking, as old as the cycles of wind and rain.

"Who was this creature a sickling girl had birthed?" Teresa asked herself.

The aura surrounding the child, a visible glow, was most strongly seen at the birth itself, and had shocked the midwife who sat between Teresa's legs.

"*Madre Maria!*" the coarse woman had exclaimed, "*Mira!* Look – the child is made of light!"

Teresa had looked down in the midst of her pains and had also seen this light. Was her womb not the darkness from which a blind child had come, the same as all other mothers? The child emerged as Teresa watched – face towards the heavens, her open eyes, deep brown, held questions and riddles Teresa knew she would never answer.

"You will tell no one of these events," she said to the midwife. The people were strange in regard to births. They saw the miraculous in tortillas; surely they would gossip about the child who came from a womb of light.

The midwife, her mouth still slightly opened from shock, nodded her compliance. She knew the people would think of miracles or witchery, either of which would mark the child for life.

Teresa suckled her child herself, to the consternation of both Gloria and polite society. When Ruiz came to look upon the child, he did not see himself in her features. He knew immediately she was not of his seed, and more – that she was not of this world.

"My daughter," he said, holding out his hands for the child.

Teresa shook her head and clutched the babe. "Go back to my sister, Jorge. This child stays in my arms."

"You would deny me my daughter?"

"Look in her eyes, Jorge Ruiz. This is no daughter of yours."

He bent down and looked into the newborn's eyes, and could see no familiar reflection in her large chocolate eyes. They held an intelligence and understanding of the world that he himself had never possessed. And yet, he could not look away from her. It was then that Jorge Ruiz fell in love with his wife's child. He yearned to be accepted by her and allowed to enter the garden behind those enormous glassy eyes. He knew his entire life would be spent in pursuit of her, spent trying to win her love or force its assurance. He was content to stare into those lovely brown eyes until he himself departed the earth, caring not that he lived in the vainest of hopes – that this child would love him.

"*Ja*," he said to Teresa as he tore himself from the baby's gaze, "You are right. That is no child of mine. But woman, listen to my words: In the eyes of God and country, you are my wife; this is my child, and unless you want to find yourself living off the charity of distant relations, you will not reveal this child's paternity to myself or anyone else."

Teresa agreed, and Ruiz went back to Gloria.

Gloria had never wondered how much her sickling sister knew of her affair with Jorge Ruiz. She agreed with prevailing thought that Teresa was an idiot. She could quarrel all day with Jorge, complain about the lack of servants (delightfully funny to Gloria) and dote on that dough-faced baby, but Gloria knew – none of it would ever matter, for none of them was without fault.

She knew Teresa and Jorge argued, but he was always clever to keep the topic to the never ending circle of work, Teresa's faults, and his daughter — who ran from the very sight of him.

It was that Maria Eugenia who made all the trouble. That Maria Eugenia who threatened to take Jorge from her, expose him to the society as a fraudulent, deceitful pretender. Jorge told Gloria about what she had said to him at the Sunday Mass.

"I have a distant relation who says you are a convict," Maria Eugenia had told him. "Truth will out," she promised.

"I will get rid of her," Gloria swore upon hearing this.

"Don't be stupid," he responded. "That woman is a pillar — she and her husband own half of Oaxaca City."

"Then she shall suffer," Gloria promised him.

Gloria could not look at Teresa's white-faced baby without wondering — who is your father? Is his blood thick enough to take away the curse of your mother's illness? The child, as yet, seemed healthy — as though she had escaped the dreaded fate of the Montelejos women. Portensia lived in strict austereness and Teresa would be moldering in her grave soon enough but already Gloria could see this one was stronger than Teresa had been at the same age. Her eyes sparkled, her laughter was boisterous and her legs, while unsteady yet, stepped with assurance. She did not cry when she fell and could easily manipulate knife, fork and spoon at a remarkably early age. Surely, Gloria realized, this child was no fool. She would one day learn her Papa was not the man she already treated with indifference. This little Paulina would know the truth.

Only then could Gloria finally dispense with the Montelejos and take Jorge far from this accursed hell. Let her old fart of a disgusting, coddling baboon of a husband die in a pile of his own feces. It would only be fair. How she longed to see her step-mother Portensia's face when she learned the pair had fled (after first feeding Guiermo a mouthful of his own shit, of course) when it was Portensia who masterminded her entire tortured life. Portensia who had convinced Guiermo — a widower — to remarry, this time "for pleasure" she had said. It was Portensia again who had so strongly objected to Teresa's marriage, and it was Portensia who took her father Hernando away from her.

And, Gloria convinced herself, probably even Portensia who killed her mother Evelyn in jealousy. All her life, Gloria had been sure Portensia had taken her mother away. If she took Jorge, it would only be fair.

Teresa was fawning over the toddler's honey blond curls. When Gloria caught the little girl's eye she smiled slightly and narrowed her eyes; that little girl too would know what it was like to lose her papa, if Gloria had her way. Paulina burst into tears.

"*Ay, bebe, amor* — don't cry!" Teresa apologized to her sister, thinking Paulina was fatigued.

"I understand completely," Gloria answered, and calmly finished her café, drawing magic patterns in the sugar. "Perhaps tomorrow I will bring Jaime," she suggested to her sister.

"Yes," Teresa answered, "he should not spend so much time with his nurse."

Gloria puckered her lips sourly, "He has become too soft for my taste," she said, "He thinks he hears voices."

"Perhaps he does, sister."

"Perhaps he has a rotten brain." Or perhaps, Gloria thought, he is being tainted by your own brat.

Teresa stroked Paulina's hair absentmindedly and shook her head. "I do not think he is rotten, Gloria. I think he is imaginative."

Gloria did not like this new mother her sister had become. She argued more, she held herself with new confidence – and though Gloria was still sure Teresa was an idiot, she was now an idiot who spoke her idiot mind.

"Perhaps," she responded. "But I do not encourage him to speak with me about his imaginings. I wish he would grow out of them with more rapidity than he has since displayed."

"He is but three years old, Gloria."

"I was four years old when we left our home in Coyoacan. If my childhood could end at that time, certainly his is too prolonged."

Teresa, shamed at this mention of her mother's famous cruelty, the flight they had made from their homes outside Mexico City during the Revolution, the death of Gloria's mother Evelyn, ashamed that she could not even defend her mother, was silent.

"I catch him speaking to these voices in the trees," Gloria continued, smug at having caused her sister's silence, for although the past no longer pained her, she found it still pained Teresa - for what reasons she did not care to ascertain. Teresa had been but an afterthought of her father and that usurper step-mother – that she should feel any guilt at all Gloria thought moronic.

"He says they are birds to which he speaks, but I know he is speaking to himself." She grunted and rubbed a delicate fingertip against a large pearl ring to feel its creamy coldness. "A strange child."

Teresa had looked down at Paulina, who seemed to be listening to her aunt with skepticism and worse – disdain. She handed the child a sugar cookie. "Perhaps you are too harsh with him."

Gloria smirked at her sister. How else will he lose that infernal piety, that hateful love of Mass, that purity which shone from his eyes unabated – to have such a son come from Jorge's loins, such joyfully cruel origins; how could she bear it? She could not see her beloved Jorge in Jaime. She could only see her sister's goodness there, and she found this insufferable.

"He must become a son to be proud of, not a weakling," she told Teresa. "He must learn to become a man."

"I must go home. Jorge expects me there."

Gloria smirked and anticipated a very long wait for her sister to enjoy her dinner; she and Jorge had arranged to meet that evening.

Four days later, Teresa Montelejos laughed unsmilingly and posed for Jorge's new camera. "I will need one for Maria Eugenia," she said, setting Paulina back on the living room floor.

"Yes, of course," her husband replied, rummaging in the drawers for the old lens cap. "You always want to include that old woman in everything," he said.

"You'd even deny me my friends," Teresa said, shaking her head and rising from the sofa, her housedress a formal brown. "How dare you, Jorge. I have so little pleasure. What a selfish man you are."

Jorge Ruiz bent over to pick his daughter up off the floor.

"Don't exaggerate, Teresa," he said, squeezing the girl too hard, trying to make himself comfortable with Paulina in his arms. "I was kidding. *Fue una broma*, woman, a joke. Lighten up."

"*Mierda*," Teresa said, "and put *la niña* down, you will hurt the child again, and that I cannot stand for."

Ruiz tucked the little girl under his arm like a football, her white-fringed dress flattened like a misfortunate tutu. "I have never hurt this child. She is my life, *mi vida* itself."

Teresa snorted. "She's terrified of you and you know that. Put her down before I get angry with you, *Naco*."

Jorge did as he was told. Teresa's anger was not something he enjoyed dealing with. "You are too controlling," he said, watching Paulina walk on steady legs to the bottom of the staircase. "But let us not fight." He made his voice soothing and placed a finger on his wife's chiffoned hair. "Take the child to that old woman and let us go upstairs."

"So that you can put me in one of those hideous dresses and pretend I am also your servant in our own bedroom?" She scoffed. "No, I will be the servant of your house, but not in my own bed."

"I did not intend that, Teresa!"

But she shook off her husband's heavy, twitching hand. "For the last time," she said, and rising to her full height she spoke each word separately, "Wear those dresses yourself." And she walked into the kitchen to start their dinner.

"Jorge, I cannot do all this work. It is too much," Teresa said later that week.

"Ay, Teresa," Ruiz murmured, resting himself on the sofa, "Can we fight about this later? I have a very hard day ahead of me."

"And not I?" Teresa's eyes burned at her husband. "I cannot relax. I cannot put my feet on the sofa, for when you get up, I must beat your dust off it!"

Ruiz got up stiffly. "I will not have strange people in my home, Teresa! In *Los Estados Unidos* the women do their own work, you can do yours."

Paulina peeked over at them from the stairs, her eyes as dark as the hallway where she dropped her doll.

"Ay, Jorge. This is not, will never be, your *Estados Unidos*. We are not that way. We have much work. I need a servant. The *bebe*, the cooking, the cleaning. I grind and sweat and bend. It is too much. You have me here like an *indio*. It is disgraceful."

"No," Ruiz said simply, and started to climb the stairs, calling out Paulina's name. "*Mi amor*, where are you? Your Papa is leaving."

"You do that to anger me," Teresa called from below. "You do not speak with her unless I yell at you, Papa," she said with an ugly sneer. "And she does not know you!" as Ruiz looked around the upper floor her voice followed him.

"You are no one's papa!"

"*Que vayas al diablo!*" he finally yelled back, angry that he could not find his tiny daughter, angry that she hid from his footsteps, angry that his wife was right. "Go to hell!" he screamed, frustrated. He tripped in the dark hallway and cursed. His face turned red. He looked down to see Paulina's doll on the floor and bent to pick it up, intending to rip off its boxed shirt and skirt when Paulina peeked out from the corner bath.

"*Venga, mi vida*," he softly said, calling his daughter like a dog, forgetting the doll. "*Venga*," he said soothingly. "We will not fight anymore, I promise you." Paulina finally tiptoed closer and let herself be swung up into his arms.

"Make your own breakfast," Teresa shouted beneath them, wrapping her shawl as Oaxacenias do, flipping each side deftly over the opposite shoulder.

Paulina wriggled, knowing her mother was about to slam the door behind her for the night to see her friend Maria Eugenia, the woman with soft hands who smelt so good, like sweet onions and fried peppers.

"Hold still!" Ruiz shouted as Paulina managed to break free and tumble down the wide staircase calling in a voice larger than anyone would have thought, "Mama! Mama, Mama, Mama!"

Teresa caught her daughter in her arms and gave Jorge Ruiz a final withering look. "You are no Papa," she said quietly and slammed the door as hard as she was able.

"I do not know what to do, Maria. This thing with Jorge and my sister – it is a sin."

Maria Eugenia poured her friend a cup of coffee with cacao. "Yes, this is true. And while not one of us has not sinned, some of us have sinned more than necessary, yes?"

Paulina and Jaime squatted together at the edge of Maria Eugenia's courtyard, plucking weeds from her potted plants, whispering like conspirators.

"They play together well, do they not?" Teresa smiled at the children who fell silent under her gaze. "They are like twins, do you see?"

Maria Eugenia did in fact see – and wondered at the coincidence. Two children who only shared one grandfather should not look so alike in countenance and yet their movements mimicked each other like two sides of a coin, their features moved like two fish in a stream.

Teresa glanced at the grandfather clock in Maria Eugenia's living room through the open door. "*Ay*, Maria! Is that the time?" She hurriedly drank her coffee and ran to scoop Paulina up in her arms. "I am late – Jorge will come demanding his lunch and I have yet to make it."

Maria Eugenia held the heavy door for her and clucked her tongue. "Teresa, why do you not yet have a servant? Not even one? This is Mexico, *Teresita*! Who doesn't have even one servant?"

"Ja, Ja, *Mai Te*, I know. I will speak with him about that again soon. But now I am late." She kissed Maria's cheek and ran, breathless and clutching the child to her aching chest, to her own home.

Teresa had learned to make *tamales, tortas, chiles reyenos, sopa caldado,* roasted leg of lamb and sauté a chicken. She learned the tricks of the marketplace and how to choose the best fruits. The woman she had become when her daughter came into the light had learned to argue and defend, bicker and cook. She did not like to clean, but again, who liked to clean? Even the servants of her mother's house would procrastinate in their duties if Portensia had not watched them so closely.

Her child, a constant reminder at her side of Guiermo Fuentes de Solis, chattered nonsense to her imaginary friends and passing ghosts, or played with her toys in the courtyard. Teresa had learned to listen to her heart when it could bear no more strain, and did not venture far from her home. But a damaged heart is like a ticking clock and would wind down soon enough, although no one is ever ready when it does.

She was grinding corn in the kitchen when a sudden pain, like a sickle slides through stalks, pierced her. She stumbled into the courtyard as Paulina jumped to her feet, her doll lying on the stones, forgotten. "Come, *mi'ja*," Teresa gasped as the child ran to her side. Her mother's blue lips trembled as the little girl helped her lie down at the foot of the staircase. "I want to hold you one last time," she caressed the little girl's face and kissed her as tears fell down Paulina's face.

"Shall I run for the doctor?" the little girl asked her Mama.

"No, sit with me a while," her mother answered, shallow breaths to mitigate the pain. "*Mi hija querida*," she said softly, "Do not be afraid. This body will soon be gone, but I will be with you always. Remember me with your heart and know – one day I will return for you." Teresa cried out as her heart shuddered; its agony at leaving her daughter alone in such a dark world was more than it could bear.

The little girl held her mother tightly until the heat of her body began to grow faint. "Go, now," Teresa whispered. "Go tell Maria Eugenia."

"Teresa loved you very much, *mi'ja*," the man said to Paulina, looking down into the casket at his wife, dressed in a white satin gown, as if she were to be christened later in the day. "*Te digo*," he continued, "I tell you, I never knew your mother. I will never know your mother. Even from the grave she does not smile for me, *mi vida*. She only smiles for you."

Paulina looked up at the man, unblinkingly and still. She knew he was an important man in the city, but being so small, did not know many things about him. Attentive, always attentive for this man, she listened but did not understand. The man was her father, but such an important father that Paulina rarely saw him. Señor Ruiz sighed and gripped his daughter's shoulder, the black strap of her dress slippery but dry.

"The sundress should not be funeral attire," the old women had told him.

"But she looks so lovely in sundresses, leave it alone," he said. "Just make it; it's none of your business."

Ruiz wanted to dress his wife in the traditional Oaxacan costume for her burial, but the colors were so bright, their embroidered flowers mixing fuchsias, oranges, purples, and yellows, he feared Teresa would not have approved.

"You want me to be your Frida," she had said when he brought them to her as gifts.

"You are from Oaxaca, aren't you proud?"

"Yes, of course," she would say, "and where are your spurs and hat? Aren't you proud?"

"Fine. Don't wear them."

Paulina wore anything that was put in front of her then. She was not only obedient toward her father, but to anyone she had ever met, whether they spoke to her or not.

"Do you want to kiss her goodbye, Paulina?" Señor Ruiz lifted her over her dead mother. "Kiss her goodbye, *cielo*. She is going to God now." Paulina kissed Maria Teresa Montelejos de Ruiz slowly. Lowering her neck deliberately and softly, she kissed her mother's lips, only to fulfill her father's wish that she do so.

He set her down on the cold marble floor of Santo Domingo, her leather sandals kissing the stone as passively as she had kissed her mother. The large funeral gathering continued its prayers, dusty Mexican voices straining to sing for Teresa's soul and its journey to the sky.

Paulina was unmoving, but this was not because of the dank cathedral, her father's immense presence, or the fact that her mother had died on Tuesday and was now going to God. Paulina Ruiz was always still. Still because she was continuously listening, trying to hear what she knew were the voices of God. Voices whispered from the saints' stony upturned faces, unheard by the singing *pueblanos* beneath their ornate prayers. Only Paulina's eyes were never still. They moved to hear person after person, from one soul to the next.

"*Tengo miedo*," one boy's soul told her. He looked towards his *abuelita* holding him tightly against her *sarapé*. She will go to God soon too, thought Paulina, her eyes moving from the boy to his grandmother.

The Mass ended, the priest blessed those assembled, and many hands came to pat the little girl's head, shake her father's hand. One hand, which smelled faintly of fried onions and oil, but sweetened with a flowery lotion, lingered on Paulina's head long enough to get her attention. "Come now with me," Maria Eugenia whispered to the girl.

"She will not come with you," Ruiz said quietly, angrily snatching up Paulina's hand. "My daughter will come home with me."

Those surrounding them made polite excuses and left, quickly but reluctantly, knowing they were too well-bred to gawk.

"This isn't your child," Maria Eugenia said quietly when they had retreated. "She will come with me to live with my children."

"You are an old woman, Maria. Perhaps you have reached the age of senility? Of course this is my child, what makes you think anyone would disagree?"

"I know you are a bad man." Maria Eugenia jabbed at his chest with each pronouncement. "You are a philanderer, an adulterer, Catholic in name only, and God-knows-what-else. This child comes with me or all of Oaxaca will know you are a fraud."

Ruiz leaned down threateningly and gritted his teeth. "Bring the constable if you want," he said, "and take her by force from my fatherly embrace." Maria Eugenia hardened her features.

"Teresa told me everything," she said.

His blood froze. "Even if she did," he said, recovering from the shock, "you are the only one who can make such a claim – therefore, who would believe you?"

"This child is not your own."

"Bring the law – and then we will see how much of a right you have to take her from me," Ruiz grabbed the little girl's arm and hurried away.

"*Te digo*," the man said to Paulina when they were again alone, "it is too excessive here in Mexico," Señor Ruiz said aloud to himself, Paulina's large chocolate eyes concentrated on his emphatic face. "Everyone always in your private affairs. Texas is not like this." He took Paulina's shoulder again and played with the dress' soft, satin strap. "They know discretion in Texas. We will go there soon," he said, the strap reminding him of Paulina. "You will like it," he said down to her, smiling into her seriousness. "The children ride horses to school and eat oranges all day. You will be happy, Paú."

Paulina did not smile for Señor Ruiz. "She only smiles for you," her father had said. But Paulina Ruiz did not smile for anyone. He is in pain, *le duele*, she thought, unblinking. Señor Ruiz, still muttering to himself on the subject of excess, began pulling Teresa's many dresses out of the closet, all smelling of the perfume of her skin, her closet, her life. Those sleeves once held arms that held Paulina; the collars had scratched her face.

Twice a year, Teresa had put on one of the Oaxacan dresses. Paulina had worn one too, her own full embroidered skirt and tapered boxed shirt alive with flowers and leaves, vines wrapping themselves around her small brown body.

Teresa would twine ribbons and flowers in Paulina's long hair to match the vines and they would walk along the Zocalo with the others.

"Stop touching them," Paulina said quietly.

Ruiz stilled his hands in the closet at the small, clear voice of his daughter. "*Que?*" He asked, after the initial shock he always felt at the sound of her little voice.

"*Por favor*," Paulina asked, and motioned for him to close the door.

"Oh, I see," he said, "*Ya veo*." He closed the cedar door and knelt beside his daughter. "You don't want to see them? They remind you of your mother and me?"

Paulina looked at the man. He took her in his arms, crushing her against his starched shirt and Spanish tie, his tobacco pungent near Paulina's forehead.

"I'm sorry I fought so much with your mother," he whispered. "It did not mean that I didn't love her, *mi cielo.*"

Paulina could still see a housedress, light blue, through a crack in the closet door. She had worn it that day, Paulina thought. Tuesday. It was a Tuesday.

"My chest hurts," Paulina told him.

Alarmed, Ruiz demanded the doctor see her that very hour, though it was past four. The old man listened to her chest, thumped her, listened, thumped again and sat back in his creaky metal chair. "She is sick, Senor, she will need care," the man in the white coat said.

Ruiz held his head in his hands. "How sick?"

"It is too soon to know. Don't excite her, Señor Ruiz," the man in the white coat said, "As she gets older it will become clear how bad the problem is." The man leaned toward Jorge Ruiz's little daughter, "How you look like your mother, child. Everything will be fine," he said again, blowing up one of his gloves for her.

Tristesa, sadness, the balloon said to Paulina as it grew larger. *Cosa dura*, a hard thing. Paulina did not want the doctor's funny balloon, not even after he drew a silly face on the fingered glove.

That night, the child had heard movement in the living room. Things were dropped against the cold stone floor, and she walked downstairs toward the hollow echoed sounds. The man, her father, was stacking boxes by the door.

"Eh? Oh, it's you. Go back to bed, little one."

She heard a small voice say from somewhere in the room, "These were your mother's things."

"These aren't important, *mi vida*," the man said. He didn't hear Paulina's voices. He was bending over the boxes to write on their sides. "They are only trinkets and letters. Nothing. If you don't sleep you will be tired tomorrow."

"Don't let him," said the voice, closer, from a dog statue next to her on the staircase, almost at her shoulder. Paulina stood still, her eyes darting from the boxes to the man. Slowly he straightened up and looked at his daughter, unmoving on the last step of the staircase, her eyes large and black.

"Why are you frightened, *mi vida*?" He asked, moving as though to come closer to a wild animal. He held out a hand as if to keep her transfixed.

"Go away from here!" barked the dog statue; it shouted in her ear, it cried out from all over the room — behind the man, above her head, inside the boxes. But Paulina did not move. She was trapped by the man's staring eyes and his outstretched hand. He reached her and picked her up into his arms. She couldn't breathe. She squirmed. He was trying to cradle her on her back like a baby.

"They don't matter," he whispered, rubbing her stomach in circles, moving lower until she loosened the grip on her muscles and relaxed. "They are dead things, and we are living." The man did not hear the voices of warning. His eyes were unfocused. They did not see the living room or the boxes. They looked into the future, where he and his beautiful silent daughter sailed on white ships and lay on green lawns. Where no one could tell him what to do.

And so, while Jorge Ruiz never knew the paternity of his only living daughter, he did know from the moment he saw this beautiful girl that she had been made for him alone. To be a Montelejos, with all the advantages it afforded him; the lovely old stone house that would one day be his when the old mother died, the business men who knew his father-in-law, a sickly wife he was now rid of — all these things paled when he held his Paulina in his arms, her sun-warmed shoulders soft with baby-down. He could not allow them to take her — she was his beloved. He was already well-versed in escape.

The circles reached lower and lower until the motion became intimate and the voice that had been shouting went silent.

When Ruiz was found to have absconded with his beautiful daughter to far more foreign fields, Gloria kept her word, though she knew Jorge had chosen Paulina over her. When he left without giving her the chance to retaliate, she chose the only target that made sense – the woman responsible for his absence. Maria Eugenia never knew the source of her pain; that a curse placed upon her by Gloria could possess her as long as she and Gloria drew breath.

"My spine of late is quite tight," she complained to her husband. "It creeks as though I were a *vejita* of ninety years old."

Doctors were called, remedies prescribed, but nothing could be found to take away Maria Eugenia's pains.

"Señora, I cannot explain your pain," one such learned man told her, "But perhaps you are familiar with the theories of Dr. Sigmund Freud?"

"I am not," the good woman replied, "but if he can prescribe a better poultice than the last doctor I would be most appreciative."

Without his closest friend, his favorite cousin at his side, young Jaime Vasquez Fuentes de Solis was punished with greater frequency. For no longer having a mother who was as absent as she had previously been meant she was freer to steer him to manhood. And that she would do with the sheer force of her determination. His two older brothers, products of careful planning and the Church's admonition that man "be fruitful and multiply", were already at school when Jaime came. For this reason, he supposed, his mother found fault with all he did. She kept a rosary of strangely color-coded beads and had a habit of whipping him with these when he was found trespassing her moods or in innocent ignorance of her unspoken rules.

From his earliest moments he understood that his father, the Señor Fuentes de Solis — a frail man who made quite an inadequate playmate — looked upon him with sadness. The Birdies who spoke to him (which was alright, according to Aunt Teresa before she went away, though his mother vigorously disagreed) explained to Jaime that the Señor Fuentes de Solis was sad over his legacy and its final failure. This never made sense to Jaime, for the Birdies always used language too arcane for his young ears. Had the voices simply come out and said, Jorge Ruiz is your father and mother despises you because he left her here in Mexico with you, Jaime would probably have fewer personality conflicts and delusions of the heart.

It was a secret Gloria jealously guarded. The man Jaime knew as 'father', the Señor Fuentes de Solis, was at one time an imposing man — prosperous, gifted, handsome and well spoken. But as time went by, as around him his sons grew and rose in stature, Guiermo Fuentes de Solis' silence increased in proportion until the occasion of hearing his voice was rare. Once his sad eyes beheld his last child, he knew he had been cuckolded, and he gave up speech indefinitely.

Jorge Ruiz, before leaving in the dead of night with Teresa's daughter Paulina, and preoccupied with the questionable paternity of his own child, neither noticed the Señor Fuentes de Solis's complicit silence nor that young Jaime bore a striking resemblance to Ruiz — especially about the eyes. Portensia did notice, but said nothing, as she herself was preoccupied with keeping her "oath before God" and not laying an eye on her granddaughter, for had she, she would have seen the truth of her paternity in a glance.

When Jaime had been small, dressed by his nurse in saddle-shoes with satin ribbons in his long curled hair, he had heard an argument between his parents; shouting, slapping, glass breaking. The kind Señor Fuentes de Solis' voice rose for the last triumphant time: "Slut!"

"Penis-less phoney!" his mother returned.

There was a sudden silence as Jaime crept to the open door and saw a sight that had paralyzed his terrified little soul: His mother standing over his father's lifeless body — her face contorted in joy. When she looked up to see her youngest watching her, she had smiled and beckoned him to her. His legs, rubber jelly on beds of iron nails, had propelled him closer.

"Look well," Gloria had said to her son, "This man was a sinner and has paid for his sins. See how great they were? God himself has smote him."

"Mama, what did Papa do?"

She shoved the small body away from hers, repulsed by the close smell of a child's fear. "He was an evil man who hid and lied to me. Me. You see what happens when you lie to me, Jaime?" She leaned down to whisper in his face, her breath hot and wet. "God will strike you dead just as he did your Papa."

Jaime drew a ragged breath as he looked as his father, unconscious from a stroke.

"See what happens?" she had asked again, turning her back on her son. She went to call the doctor as Jaime inched his hand toward his father's face.

He felt a miniscule tingle of hair and his arm instantly gave up gooseflesh.

"See?" his mother called from the other room. A mixture of feelings flooded his brain: fear of his mother, shame and love for his father, and the overwhelming need for comfort.

When his father's eyes opened suddenly, Jaime Vasquez screamed as shrill as a whistle and ran for the nearest hiding place between two very large pots in the far patio. He wished fervently to be magically invisible, for death to come to him at that moment, for his mother to suddenly laugh at the outrageousness of such a prank.

Jaime's small, grimy hands clutched his mouth shut as his frantic breath moistened his palms. He listened to her high-heeled shoes click on the tile. From behind the pots Jaime watched his mother bend down and whisper something to his father, her voice a distant sing-song like chant. "And no one will ever know," she said, standing as she smirked down at him. "If you ever speak again it will truly be a miracle, and I will eat my own liver." She suddenly turned her attention to the pots. "Run, Jaime, before I curse you for your father's neglect."

The young boy had done so, as quickly as three-year-old legs could take him.

Part 2: Escape to Egypt

    Hernando's old train lumbered North, puffing with an exaggerated whine like an old woman who knows no one is listening to her complaints. The worn velvet seats, once red and luxurious, were faded with use but comfortable and familiar. Jorge Ruiz and his daughter Paulina sat watching the dusty plains give way to green, lush fields, then mountains, ruins, and streams. They pushed through the commotion of Mexico City, like a disturbed ant hill at high noon, and farther toward the US/Mexico border without stopping for other passengers, supplies, or to stretch their legs.

    Paulina sat in a state of silent shock, the voices having grown more distant the longer she sat on the train, until they fell completely silent near Laredo, their whispered menace and warnings merely traces of echoes in her memory. Her tiny legs and plump, dimpled knees peeked through gingham and lace, and dangled far above the floor as her eyes stared out, vacant and unseeing.

    "Where are we going?" she asked after several hours of silence.

    "Texas," Ed Collins replied.

    "What's in Texas, Papa?"

    "Your grandfather. His land. My inheritance." Abruptly reverting to his old self, that two-bit ex-con, Ed smiled at his daughter and patted her hand reassuringly. "I'm from Texas, Paulina, honey. They call me Ed there. It's where your Grandpops lives."

    Again he saw his father in his memories; tall, imposing, fearless. He saw himself in his mind's eye – also tall and now imposing as well. A man in his own right, with his own trains, silver, cattle, and family. Would his father kill the fattened calf when his Prodigal Son returned? Would he rather, as Ed hoped, be forced to shake his son's hand as an equal? Ed Collins sniggered just to think of it – his father shaking the hand of his son. A son done good, a son gone his own way to return a self-made man. A son a father should be proud of; the next generation of Collins.

Ed had not bedded with the swine and skulked back to his homestead with their filth upon his back, no. Ed Collins had left in disgrace, yes, a convict who'd done his time. But he had returned a respectably widowed man with a beautiful daughter at his side, sacks of silver at his feet, a conservative and well-made suit on his person. And with him – the only heir his father would ever see.

Ed Collins knew he was now a man to answer to.

Their hotel was on Main between a five-and-dime and a barber shop. The First National was across the street and beside that was a lunch counter. The street hustled with activity, people rushing to get done what needed to be done before the sun became too strong for them to stand it. Ed Collins held his daughter's hand tightly, unable to make up his mind.

"Do we see Grandpops now?" Paulina asked him in a small voice, wide-eyed at the people, the cars, the shops and other strange sights. There was an order and sterility that frightened the little girl. What kind of road had no dirt? What kind of people were these who wore so many layers of clothes in the hot sun? Why were they such a blur of white – colorless hats and shoes, gloves and lace, marshmallow faces with bright red dotted lips? When would her mother come and take her home?

Ed Collins, in his new suit and pork-pie hat, sucked his teeth and looked about him at the people who had rushed ahead into the future while he exploded mountains and crawled into mineshafts for silver far to the south. The women wore tiny new wrist watches, slick coats and elaborate hair styles while their men seemed worried and harassed, impatient without wanting to appear so. He dithered on the corner beside the car they had purchased, unsure about the confident thoughts he had on the train only the day before. After all, Judge Collins was the Real McCoy and what was he? A pretender, a man built upon a lie. He knew what the Judge would say: "You might wear those fancy clothes,

Ebner, but you're a naked liar underneath." And yet, Ed Collins yearned to see his father, to see if his beautiful little girl would move the old man's heart. This, his only grandchild, a lovely vision of childish sweetness and honey brown hair. Surely twelve years of absence had softened the old Judge a little; surely he would not turn his back on his only son – returning a better man than he had left. Was that not what his father had wanted of him in the beginning?

"Let's take a trip," he answered her. "I want to show you where I lived when I was your age."

They drove in silence, the brittle grass of August brown and thirsty, blurred against the black tar of the road. The town had grown nearly to the outer limits of Judge Collins' ranch, encroaching upon his grasslands, herds, and rusted farm equipment. The old shed, the hay barn, the rickety waterholes and hay troughs whistled in the wind; beat down by that harsh sun, paint-flecked and water-stained they quietly fell apart. Ed Collins slowed the Buick down to lean out his window and gape open-mouthed at the homestead; once grand, once solid, larger-than-life in Ed's mind, it was now a crumbling shell of brick, wood, and iron.

In the distant side field an old man bent over wilted leaves picking mole crickets and larve, both man and crop stooped and sickly. It seemed the Judge had tried his hand at growing tobacco. Half of them withered in the stale air, and the other clung to life irrigated as far as tin pipes could reach. Ed stopped the car and sat watching his father work slowly and laboriously, intent on the life of his plants. The old man finished and snapped the tin lid of the coffee can shut – crickets and larve writhing inside. Feeling a stranger's eyes upon him, Judge Collins turned to see a shiny new Buick pulling away in the distance.

"I have to go to the bank," Ed told his daughter as they pulled up again in front of their Hotel. He lifted her out of the bucket seat and set her upon the wooden bench outside the large bay windows of the First National. "You sit here and don't move, hear?" He shielded his eyes against the glare. "And don't talk to anyone either."

Paulina sat still and put her hands on her knees. The strange white people in their odd clothing and hurried steps minced past her to their cars and homes, store fronts and businesses. She looked at the people who did not see her, and watched the clock on the town hall click past three in the afternoon. There was an odd silence to their activity; even as they greeted each other in an unfamiliar language, wide smiles and cold eyes.

"Hello there, little one," an old man creakily sat down on the wooden bench. "Waiting for your Daddy?"

Paulina's eyes widened with fear. What if her papa saw her disobeying him? He would be angry with her, she knew. She did not understand the old man's words, but his eyes were not cold and he did not smile as falsely as the others did. He looked stern but kind, an honest man. She smiled at him timidly.

"What's your name?" he asked her when she did not answer. "You aren't lost, now, are you?"

It was then that her father stepped across the threshold of the bank, and stopped. The old man stood up with painful difficulty. "Arthritis in my knees," he said by way of greeting. "Getting old is a pain."

"Hello, father," Ed said in a voice Paulina had never heard before.

"Hello Ebner. Heard you were back. What brings you to the bank?"

My money, he thought, but said, "I see you have met my daughter," instead.

The old man squinted at the little girl on the bench. "Your daughter?" he asked. The judge leaned on his walking stick and tilted his head toward her, squinted his eyes and looked at the little girl again more intently. "Now, I'm an old man, Ebner, but this little one is no little girl of yours." Judge Collins peered at his son. "So, are you stealing children now besides what else other nefarious business?"

Ed frowned and shook his head. "This little girl is my daughter, you stubborn old fool, and if you had any real sense you'd want to be her Grandpops."

"This is someone else's kin, Ebner. No relation of mine."

"Paulina, this is your Grandfather," he told her in Spanish.

"She doesn't even speak English?" the Judge asked, incredulous. "Now, why doesn't she speak English?"

"Because her mother was Mexican. She's lived her whole life with us in Mexico. They don't speak English in Mexico."

His father grunted and hardened his heart. "Well then you take her back there, pronto. I haven't forgotten your ways, son, nor become senile enough to think you've made good. What? You think by dragging some child up this way and making out to be her father that makes you a man? It most certainly does not." The old judge jabbed his son in the chest. "You are not welcome here and would be wise to remember: Those who take what is not theirs will find that everything comes back to its rightful place in the end."

Ed snorted in derision and brushed his father's fingers away. "You always were good for a one-liner, weren't you?"

"Get out of here, Ebner. This is no place for the likes of you. As for that child, whomever she belongs to, for her sake," the judge said as he turned his back, "I hope you send her home to her people. And I hope you do so before I call the police."

The old man walked away, stooped and nursing his bad knees, leaving his son to grit his teeth in consternation.

"Fool," Ed Collins spat out. "Damned fool."

"Papa, that man was my Grandpapa from my mama or from you? Will we see him again?" she asked innocently.

Ed yanked Paulina off the wooden bench. He looked down at her furiously and saw Teresa in her eyes. Teresa, mocking him, saying, "You are no one's papa!" His father, that vile old man, calling out, "Police! Here he is; the liar in the new suit!" Ed Collins ran from them, the voices within his own imagination. With the little girl swept up in his arms, he rushed into the hotel, up the stairs and into their room, slamming the door behind him.

"Now you listen to me," he yelled at her, as she tumbled out of his arms. "I am your father and you will do as I say." He shook her until her head snapped back and forth like a stalk of wheat. "You will not speak until I ask you a question, and you will learn to obey!" And yanking her bloomers down he began to spank her. "I told you," he screamed between smacks, "Not to speak to anyone! And you disobeyed me!" Furiously, he spanked her again and again until her soft skin was bright red, and her screams brought agitated knocks at the door of their room.

"Sir," a voice pleaded, "Sir, I realize you are only doing your Christian duty to a wayward child, but the other guests are complaining of the noise."

"That's fine," Ed Collins said calmly, as he lifted the whimpering child to the bed, the voices now silenced. "I'm finished."

That night, Ed Collins led a silent, red-eyed little girl to the offices of Franklin Larrington. Having checked out of the hotel amid the angry faces of the staff and the guarded stares of several guests, Ed Collins was subdued, drained of all emotion. He felt trapped, bitter, broken. He would not inherit the ranch, his father's money in the bank, or the brick house falling to dust on the homestead. It would all go to some University, he knew, the Judge Collins Memorial Library or something. What a waste.

The pair waited as Franklin's secretary let them in. "He's waiting for you in the inner office," she said and gathered her things together for the night.

"Thanks for seeing me, Franklin," Ed leaned over Paulina to shake his friend's hand.

"Least I could do," Franklin answered. He settled himself back into the leather chair and poured Ed a large drink. "Anything for the little one?"

"Water's fine for her."

"Alrighty."

Paulina looked at her father as the strange man offered her the glass. Ed nodded at her and she took it and drank deeply.

"Now. What brings you by?"

Ed's shoulders drooped and he slumped back in his chair. "I need work," he said. "Preferably, work that takes me far from here."

Franklin, visibly relieved Ed didn't want to hang about nearby, smiled and winked at Paulina. "Perfect. I've just the thing," he said. "Ever been East?"

"Been to New York a few times."

"More east." Franklin leaned forward and pushed an object on his desk towards Ed. "See this?"

Ed took it in his hands and turned it around. It was a knife made of bronze, snuggly fitted to an ornate gold sheath.

"That comes from none other than the tomb of that Egyptian King they just found over there outside Cairo."

Ed turned the object around in his hands again, but more carefully this time.

"I collect now – what with all this extra money made with your operations down South I decided to invest in my future."

The shelf behind him was loaded with objects, rocks, small artifacts and rolled-up documents. "There is a virtual fortune on this shelf, Collins. A fortune," Franklin shook his head, "that was hard to get, and comes with certain risks." He poured them both more whiskey. "The man I used to have go get them for me, my man in-country, was shot. Shot dead over, you won't believe this, defiling a mosque. That's where they go to church in the East, a mosque."

"And you want me to replace him?"

"No, not as yet. I want to see if you can do the one job. Just oversee one shipment and we'll take it from there."

"But I don't speak Turk, Frank."

"They don't speak Turk in Egypt, Ed. They speak Arabic. You picked up Spanish from a bunch of cons, I expect you to pick up Arabic just as fast."

Ed Collins looked at his daughter, holding her empty glass carefully. "When?"

"I'd need you to leave within the week."

"We can leave tomorrow."

"Sounds good to me." Franklin shrugged. "Nice place, this Egypt. Cairo like a modern city – or beginning to become anyways, so said my man before he was gut-shot."

Ed Collins, the broken edges of his self-respect beginning to mend, lifted his glass and swore. "Hell, might even be fun."

Part 3: A Reluctant Saint

1952
Garden City, Cairo

After the 23rd July Revolution drove away the Baxters, the McAlisters, and the rest of her British classmates, Paulina Ruiz's studies ended with little fanfare. A grown woman, she spent her days reading through the vast library some other family had left behind in their home in Garden City during the Revolution, before her father had acquired it, and waited for him to return from his long trips. Empty and sad, alone as far back as her memory could reach; hatred for her father slowly smothered itself from a living flame to a smoldering ember in her tiny breast.

Each day was the same as the last. She awoke, dressed, ate in the dining room alone, and went to the library to read. The light would dim, she would yawn, wonder when her father would return, and go to her room to undress. Some days she went out for quiet lunches with friends or friends of friends, but these were exceptions. Some days she went shopping or to the tailor for a few new clothes, but this was even less often. Most of her friends had been British, and as such, were now gone. The excuses to leave the library became fewer and fewer until one day they seemed a distant memory.

It had been early in the afternoon when Sharia knocked at the library door and wiped her wet hands on her apron before handing Paulina a letter. It sat, unopened, a strange thing to her – a letter in her name.

Paulina glanced at it on her desk amid the old books before shoving it into her knapsack. It was addressed to a Señorita Paulina de Ruiz, postmarked Oaxaca City, Mexico. She could not read it as she sat within her father's house; if he found her with it, he would surely take it away. She decided to go out into the street and walk to the bus stop (which only saw a bus every hour and a half). In relative isolation, Paulina drew the letter out from her pocket, now crumpled and slightly torn. She opened it and read:

"*To Señorita Paulina de Ruiz,*
I write as an emissary of your cousin Jaime Vasquez Fuentes de Solis who has appealed to me to write this letter. He apologizes that he cannot write to you himself in view of his lack of English writing skills but wishes you to know that your godmother, Maria Eugenia de los Cruces, has requested you come to Oaxaca City, Mexico. He wishes me to inform you that this woman, Maria Eugenia, was once a very good friend of your mother's, and has many things she wants to speak to you about. She offers photographs of your mother in exchange for this meeting. One of these photos waits for you in my bookshop in the Zocalo. Jaime also wanted me to inform you of the very serious illness of his (and your) grandfather, Hernando, of whom is it said, may very soon join Jesus, Mary, and the Disciples in their eternal slumbers.
I am very sincerely yours,
Gary Lechney."

Paulina replaced the thin scrap of onion paper into its envelope and held her breath. Her glance darted up to both ends of the street, her father so firmly fixed in her mind she did so from a force of habit so strong as to be called dread. She stuffed the letter back into her pocket and climbed the steps to her room.

It was three days before Jorge Ruiz banged open the door of his daughter's room. "What is this?" In his hand was the letter from Gary Lechney.

"Where did you get that?"

"Never you mind," her father fumed, "And answer my question."

"It's a letter, obviously."

"Obviously. The washer-woman gave it to me, thinking it was important, which she found in the pocket of your old skirt – the one I keep insisting you get rid of."

"It is important."

"No." Jorge Ruiz held the onion scrap with both hands high in the air and ripped it in two. "This is trash. It is lies and foolishness."

Tears sprang to Paulina's eyes as the letter rained down in bits and jagged pieces, like shards of glass from a shattered window. "It's mine, you can't do that."

"You are my daughter and I'll do as I please with you and your things! Who have you been writing to? How did this find you here?"

Paulina set her jaw as tears continued coursing down her cheeks. "Who is Maria Eugenia? Why can't we go back to Mexico?"

"There is nothing in Mexico for you! Forget that place!"

"What's in Mexico? Why won't you tell me?"

Jorge Ruiz raised his hand to strike his daughter. "Ask me again," he said quietly, hand frozen in mid-motion.

Paulina covered her hands with her face and wept.

"Ask me again," her father repeated.

"What are you afraid of?"

The house servants lowered their eyes and went about their chores – laundry, dishes, dusting. The cook savored a spoonful of the lunch she had just prepared and the gardener raked up the leaves from the old plum tree outside the library window. When the girl's screams pierced the mid-day calm, each thought the same thing: *A good father spares not the rod.*

"Get my daughter some aloe from the garden," he said to the cook when he had finished. "And throw out her clothes. They are ruined."

In the middle of the night, two nights before the moon would reach its fullness, Paulina lay awake and listening to the sounds of Cairo. Not yet accustomed to the new house in Garden City which was never completely still, a place where leaves rustled and buildings groaned late into the night, Paulina had been roused from a troubled sleep. Somewhere, a wild dog barked. This was the colonial section of Cairo the Brits had built, Garden City. The buildings were beautiful, decrepit, rotting. When the Brits had left during the Revolution, no real upkeep had been done for the most part. Foreigners lived mostly in Maadi and Zamaleck surrounded by embassies and compounds, but Garden City, built by the Brits for the Brits was left in isolation. As if the Egyptians hadn't quite moved in yet, or were afraid to claim it, Paulina thought as she lay awake in the night, listening. As if no one lived there and all the buildings were rotting by themselves. Every now and again, she would catch glimpses of children playing football in the streets and old men who sat by doorways and operated elevators and intercoms, while there were people around her (she could hear their footsteps and smell their dinners) in the midst of over-hung trees like swamp vines, you never saw anyone in Garden City. They were like mice, hidden packs of families living and working.

    The old stone house had been hurriedly vacated, doors ajar where they should be shut, meals in progress attended by phantom diners, tables overturned and papers scattered. The furniture was still there, the paintings on walls, silverware in drawers and china in cupboards. When Ruiz flashed a large amount of money at a few friends they had slapped his back and proclaimed him their newest neighbor. "Those old Brits ran out like rats!" his friends had laughed, "Of course they'd expected it – why build the city out of a maze if not to scurry out when the time has come?"

    They pounded his back and congratulated him on moving up in society – a new grand house, expensive furniture, the ear of the politicians, and the pockets of foreign investors. Having spent the last twenty years moving artifacts out of the country, and replacing them with guns and provisions, bending the ear of those itching for power and those willing to do anything to keep it, Ed Collins had kept his Mexican name and learned Arabic well enough to silence anyone who doubted him.

    The door opened and a crack of light from the dim chandelier shone in her eyes. "Get up," Jorge Ruiz told his daughter in the darkness of her room. "Pack only what you can get in ten minutes. The car is waiting outside."

    Paulina glanced outside and saw the cars black curtains had been drawn but their driver wasn't in the front seat. She grabbed her camera, a shawl, some clothes and a few fountain pens and shoved them into a small rucksack. Paulina owned nothing of real value. Her lack of possessions, she had found, annoyed her father.

"Why don't you buy things like women do?" exasperated, he would ask when her catalogue-bought designer clothes had pulls and holes. "I don't want them," she said, frightened to see the pink blush on her father's face, a trembling anger.

"But when we go out with others, what must they think of me?"

"It is no affair of mine what people think of you, father," she would respond, though he knew this would only incur his wrath.

"*Mierda*," he would say, *shit*.

His girlfriends often brought Paulina clothes to wear of the latest fashions, the same styles their daughters also wore. They pitied the gallant Mr. Ruiz, a lone father in the world, raising a sullen, silent daughter – the worst company at parties or official State functions. But it was not out of pity, not really, that these women did so. They fussed over his daughter, bought her chic European clothing for polo matches and high tea (easily taken over by the upper-class Egyptians in place of their British counterparts), and advised him to cut her hair properly ("I know so many stylists, Jorge!" they would exclaim) because Jorge Ruiz was a powerful man, a desirable man. His light brown hair only made darker by the sun into a burnished gold, a rare Adonis in a land of tall dark and handsome.

They did not know where his money came from, did not eavesdrop on their husbands when the men spoke together enveloped in wreaths of cigar smoke and single malt Scotch. Deals were made in the libraries of usurped British officers, deals of which even the men at the top of command did not openly speak. Only Paulina knew her father never left home without a side pistol and a long hunting knife thrust into his sock garter.

He came back into her room as she was pulling the knapsack string tightly closed. "*Ja, ja*," he said, slipping into Spanish, "Let us be gone, we have a far way to travel through the blockades before anyone can find us."

She scooped up a few books.

"We're going to the house in Sharm el Sheikh. Our boat waits on the Red Sea."

Paulina did not ask why they were going to their vacation house in the dead of night, or why their yacht which only patrolled the Nile for dinner parties or to impress long dead friends and colleagues would have found its way over so far a distance as to the Red Sea. She knew not to ask her father such things.

The road over the Sinai was a winding ribbon, a dirt path in some places – kept this way so as to control it better from invaders or pretenders to its rugged beauty.

Once, when the roads were open briefly, she had gone to see St. Catherine's monastery and because she lacked the fervor to enter, she climbed Mt. Sinai instead.

The mountain was dusty, the rocks worn by countless pilgrim feet. She had climbed for two hours in a long upwards spiral. The path, well worn and deserted was peaceful. But then the trail became narrow and steep and she began to sweat and shiver in the night air. People on camels passed by, and Paulina began to resent them. After three hours she stopped by the side of the trail and sat down on the rocky ledge. She looked down and saw Sharm el Sheikh in the distance by the sea. Only a few lights were blinking, and she didn't want to continue climbing. She wanted to die on this holy mountain, far from her father, his influence, herself. She had a cramp in her leg, and from months of smoking, could not catch her breath. Her lungs filled with crystalline razors. She shivered and watched people pass.

"Camel, Miss?" a man asked in Arabic. She climbed up and took the camel's reins tightly as they started walking. Familiar with their lumbering gate, their gliding strides on cushioned hooves, she was not afraid of the camel. She was afraid of falling. She looked up at the stars above the Sinai, hundreds upon hundreds of billions of stars that glittered like a bed of the smallest diamonds.

But then the camel could go no further and the man helped her dismount beside the sacred stone staircase cut into the side of the mountain. Paulina sat down, again dismayed at herself for this stupid expedition. But then a grandmother passed by, her face a map of criss-crossed roads. She had more faith in her pinky than Paulina had in her entire body.

Paulina grunted and pulled herself off the stone step and wrapped her thick, woolen poncho around herself. Her mind numb, she joined the line of pilgrims climbing the last steps to the summit, and then among the large boulders at the top, Paulina found a place to sit. She dangled her legs at the edge of the precipice and pulled the poncho close. Far below her lay the foothills of Mt. Sinai and farther away, the dunes of the desert hills. They looked like crumpled construction paper, lengthened shadows of moon and star-light. With her head on her knees, facing Israel at the summit of Mt. Sinai, she slept.

"Oooh, ahhh," the people said and Paulina awoke to see a pinprick of light in the distance. There, crowning the foothills was the sun. It grew until it blinded her, it grew until it touched the desert sands which sparkled like the stars had done, and then it was day.

The road-blocks would certainly be up now, and this was not a vacation, Ruiz reminded his daughter. "I am prepared to pay our passage there, but you will not speak, unless they want to hear your Arabic – though I do not think this will be the case." Ruiz checked the ammunition in his pistol and started up their Rolls.

"What about our things?" Paulina asked, knowing this would only infuriate him, her curiosity was greater than her fear.

"No one would dare enter my house, Pau. I am not just some piddling official, to be tossed aside and trampled."

"Then what are we running from?"

"We aren't running." Jorge swiveled in his seat, one outstretched arm bracing the passenger side headrest, and backed out of their driveway into the deserted street. "And mind your own business," he muttered.

They left the city and began their journey through the blackness of the Sinai. The trip took a long time; Paulina remembered only the rocky, grey landscape when dawn approached. The heat, the swaying motion, the soft seats of the Rolls put her to sleep until they got to the first checkpoint.

"*Ma'salama,*" Ruiz, jovial, held out fresh cigarettes to the soldiers posted there. There were no houses in the Sinai, only the desert tribes of Bedouins Ruiz knew from his business transactions (men whose only loyalty was to their own families and who despised Jorge Ruiz, who only worked with him for money to buy more camels). There was no other way across the desert. Should one be lost on this road, he would never recover – he would die of thirst in a matter of hours. The air was palpable but salty, unlike Cairo where the heat tasted like sand and smog.

"Where to, friend?" the soldiers asked her father.

"Sharm," he said, the small fishing village whose best parts faced the Red Sea. There, the houses and inns were painted with thick white paste and surrounded by tall skinny palms. There was a long wooden boardwalk and tents on the sand.

"Nice weekend to relax," they said and returned his papers.

Paulina wondered where the Bedouins could be found – and who it was that could cause her father such anxiety. If only she could find the desert nomads and barter passage back to Cairo, her life for his – even she knew her father had many enemies among them.

Sharm El Sheikh, Egypt
(on the Red Sea)

The rocky landscape of the desert behind her was lit a ruby red by the setting sun when Paulina stepped out to the balcony to smoke a cigarette. She inhaled sea spray and fire, her back to the magnificent white villa that glowed in the light of sunset. Often when Paulina smoked on the balcony, she felt as if she would never leave this place, its forgetful location in a small town by a blue-topaz-colored sea. Waves pounded beneath her, spray filled her nostrils, and smoke filled her lungs. She closed her eyes and imagined fingertips in her hair, the nails lightly grazing her scalp. She imagined her hair washed as she lay in the bath. A man she did not know would come and lovingly acquiesce; he would make the foam of the shampoo a soft cap of suds. Firm hands would ease away her thoughts, wipe them away and leave her with nothing to think or feel.

She stood on the balcony and imagined these things, but soon the air grew too cold for standing still, and the sea spray made her clothes wet and clingy. She smelt of musty sea urchins and salt. Paulina stopped and listened for her father. She entered the villa and paused beside the living room door. The distinct crackle of their old rotary telephone rustled beside her. Someone else was now using the line from another part of the villa. She had noticed some time ago that when someone was on the other line, the conversation was clearly heard from the frayed wires, like the faint memories of mid-morning dreams. Ghost whispers. She leaned in to listen.

Jorge Ruiz was a very unpleasant man when displeased. The yacht had not been on the Sea as promised, which made Jorge Ruiz an extremely unpleasant man. He saw no problem doing a few favors here and there, so long as they were returned in kind and in equal proportion. He supplied a few boys in Cairo with the difficult to obtain wares they requested so long as they paid him a profit and kept their mouths shut. He only asked two things: discretion and complete reliability. There was nothing of greater importance to Jorge Ruiz. And now his man in Alexandria could not work with his man in Cairo to produce a simple chain of events – bringing his boat to Sharm el Sheikh.

He mixed a Scotch and soda before calling Sabina at her embassy house in Zamaleck. She would be just now climbing out of her pool, ordering cocktails of more fruit juice than liquor, a sheer robe covering her frilly bathing costume.

The line only rang once. "Tell your husband to leave me alone," he said menacingly.

"I will do no such thing," the woman replied, this wealthy wife of a diplomatic imbecile.

Paulina crept closer to the telephone in the living room.

"Tell Akmal he is only compromising his interests."

"Unfortunately," the woman's honeyed voice replied, "he doesn't care."

"He should care if he wants to live out his days in that position that affords him such a wife as you."

The woman sighed melodramatically, and Ruiz could imagine her, a softly bronzed statuesque beauty queen wrapping the telephone's cord around her finger as she had done to her men, "Darling, I've tried. You know Akmal is not one of those who will stand for his wife to keep lovers."

"I am not just your lover," Ruiz growled, "I am the best business man your husband has." He shifted the phone closer to his mouth, "For the sake of national pride, he should leave me alone."

The woman laughed, "For all the money you bring, he could not care a fig, Jorge. He is angry. Let him stomp about the Sinai a bit, hmm?"

"You don't understand, Sabina. I haven't got my boat handy. He knows where I am."

"Listen, Jorge. I do not control my husband. If Akmal al Sofian finds you, I advise you to turn and run. He would shoot no man in the back."

Jorge Ruiz did not dignify this with a response but hung up the telephone and cursed. He paced the living room for few moments before setting off to the marina himself. He would have to find another boat, or there would be no escaping a cuckolded man's wrath.

His daughter listened to the fading footsteps tread away upon the hallway's stones. She heard him quietly close the door and went to pack her rucksack and had but shouldered it when Khaled, their man servant in Sharm, found her stealthily leaving the villa a half-hour later.

"I have taught you well to walk without sound, Miss," he whispered in Arabic.

"Hello, Khaled."

"Where is the Miss going on this moonless night?"

"I seek the Bedouins father does business with, Khaled." As quietly as he, Paulina whispered, "You know where they can be found."

"*In sha Allah,*" he answered.

Yes, if God is willing, she thought, knowing this was her only way out of the Sinai, the only way she would survive the journey, the only way away from her father.

"You must help me, Khaled, I beg of you."

"The Miss knows I am but a loyal servant of your father's."

"The Miss also knows you are privy to his secrets."

The old man sighed inaudibly. His employer had influenced more wars than he cared to remember, and though grateful for his country's sake, it was a slap in the face each time he had to wait upon another strange woman in their home, her flashing glances at the table, her insistence that he call her "Madam." Khaled could not simply shut his eyes and forget his employer was a dirty pig.

"But Miss, these men you seek are without concern for you. They will keep you hostage when you find them. You have nothing they want."

"You are mistaken, Khaled."

The Egyptian regarded his position, careful not to look the girl in the eye. She was leaving whatever he said, and he could not bear knowing that she would die without his help in the desert. He had cared for this girl for many long years.

"I cannot keep you safe from them," he said to Paulina, "but I can help you find them."

The cold desert was pitch with night, illuminated only by starlight, accessible only by animal's hooves. Men with rusted jeeps patrolled the town, but Khaled knew from where and when they came, and the pair slipped quietly into the open sands on foot without being disturbed. Khaled told her if they blundered onto the tribe's unspoken territory they would be caught and made to explain. "It is my hope, *In sha Allah*, that you can explain," he said.

"I have only one thing to say," she answered.

He worried for this girl. What if the Bedouin traders did not recognize her? What if they did not believe she was the daughter she said she was, if they believed her to be a runaway bride, or worse, who had run away with him?

Paulina with her plain looks and arrogance could fit in almost anywhere if given the chance. She was not preoccupied in the same way her servant clearly was.

"Halt," came the order they had been expecting for over an hour of fitful walking.

"I leave you here, Khaled," she said as the men from atop their camels glared down at her in the silvery light.

"Miss, you are not safe," he said.

"I am Paulina Ruiz," she told the men in perfect Arabic with only the hint of a foreigner's tongue. "Will you safeguard my servant to return to our home?"

The men touched their hearts with closed fists.

"Will you safeguard my own safety?"

Again, the men touched their hearts.

"Goodbye, Khaled," Paulina said.

"Goodbye, Miss."

When they heard her proposal, the Bedouins wrapped her in cloths as one of them and lent her a fine camel. When they told her how to ride it (impressed she already knew), they set out north as moonlight dimmed to an early dawn.

There were no checkpoints where the tribes sailed on the desert as if it were sea. They passed the early hours of dawn trotting their beasts (showing their three inch teeth with wild abandon, happy to run, happy to hear the *tut tut tut* of their masters) and silently read the sands and morning stars. After a day and a half of riding north through mountains and then west over the wide desert expanse they lead her to the edge of Al Ababiya, a small town south of Suez, and she dismounted the camel they had lent her.

"*Akmal al Sofian*," she said and the tribe touched their foreheads and then their hearts. Yes, this was a valuable name. When this man al Sofian found what he was looking for, it would solve many quarrels.

She had only been back in Cairo a day and half when her father's most loyal servant had come looking for her in their stone house in Garden City. "Miss, your father has been shot, where have you been?"

Startled in the act of escaping, in the midst of packing her bags, with only a hazy plan of flying to Mexico, Paulina stopped and allowed the servant to hustle her to her father's side. A cloud drifted over the Nile and darkened the faint green tiles of the hospital room. Ruiz's lips moved inaudibly. Machines *beep beep beeped* beside him. He reached for Paulina's hand and gave it a feeble shake as she sat beside him, though his gaze came from cold snakes eyes.

"I thought you had gone," he said.

"Where would I go?"

"You want to go back to Mexico."

"Yes."

Ruiz drew a ragged breath. "Don't go back there," he said faintly. "It will only hurt you."

"What will hurt me?"

"The truth," he whispered.

The nurse came to adjust his wires, and Paulina breathed deeply, as if submerged. Her chest heaved, and her collarbone exposed itself, sharp as a bird's wing.

"Don't leave me," her father pleaded. Jorge Ruiz closed his eyes and sank back onto the bed, damaged by an assassin's bullet still buried deep inside in his neck – a hard price to pay in the middle of the day on a jewel-toned sea.

Paulina watched him sleep as he clung to life, unable to leave his side, so long used to his authority.

The claustrophobic hospital room, the cloying smell of medicinal remedies, the moans from the dying, and the rusty smell of blood and bandages was too much. One of the doctors had noticed her pale and shaking when examining her father and taking her aside, suggested that a brief respite from the hospital and fresh air would do her some good. He recommended the beautiful church of St. George.

"It is very close," he had said. "Your father won't even know you had gone." The doctor winked and added, "I have given him a strong sedative, you know."

Luckily, the subway car wasn't crowded and she easily found a seat, her knees weak at the unexpected freedom. She had gone to the front car, the women-only car, and sat down. Paulina had forgotten that Egyptians still thought she was an Arab. They spoke to her in Arabic; they passed their groceries to her in buses. Mexicans must look like Egyptians, she thought, though she had met very few in Cairo growing up. The car filled up the closer to the center they went. She was the only woman not in *higab*; no colorful scarf was tied artfully and traditionally around her head, hiding her hair from sight. The other women looked for the Coptic cross, and didn't find it. They looked for signs that she was a foreigner and did not find those either. So they continued to stare, and Paulina thought about Maria Eugenia. She remembered the sound of the name. She could not think of whom it represented, but she knew the feel of the words in her ears and in her mouth.

"Maria Eugenia." she said to herself, quietly, as the train passed El Zahraa station. The woman's name was not one you heard every day, or said correctly if you did not know how. The name said "*hace mucho tiempo.*" It has been a long time. The name said, "*con tu mama*"; it said, "*yo se.*" I know what you were looking for in Oaxaca and never found. In syllables, it said, "*Ma-de-oo-hen-ee-ah*"

The train had reached Mar Gris and Coptic Cairo. She lingered by the door, waiting for the old machinery to allow her into more familiar territory. But the car had become full, children clung to legs and arms, their mothers leaning against the wall of the train, handing babies and shopping bags to handy strangers. On the women's car, everyone would help. Being a woman in Egypt is hard.

"*Aiza*," someone said to Paulina in Arabic. She was passed a sleeping child as the woman shifted her groceries and other baby to her free arm. The woman was wearing full *higab*, her headscarf reaching past her knees. She motioned to take the child back, but the doors had already closed, and Paulina was in no rush; she held the child longer until she reached the stop past Coptic Cairo.

It was in walking back to her intended destination that she saw looked into one of the archways beside her. It led to a winding complex of pilgrimage sites and hidden Coptic churches.

"Mary and Joseph stop here with the baby Jesus," one hawker, a portly Egyptian, told her.

"Oh yes?"

He nodded, and walked alongside her. The jewelry and knick-knack sellers rarely bothered Paulina. They assumed she was Egyptian. But this one said, "You have seen the crypt beneath St. George?" as she wound her way toward the cellar space of Mary and Joseph's Egyptian flight.

"No," she said, surprised by herself. "I haven't." The name had always made her uncomfortable. It was too much like her father's name.

"It would be my absolute pleasure to show you, Miss; it is this way," he called over his shoulder, motioning for Paulina to follow him into the green courtyard of a nunnery, the other tourists momentarily forgotten. "Beneath the nuns is old crypt where lie bones of dragon George slew and manacles he was bound by. You know story?" he asked, stopping at the gate of the courtyard.

"Yes," she said to evade further instruction, wanting to be left in peace.

"The shrine is down those steps," the man said, pointing to a gaping hole that suggested a wide passage beside the steps up to the Nunnery. "You must remove your shoes." He called after her, holding the grill of the gate with his free hand. "Go, go." He urged Paulina, waving at her with the cheap jewelry.

Paulina felt drawn by the darkness and the mystery of the shrine. Warily, she climbed down the awkward stone steps until she came to a curtain where a Coptic priest was chanting Mass, encircled and pressed by the devout. Mothers and children, the old and sick were all bending down to remove their shoes, but Paulina did not have the courage to enter. She felt shut out from their fervor. Instead, she moved slowly around the edge of the large room, dimmed by its subterranean position, paintings and nun's testimonies framed on the stone walls. Paulina moved along the holy perimeter until a plaque stopped her.

Saint Teresa, it said, and Paulina's eyes cautiously moved upward to the mid-sized icon it noted. It was a girl. She looked shy, but softly happy and still in the first beginnings of womanhood.

"Saint Teresa," Paulina murmured; her mother's name on her lips.

"She is the patron saint of young nuns." A woman at her elbow commented, assuming Paulina was listening, though she had not been acknowledged. "You are one of these?"

Paulina started and smiled ruefully at the woman, thinking of her father. "No, ma'am, I am not one of those."

The old woman shrugged, unperturbed. Paulina continued to stare at the oil painting, cracked and polished by millions of praying lips and fingertips.

It is the Saint Teresa, she thought again. Her story was unknown to Paulina, but the saint's likeness touched her. Young Teresa's face was soft and kind, just a girl. What had her mother thought of this saint, her namesake? Paulina did not recall much of Teresa, but certainly she was nothing like this forlorn and poetic saint.

"You do not know the story of Saint Teresa?" The old woman was dressed in widow's clothes.

"No, ma'am, I do not," Paulina said, politely, repentant for laughing earlier. The old woman's attention was strangely soothing.

"Well," The old woman said, heavily setting down her bag and leaning on the cold sweating stones of St. George's tomb. "The girl was the last daughter of a wealthy man. This man adored his little daughter and gave to her whatever she asked of him. One day this girl decided to be a nun and only serve God. What could the rich father do? He had never denied Teresa anything. So, he let her be a nun, and she died soon after." The old woman scrunched up her lips and shrugged her shoulders. "The miracle only happened after the little nun died. Her body," the woman leaned forward to whisper, holding up a wrinkled finger, "did not decay!" The old woman leaned back, "And other sick girls were cured of their illnesses by Teresa's undecaying body, for her father kept it on display."

The woman studied Paulina. "I feel it is good for you to know this story, yes?" she asked. Paulina did not take her eyes off Saint Teresa's unblemished face, the faded color of an Egyptian dawn.

Carefully, Paulina moved her eyes from the icon to the old woman, her own face as unlined as the saint's. "Why do you tell me this story?"

"The saints are saints because they belong to us," the woman answered, her eyes showing a kindness Paulina was not used to seeing in churches. "Each one finds his own saint to guide him, to know his story so that we may find faith as the saint found faith." The widow crossed herself and turned to climb the large uneven steps to the sunlight of the Egyptian courtyard above. "You look as if you came here lost," she said, "and Teresa has been put here for you, that you may find your path." The old woman's body still pointed away, but she folded her hands in Paulina's direction. "I hope you find it. You are as innocent as the saint. Whatever sickness or strain you bear, the saints can help, for even in death as Teresa healed some, you will find God heals all." The old woman finally left Paulina to the icon, Saint Teresa becoming more lifelike the longer she looked.

A medallion of Saint Christopher hung from the corner of the frame as an offering, and without thinking Paulina, took it and clutched it in her hand as if the Saint had hung it there for Paulina alone. She turned and left the crypt, the Egyptian sun blinding.

She dreamed that night of a house. Empty, truly empty now that her mother had died. But it was Paulina who was the ghost, expelled, exorcised. The house was waiting for someone else to return, but not her — she was leaving to follow the man who had killed her mother.

Desculpame, the house moaned in the dry Oaxacan wind, forgive me. She breathed in and out with the empty house. *Respirir*, she thought, and the dark house took another deep breath, exhaling as she exhaled.

The little girl lay with her chest flat on the stone floor, pulsing heat and giving it to the stone beneath her.

Des-cul-pa, the stairs moaned.

Tri-ste-sa, said the stone.

I want to go to God now too, Paulina thought, like Mama. Her mother was gone, and though no one had said so, she would not come back.

Te siento, said her mother's house, I feel you.

Paulina lay out her little arms, palms downward, face to one side on the cool stone where once sat the couch, where her mother had once held her close, having coffee and cake with her friends in the morning. Paulina was never far from her. She would have slept in Tere's bed had it not been for the man, her father, lying in the place she wanted.

Ten quidado, her father's eyes always said. Be careful little one. He held her tightly, but Tere had held her as if Paulina had been part of her own body.

"*Mi mama*," Paulina whispered to the empty house.

Ya se, it said, I know. *Un coraje, es un coraje, niña.* Be strong.

Her sundress straps pulled at Paulina's shoulders. She heard her father yelling downstairs at her grandmother's maid, Guadalupe, "No! She stays with me!"

Guadalupe's voice floated upwards from the atrium, "The child needs a woman's care! Please, Señor, let me take her to Maria Eugenia's home as her grandmother has demanded."

"She is <u>my</u> daughter."

The door slammed, and Ruiz panted with the exertion of it.

"Everyone in your business," the man, her father muttered. "Back to Texas is where we will go."

Fe, the house groaned around her. Faith; the worst is past.

It is Wednesday, Paulina thought, spreading her arms as much as she could. Yesterday had been Tuesday. Mama visits God on Tuesday.

The man, her father, was calling her name.

Ten quidado, said the stone, be careful.

No te olvido, said the stairs, I won't forget you.

Fe, whispered the house.

Paulina woke easily as the call to prayer carried itself past the screen of the balcony, opened her eyes in the gray morning without effort. She remembered when she learnt the first word of the call, "Akbar" which meant "The greatest," and the rest was a list of the greatness of God's acts. She had been only a few years old, and it was the first Arabic she had understood.

"*Fe*," she whispered. *Faith.* Maria Eugenia had been her mother's best friend. Paulina could not remember her, but knew her anyway.

"We are going to Mai Te's," Teresa would tell Paulina, as she combed her long wet hair. "We will have a little party, *niña*. Would you like a little party?" Teresa would smile for Paulina, and Paulina's eyes stared at her.

"*Fe*," she whispered. Something about the dream told her it was no dream, but memory, a long memory poignant of a time when she heard voices. A time she had been confused and unhappy: the time when her mother had suddenly died.

There was a warning and a voice of caution. *Ten quidado*, she told herself.

Hazy memories niggled her mind. A tall, stern man. Her father, afraid of him. A sun drenched plaza. The smell of fried onions. Her mother, collapsed at the base of the staircase. Her father's hands where they should never have been. His voice, above her, yelling. The chandelier trembling, the voices shouting, trains.

"I want to go to the University, Papa," she said one day, many years before.

"The University is only for girls who don't want to get married."

"Can I get married?"

"Who would marry you?" Ruiz had chuckled and pulled his daughter's hair. "I didn't mean that, sweetheart. All I meant was that I need you at home. You are a valuable member of my household."

"But I have nothing to do."

"Nonsense! If you would only learn to host parties, maybe wear a shorter skirt, do your hair, fix yourself up."

"But if I can't marry then why should I do those things?"

"So that you are chic, desirable, wanted."

"By whom?"

"Me, for one. I don't want you hanging around all glum and ill-kept." He had put his arm around his daughter. "Don't you know that you are a reflection of me? That you are an extension of myself. That is an important job, now isn't it?"

"Yes, Papa," Paulina had whispered, abashed, afraid of the pincer grip he had on her shoulder.

"Make me proud," he had said that day. "And don't forget who you are."

The sun shone brightly in the cloudless sky, children yelled, unseen but nearby, and she sat up to rub her eyes. The memories, dreams, and whispers receded into the back of her mind and left only one thought behind – that she had to get back to Oaxaca City. Paulina gathered her things and went to the hospital for the final time.

When Ruiz was found dead in his hospital bed, they took his body away and gave her his remains in a steel urn reserved for European atheists and infidels. The next day she boarded a plane to Mexico; the flight across the Atlantic effortlessly fixed with his money, his pig leather suitcases, and his monogram on everything she touched.

Six hours later, the plane from Cairo to Frankfurt, Frankfurt to Mexico City was circling, and Paulina looked down at the twin mountain ranges that held the swamp city. They were brown to the eye and worn. She sighed and wished the journey was over.

Oaxaca City, Mexico

The streets were very old. They were cobbled with bumpy stones that easily tripped you if you weren't watching. That was Paulina's first thought. The second was that it was much too bright. The city was obscenely bright in every way. The sun, the buildings in triple layers of loud paint, the people's meticulously embroidered dresses and frayed jeans. It was concentrated and intense, dazzling but impossible to ignore.

She had not been to Mexico in such a long time that at first, driving from the airport of Oaxaca City, she had expected the city to be as bland as the countryside had been. The rocky desert, the small villages populated by donkeys and half-naked children, playing or winding leaves around their fingers were dusty green and tan, the air clear, fresh. That she had expected for the southern mountain region. But cities were always dirty, she thought. Cities were smog-ridden and garbage-filled, gray buildings and gray people. But by the time Paulina had reached the outskirts of Oaxaca City she knew she had no idea what this place was like. She saw houses of every color in her mind's palate, from pink to blue and yellow to orange. Whole homes and buildings were painted entirely in some loud shade and trimmed with a different but equally loud shade. The city was carefully neat, the many trees large and healthy. It was a beautiful place despite the intensity. She had not expected that at all.

"I have always heard how dirty and poor Mexico is, that it's a third world country, that people starved and lived in slums," Paulina said to a fellow travller as they entered the city on the bus.

"They do," he answered. "But not here."

Some of the historic district streets were blocked — they had to wind their way around in circles, the little bus bouncing unhappily on the old cobblestones. There must have been twenty hotels to a one-block radius, she thought, all simply designed and old-fashioned, their square blocks well preserved.

Paulina disembarked at Pina Suarez, at a nice small hotel smack in the middle of it all. She was apprehensive, moving purposefully as if she had a job to do and it would be over as soon as she got to it.

"*Las Pinas*," she read on the ornate sign. They were off a small square, "*la Plaza de las Artistas*," the driver had said it was called. Men with carts and card tables rolled out carefully packed boxes and rugs to set up their paintings and jewelry, shirts, blankets and fantastical wooden figures.

"What are those painted wooden sculptures?" Paulina asked the bus driver carrying her bag. They seemed aboriginal, white and colored dots crammed in straight lines onto the cats and birds. Some were bright blue, some pink or purple, all very detailed and complicated.

"They are called *Alebrejes*, Señorita. The more intricate and large, if made from one piece of wood, the more expensive and skilled the artist who made it," he replied. "It's an art form that is native to Oaxaca." He paused. "Each region is famous throughout Mexico for something, and Oaxaca's got gold, and useless pieces of wood." He handed her father's old Italian luggage to her, accepting a modest tip.

Paulina looked across the square. *Oro de Oaxaca*, said the shop sign next to three identical shops, all the windows still shut.

The wealth of the city was obvious in its simple but lavish architecture, its well-laid streets, its impressive cathedral. It was still early, and the street sweepers were out with their branch brooms, palm leaves tied together with string. The shops weren't open yet, but sales people slowly shuffled to work, stopping for vending machine cappuccinos and a word with their friends.

Paulina rang the bell, calling out, "*Hola! Señor! Tengo reservaciones, abrame, no?*" Finally, a bolt slid open, rusty steel on old iron.

"*Sí?*" the old man asked as he tucked his beer gut into his Lee jeans with dignity.

"Paulina Ruiz. I have been waiting for quite some time, *Señor*."

"Apologies," the man said, trying to hide that he was giving her the eye as he heard her name. "Ruiz? *Si, claro. Beto! Venga!*" he shouted behind him, summoning a tall boy of about thirteen. "Help the *Señorita* with her bags. I'll get you the key to your room," he told Paulina while leading her into the courtyard of the hotel. The walk was lined with pink geraniums, a café with white iron tables and chairs set up on the grass. To her left was a lounge room and a car rental shop. On her right was an artsy, folk style bar attached to the outdoor café, furnished in mostly wood paneling and tapestries. She poked her head into the bar, looking at the strange paintings and photographs, large balcony windows framed in iron bars open to the sidewalk. There were heavy chairs on a sort of landing next to the windows. She made a mental note to sit in the window seat and watch the jewelry sellers of the Plaza when the boy called out, "*Señorita, el cuarto esta listo!*"

The October air was crisp and cool, even this far into the mountains of the south. "*Calabera!*" venders shouted. "*Pan de muerto!*"

She left the hotel and passed general shops, festive with bread, candles, sugar cubes of grinning skulls in preparation for *Dia de los Muertos*, Day of the Dead. Some shops had even built huge pyramids of skulls, all sizes, some chocolate, some white cane sugar, some pink and purple or blue to accompany the paper cut-outs and clay masks.

"Morbid," she said, passing one of the shops. "Why does it have to be so morbid?"

She stopped to examine a stack of tiny skulls, each only about an inch tall, perfectly made and bright with microscopic detail.

"*Le quiere uno, Señorita?*" she was asked. "*Son para el dia de los Muertos.*"

"Oh, no, no," Paulina backed away. "I really don't want one, thank you."

"Sure, here, get one," the man beside her handed the shopkeeper a few pesos and chose a chocolate skull from the top of the pyramid. "Eat it; it's good," he told her, holding the skull to Paulina, its eyes glittering with sequins.

"It's only chocolate," the man said, laughing at her horrified expression, and popped one into his mouth. He stuck out his hand. "Gary."

She took it and said, "Paulina."

Gary nodded and told her he already knew – the town was still small enough that news travelled quickly.

Paulina looked again at the store's goods. "How could a people so religious eat symbolic representations of the dead?"

Gary shrugged and began walking. "I don't know. It's very Catholic, you know. Eating the body of Christ makes it easier, maybe. But maybe it's just they don't take everything so seriously."

"Death is always serious."

"Not if you aren't afraid of it."

"Aren't you?"

"Sure," he said, leading her farther down *Calle Reforma*. They passed tourist shops selling clothes and big stone jewelry. "*Tamales!*" a woman cried as she passed, the stack of corn wrapped maize balanced on her wrinkled neck, the aroma wafting two steps behind her.

They sell everything on the street here, she thought, carts of useful things rolling past her, sandals and hair clips. *Oro de Monte Alban*, one store was called, *Puerto de Plata*, another on the cobbled street of Reforma.

"*Mira, hija,*" Gary called to one little girl balancing herself on the curbs and cobbles of the tourist street, selling seeds in long thin bags. Gary dug into his pocket and held out a balloon. He began to blow it up, his cheeks puffing out. Paulina had no idea what he was up to. Neither did the little brown girl, who wandered closer cautiously, her eyes lighting up with the attention and the sight of the balloon. Gary blew until the balloon had grown to the size of the girl's head and then Paulina understood.

It was a globe. He tied it and said, "Here is Mexico, *mi hija*," pointing.

The little girl had come to stand where Paulina was standing. She put a thin grubby hand on Paulina's linen pants, pointing to where Gary had pointed. "*Aqui esta Mejico?*" she asked, incredulously. Paulina wondered if the child had ever seen a representation of the world before.

"Yes," Paulina answered. The girl's mother finally noticed that her daughter had caught a couple of tourists and slowly began to wander closer, another baby on her back. "Here is Mexico," Paulina repeated, laughing and handing the girl the balloon, which embarrassed her mother now hovering nearby.

"What have you got there?" Paulina asked, her eyes on the girl's mother. The little girl suddenly remembered her job and held out the seeds. Paulina handed her some pesos and took a packet.

"Thank the gentleman for the balloon," the girl's mother called, rearranging the bright purple *sarape* she wore around the sleeping baby on her back.

"*Gracias, Señor,*" the girl said, shyly, pulling at the red yarn in her braids, Mexico's place forgotten, and scampered off, the world clutched in her hands. The mother showed her good gold tooth in a nod to Paulina, following her daughter to look for more tourists.

They walked down Reforma past Santo Domingo's courtyard. Paulina's back was straight; she walked without seeing. Past the cathedral and its monastery's high walls there was another square, shaded by the old buildings that surrounded it. It was a small plaza, occupied only by an old Indian man in a heavy poncho and wide hat.

They sat down on a stone bench by a sun-bleached wall and Gary reached into his jacket as Paulina slouched against the ivy and lit a cigarette. He opened the envelope and handed it to her. She took out the photograph, and Gary looked away, giving her a slight but decided moment of privacy.

The woman in the old photograph was small, wearing an old-fashioned hairdo, a swift uplifting of dark hair. She wore a brown dress, but not much of it was visible because of the child she held on her knee. The woman's face was unsmiling — large stern eyes held in a long oval face, her plump lips set straight, but held loosely. She was not exactly a pretty woman – not by Paulina's standards, at least. The child in the photograph wasn't smiling either. Her own large eyes came at the camera quickly, much faster than the woman's steady gaze. The child's eyes were penetrating and sharp. They seemed about to look away after their quick deep glance at the camera.

Paulina let out her breath. "I know this place," she said. "It was the living room of our house here in Oaxaca."

Gary looked at the photograph she held and then Paulina turned the photo over. There was an address scribbled out in Spanish. "Mitla," Paulina mumbled, "is a little pueblo about an hour's bus ride from here." She looked up, squinting.

Paulina took out her guidebook and looked it up. She had bought the book in the airport – mostly for the maps. The book told her that on the way to Mitla there was a tourist spot called Tule. Amongst other attractions like a beautiful cathedral, a market, and the quaint café's offering the best café de cacao around, there was a very large old tree, Tule, and apparently it was the size of a house.

Paulina stood and shook Gary's hand. "I might see you again," she said.

"Say hello to your cousin Jaime for me when you meet him," he replied.

Mitla Village, Oaxaca, Mexico

The desert was red here, plateaus obscured villages and mud homes. More Indians walked down the highways in their shuffling way, carrying their wares or their children. It was like Mars, she thought, so unlike anything she had ever imagined. Every so often she would catch a bit of a Zapoteca pyramid, buried by the dirt of the desert, temples neglected by the tourists, crumbling into the desert that had built them.

Paulina stared ahead at the back of the seat in front of her, occasionally taking out the photograph. When her stop came, Paulina paused, one leg stretched out long before the other one on the last step into Mitla, the tourists in front of her gazing at the postcard village and its streets of Indian shops, selling mostly clothes and fabric, knick-knacks and bags. Mitla's main business was textiles.

"*Calle Ciento Veinti-ocho?*" She asked an Indian woman struggling with a bundle of soft cotton pants. The woman pointed to a long dirt road to Paulina's left which led away from the town, uphill to small ranches and sets of simple white houses in circles. She nodded and started up the red dirt road, the dust flying up behind her as she set her face forward.

The jagged mountains in the distance behind and in front were clear and rusty. Donkeys brayed in their pens, two children ran past, laughing and pushing each other to go faster, their sandals flapping loudly.

Maria Eugenia's home was in a small group beside a half-collapsed barn, lightly whistling in the wind. The barn housed a cloth spinner and a large rickety wooden loom. Paulina looked in and saw stacks of cotton and spun fabric ready to be dyed.

"It is my son's place," she heard a woman say. Paulina turned slowly toward the sound. She was much older than Paulina thought she would be, holding a little boy's hand and plucking at her hair with the other. "Come in, I've started the *café*."

Paulina followed the woman as she went inside the small home, neat but haphazard. A chicken ran past her as she looked for something to say.

"I used to live with *mi esposo* in the city," the woman said. She put cups and a china set of *café* on a tray. "He used to own shops and hotels downtown, but died about ten years ago so I came here to live with *mi hijo*, my son Ricardo. Ricardo doesn't like the city." She shooed the little boy outside and invited Paulina into the living room. "But I kept the house," she said, and sat in an old chair, groaning. "It is another hotel, I think, now," she waved her hand. "Ricardo takes care of all that."

Paulina was uncomfortable in her chair but tried not to pull her knees up for the benefit of this old friend of her mother's. "Your father never told you what happened," Maria Eugenia said.

"No," Paulina replied.

"He was a snake, an ego bigger than the Yucatan. He wouldn't let me see you after Teresa died." She poured the coffee, adding sweet milk to Paulina's cup.

"*Te digo*, the things she did for that man." She shook her head, "and he left in the dead of night the day after. I just heard you came back to bury him. *En fin! Gracias a Dios*, the man is dead. He killed her, *mi amor*. She wanted to please him by having a baby – and this is what killed her."

She handed Paulina the cup and patted her knee. "Excuse me, *niña*. I didn't mean to hurt you, but she was too sick for *bebes*. Especially back in those days. You know that. And he made her care for you herself. He said he didn't want servants in the house, that they stole and didn't respect his privacy. *Respeto*! For that man! Pah! Of course servants steal; they are a bother. But we women, we need them. Your father, *el gringo codo*, excuse me, mi *corazon*, but that cheap lazy American," she said, hitting her elbow. "I have not been able to speak with you for so long, I am full of bitterness, here in my heart, en *mi corazon*." She stopped hitting her elbow and instead hit her heart, as one does for the *Mea Culpa* in Mass. Three times she beat her chest, and then stopped to sip her coffee.

"Look at what a woman you are," Maria Eugenia said quietly. The old woman leaned back against the faded chair to look at Paulina. "How we adored you, *princesa*." The old woman got to her feet, pulling out shelves and drawers. "Here, I will show you your mother and me," she said.

Paulina didn't mind the harsh words; they were peppered with sweetness. Even as the old woman had beat her heart in grief, Paulina hadn't minded.

"Teresa was fierce in her love for you." Maria Eugenia handed Paulina a few photos. "Look," she said, "here you can see us in the Yucatan at Chichin Itza. Aren't we good looking?" The old woman sighed, tipping her head at the old photograph. Teresa was saying something to the camera, but Paulina did not know what it could have been.

"*Ja*, her heart, *mi vida*, it was not as strong as her spirit." Maria Eugenia glanced at Paulina sipping her coffee, holding the old black and whites.

"He did not tell you anything at all. That snake, he did not." Maria Eugenia sat back, shaking her head, letting her own coffee become cold, unattended. A film began to creep over it as she gathered up what she wanted to say in her mind.

"Ahh," she finally moaned. "*Pobrecita.* Your mother, like her mother before her and before her, had a weak heart. She knew this."

Paulina frowned, putting down her cup, and the picture of the woman who now sat in an old wicker chair.

"Many lost *bebes*. And Teresa, she wanted so badly. But the doctors, they told her to stop. She was sick in the heart and it was too late. But your mama, she wanted you so much, even more than the love of her life she wanted you, *Tesoro.*" Maria Eugenia shook her wrinkled head, her black beaded earrings clinking together with the sound of plastic. "And that Jorge would say, Teresa, if we had a *bebe* I would be a good husband, a good father! And she tried, *mi vida*. She really did." Maria Eugenia thought back and sat still.

"So, here you were finally, and for her - weak heart, new *bebe*, and no servant. This was difficult for your mother Teresa, but she is an ox. She say, 'Jorge has no trust for people in the house. I care for the *bebe*, I work, I cook, I clean, it is not so hard.' But I knew, *amor*," the old woman leaned forward to look into Paulina's face. "I knew it was too hard: it killed her, all this work. All for him. And him who went back to his whore anyway." The old woman sipped cold *café*, remembering the little girl beside her. "But you were everyone's favorite." Maria Eugenia looked over again at Paulina, still touching the cup, but slightly as the taste of the coffee was gone from her mouth. "So quiet and polite, even as *un bebe.*"

"What was she like?" Paulina asked, her voice devoid of inflection, afraid of the memories Maria Eugenia could give her. "With me, what was she like?"

"She loved you, *amor*, never doubt this. She loved to dress and pet you. She never told you to 'Go play, get out of my hair little girl,' as other mamas told their *bebes*." Maria waved her hand again, poking her hair. "You were always with us. I remember," she smiled into the past as Paulina did not do, looking far away, "I remember once we went to Riviera Maya, where I took those pictures I show you. Just us, not your papa, that snake, and you played in the sand as we drank our *café* and spoke of things very serious." Maria Eugenia looked away from the past and saw Paulina clearly, this grown woman who smelt of men and money, of books and airplanes. "She spoke of her pain only to me there that day in Merida. *Puerto del Sol*, our hotel. Many *gringos* there. They looked at your mama and me. Even me, those dirty dogs! I always hated *gringos*. They think they can buy Mexico, *niña*. But they cannot buy *alma, tradicion, historia*. We were not beautiful women, *niña*, not even then, but we owned our own souls, and that is what makes a woman desired. It is what sets a woman above the corruption and disgust of our *nacion pobre*, this poor lying whore of a country we have." Maria sat back in her chair.

"And as those *gringos* looked at your mother and me, as Tere told me of the pain in her chest, her heart, you made sandcastles on a beach that belongs to *nuestra Mejico*, our Mexico. I knew I must keep you from that man, your papa, when Tere was gone. I did not tell her, but I told you *niña*. Do you remember I told you this?"

Again the old woman looked at Paulina, her eyes soft with age and failure. She knew the neatly dressed half-*gringa* knew nothing of her or her failures and promises, the battle she had fought for that beautiful little girl with huge brown eyes - windows that reflected nothing now, this old woman's lifetime later, when they had once confessed of saints.

"I am sorry, *niña*," was all Maria Eugenia could say, taking her glasses off her wrinkled face. "I could not keep you. I had no rights against that man." Tears began to fall into the wrinkled folds of her cheeks, and she wiped them away, her earrings catching on her fingers. "I have felt such grief and *coraje* at what that man did to you, *corazon*."

Neither spoke for a moment. Paulina did not breathe, did not stir or speak. This woman knew her life. This old woman who had no one but her son to care for her, surrounded by chickens and an unknown *primo* in the city, she knew what her father had done for so long.

"Teresa kept you far away from that man. She tried, *corazon*, as did I. But he took you away. I could not, I could not," Maria Eugenia turned her face away from the memory. "Save you. And I have never spoken of this to anyone. I have lived many mornings since my little *niña* has left and prayed to the Virgin that he find a woman to care for you. To protect you, to save you from that man as I had failed." The old shoulders did not shake, but the tears were clear in the years of lines on her face. With no glasses, the woman was nearly blind. She did not see Paulina, rocking slightly in her chair, flinching, her jaw working in hatred of the feelings that were all that was left of her life with her father. Revulsion, fear, an engulfing sense of guilt.

Maria Eugenia wiped her glasses, no longer apologizing, no longer bathed in regret. It had been said; it was over for the old woman. "Maybe if I had not tried so hard he would not have left."

"Yes, he would have," Paulina answered the undressed recrimination. "Papa wanted a world that did not exist. He wanted to be a part of a life he would have to create. And when he couldn't, he decided it had been better before. Papa was a stupid man." She looked at Maria Eugenia and the old woman looked at her. "Papa was a selfish lover of himself. Let us not speak of him *jamas*."

For the first time, Maria Eugenia smiled.

"Tell me more about my mama," Paulina said and sat back in her chair, now pulling up her knees in an attitude of intimacy.

"She made delicious, *sabrosas*, pastries. She sang for you, danced for you. She brushed your hair five times in one day. We went to the *Mercado* where the men with their carts knew us. They gave you sweets dipped in *miel*, *azucar* and nuts. You never wanted for anything with us. Your Mama was so proud when you began to say your own little prayers, and how you loved the Mass. Until the day she died, you were her *niña*, her best moment, the reason she made up her bed and why she fought the pain to get out of it each morning. For you, *nadamas para ti, Niña*. For you she lived four more years. And no one can take that away from you or me or my friend Teresa."

Maria Eugenia poured them both more *café de cacao* and patted Paulina's knee. "The memories will come, *chica*. You stay here in Oaxaca, walk the Zocalo. You will see your Mama in your mind."

But Paulina was not ready yet for her mama. Her chest did not ache - it raced. She breathed easily and was a young woman.

"What is this weak heart?" Paulina had to ask. "Where does it come from and is there something I can do? Do I have it too?"

"I don't know, *mi amor*. Don't you have your own doctors? But I do know this: it has killed many of your women and made many orphans. I do not know its name. Teresa did not speak of doctors to me, *mi vida*. But there were days she would stop what she was doing to lie and rest."

Paulina looked out Maria Eugenia's window, the Mitla ranch ringed by desert plains and the flat distant plateaus. The air was dry and the sky was clean. She saw an old *pueblano* walking down the shifting dirt road, his ragged jeans dragging behind his plastic sandals. She needed time to think, to be alone. "Do you remember which doctor she went to?"

Mari had to think. "Maybe Dr. Sanchez on *Independencia*. But that was many years ago, *niña*."

Paulina trembled in her light jacket. They sat quietly, Maria thinking of her friend who this child did not resemble, Paulina for the first time considering her own mortality.

"Next week is *Dia de los Muertos, Niña*," the old woman said, filling in the room's unspoken sadness with the soft melancholy of her voice. "You know this?" she asked gently.

Paulina nodded.

"Go and see your mama. Go to her grave and pray to her that she finds you. Keep the vigil your *primos* never do."

Paulina looked down at the old woman's hand on her knee. She followed it up to her elbow, her shoulder, until Paulina could see Maria Eugenia's face. It was full of compassion and pain. It was full of unspoken secrets and the one woman's laughter Paulina could not remember and would never hear, though she would have given her own life.

Oaxaca City, Mexico

With the phone book in her lap Paulina dialed the doctor's phone number.

"Doctor Sanchez?" she asked. "Do you remember a patient named Teresa Montelejos Ruiz, about twenty or so years ago?"

She listened and continued. "His son? Oh. I'm sorry to hear that. Files on record? Yes? Oh. Yes, I'm her daughter," there was a pause. *"Independencia?* Tomorrow? Thank you, Doctor. I will, absolutely."

She hung up the old yellow receiver and stared at the wall, trying to process her thoughts, what Maria Eugenia had told her from what she dimly remembered as a child in Oaxaca, the only time she had ever seen a doctor.

"It's down here somewhere," Dr. Sanchez said, leading Paulina into the maze of boxes. "We never cleaned it; it is as the old man left it."

They found the old files and went to the clinic where the doctor listened to the beating of Paulina's heart. "Deep breath, please," the doctor said, his cold hands on her chest. "One more please," he quietly repeated, listening to her body, air moving into her lungs, her rapid heartbeat fluttering into the metal poked into his ears. He pulled away from her to the desk where he glanced at her mother's old file.

"So? How long will I live?"

"How long will you live?" the doctor sat back on his swiveling chair and crossed his arms. "I do not know, Señorita. You are not yet ill. There is no way to predict a thing like this. All depends upon the care you take for yourself. Too much stress and activity means possible heart palpitations, murmurs, gradual weakening. Don't climb any mountains; take life easily. Do not be so active. No more cigarettes or coffee." The doctor stood and shook her hand. "Well, that's all I have to say. If you want a diet and light exercise plan, come back here to see me."

The next day she chose a café that opened to the Zocalo; the Doctor's words sat on Paulina's shoulders like a wooden yolk. The people of the Zocalo weaved past each other. She stopped one of the necklace ladies floating past their table and bought a green stone necklace. Paulina spread out her limbs, man-like, and waited for Maria Eugenia to come.

The old woman walked bent but proud, small, but somehow she was dignified with slow grace. Maria Eugenia put down her large leather purse next to the table, summoning the waiter who stood behind them at the café's iron barred window. "*Chocolate,*" she said.

He bowed to her, knowing Maria Eugenia as did most of the city, and her charity, her old world mannerisms.

"Make an old woman happy, *mi cielo,*" Maria Eugenia said. "Come back to Mexico."

"Stay here?"

"Where else you going to go?"

Paulina sat and thought. There was nowhere else to go, Maria Eugenia was right. "I have come back," she corrected the old woman's previous statement. "So maybe I'll stick around."

"And where will you live?"

"My hotel is very nice."

Maria Eugenia smiled through the pains of her seniority. "I know the man who owns it," she said. "Maybe I can get you a discount." And the old woman winked at Paulina naughtily. "Do you know where your Mama's grave is, *nina*?" When Paulina shook her head, Maria Eugenia took a long drink of her chocolate and nodded. "I will take you there."

At the old French cemetery, Maria Eugenia found her friend's grave easily. She instructed Paulina to put down her bag loaded with candles, *Pan de Muerto*, the icons of Teresa's favorite saints she had bought in the street and set her to work cleaning the neglected tomb. Maria Eugenia had bought *calaveras*, the paper mache skeletons engaged in living life in death, and a bottle of *Rompompe*. Every woman in Mexico has a bit of the witch in her, Paulina thought.

"Your mother loved a nice cup of cacao," Maria Eugenia told Paulina and poured a cupful of steaming chocolate into the vase holders, the liquid quickly sinking into the old thirsty dirt. She then instructed Paulina to clear away the old plants. The scrub beside the tomb and in its vase holders were brittle from the lack of water that once fed the flowers Maria Eugenia had planted many years before. Paulina had filled a garbage bag when she finally got up off her knees to embrace the old woman.

"I will leave you here with your mother," Maria Eugenia said to Paulina. "Go with God."

Paulina Montelejos sat on her mother's grave and drank chocolate coffee. Her father sat beside her in his steel American urn. The cemetery, *Pantheon Frances*, whispered to its dead, moving quietly to the rhythm of the old men sitting along its avenues in their *ranchero* hats and gray woolen ponchos. The people around her trailed their fingers along the crumbled walls of monumental graves and listened to the calls of water sellers and *tamale* women. Paulina unwrapped three bunches of *flores de los muertos* from the *Mercado*; vibrant orange marigolds, white lilies, and fuchsia coxcomb. But she did not arrange them in the marble vases at the head of the grave. Instead she scattered their petals into the shape of an immense cross, obliterating the middle of the inscription from sight.

> *Maria Teresa Montelejos de Ruiz*
> *Se fue con Dios*
> *Con el amor de su esposo*
> *Y su hija*

  Paulina finished her *Café de Cacao* and opened her father's urn. Carefully, she covered the cross in his ashes, the still Oaxacan breeze as calming as the endless Mexican sky. She emptied the last of her father into her palm and leaned across the white marble grave to blow him into the crucifix where Jesus waited. He settled into the crevices of God's arms, above her mother's inscription. Now he is with God as well, Paulina thought, standing. And as she picked up her cup, the urn, and the newspaper wrapping from the three bunches of flowers, she stopped to leave a small plastic icon of St. Judas, bearing his own cross.
  In the courtyard of Santo Domingo she sat among stiff mescal plants with defensive arms held like razor-tipped swords and watched the cathedral: its gaudy flamboyance, its arrogance, its utter disregard for propriety. The colossal fifteenth-century structure, engulfed in gold leaf, displayed magnificent religiosity from without while from within framed sepia portraits were glued to the saints' glass cases. The photographs, petitions to the intermingled God of Christianity and the Zapoteca Indians crumbled beside flowers wilting in the heat, their fragrances heady in the filtered sunlight of

Mass. As they had dressed Santo Domingo in gold, and continued to dress her in flowered finery and old photographs, the people of Oaxaca City would also don their own chalecos and sarapes, their finest most vibrant gold jewelry and join the Cathedral.

Paulina did not like the cathedral of Santo Domingo itself. At the siesta hour the historic center of Oaxaca City felt deceptively unreal. No one was in the plaza; the vendors, tourist police, early tourists, shop people, and bus drivers' kids were nowhere nearby. There was something artificial about this time. As if what gave the place its flow had been eradicated and all that was left were sets and the huge paper heads, their eyes unmoved by the early sun. She had come to like this feeling of monstrous unreality. It was as if she was not in the plaza either; as if she didn't exist between the cobbles of the tourist streets and the rows of mescal plants in the cathedral's outer gardens. Paulina felt then as though nothing had ever existed. That her life was not possible and had never been experienced before — for although pigeons still fluttered among the crooked arms of sainted Indian gods, an apocalypse had occurred.

But then the day cooled and the illusion rolled over to show an active human scene crossing itself piously: begging, hawking, embracing, and going about the business of a few thousand non-converging lives.

Mitla Village, Mexico

"I am sick," Paulina announced at Maria Eugenia's door the next day.

"I know this, yes."

"When will I die?"

Maria Eugenia looked deep into Paulina's eyes. "Do you think I can heal you, *niña*?"

"Well can't you? With all your herbs and remedies and juju?"

Maria Eugenia pursed her lips. "Give me your hand," she said. Paulina did, expecting her god-mother to examine it for signs or marks, but Maria Eugenia slapped it instead and the sting of it surprised Paulina. "That teach you. I am a God-fearing woman, make no mistake." Paulina rubbed the back of her hand.

"Come inside, I make you *café*." Paulina followed the old woman inside her son's house.

"*Abuelita*," a little boy called from one of the rooms.

"Excuse me, *niña*," Maria Eugenia wiped her hands on her stained apron and went to her grandson. The kitchen smelt of spring onions and fried flour. The sun poured in from one window and Paulina could see the dust dancing in the beam. She leaned back against the counter next to the stove and listened to the murmurs of her godmother and the little boy; her low voice and his moaned replies. The water began to boil, rolling waves in the small pot and Paulina turned off the heat. She didn't want to be presumptuous so instead of making the *café* she leaned back against the counter and inspected the empanadas that waited on a large blue plate. She leaned down to smell the onion and green pepper smothered with white goat's cheese.

"I am sorry," Maria Eugenia bustled back in and made the *café* in three movements. "Miguelito is sick. The doctor has said he has the feather pox."

"Chicken pox."

"Yes, this *pollo* pox. He is very unhappy." Maria Eugenia loaded a tray with the *café*, *empanadas*, and some sugar cookies and went into the living room. "We sit here," she sighed and sat down. Paulina sat down and looked at her hands. She could hear the little boy crying softly.

"You only come here to tell me you dying, *niña*?" Maria Eugenia took a sip and swallowed before she laid her trap. "No more questions about your mother and her family in Puebla?"

"What family?"

"Your family in Puebla." Maria Eugenia again took a sip, but this time to hide her smile.

"I have no family in Puebla, *Madrina*. They are all here in Oaxaca."

"You know better than me, *niña*."

Paulina slumped forward. "No, I don't god-mother. I don't want to see Aunt Gloria or any of my cousins, but if you say there are more, then," Paulina shrugged, "of course I believe you."

Maria Eugenia stood up and rummaged in her dresser drawer. Her skirt bunched and her plastic beads clinked together. "Here," she said, handing Paulina a very old photograph of a young man, his hat cocked over one eye rakishly. "That is your grandfather."

Paulina took the photograph with her fingertips, wondering at it. "Mine?" She examined the photograph. "He's very handsome. Why haven't I met him? My — no one — ever said anything about him."

"You not ask, *niña*?" Maria Eugenia's voice was accusatory, as if Paulina had knowingly refused this man. Paulina shrank back at the sound.

"No, I didn't ask. I never asked anything," she stopped. "We didn't talk much," she said after a moment.

Maria Eugenia nodded, "We not talk much either."

Paulina felt herself smiling though she felt very sad. "He is in Puebla?"

"Yes, *mi'ja*, but I don't know where. But I know he is very ill. I told Jaime this; I believe he wrote you a letter? Jaime has not a lot of contact with his grandfather but I hear many things. I told Jaime that his grandfather was ill, and by extension, I told you. But your grandmother, she knows where Hernando is. She lives in Puerto Escondido, she is easy to find."

Paulina started. "My grandmother? I have a grandmother too?"

"Doesn't everyone?" Maria Eugenia looked at Paulina's cup and said, "Drink your *café*; I put herbs in it to help digestion. Drink." Paulina took the cup in both hands and drank deeply.

"Why don't they live together?" she asked.

"Just because everyone have grandparents does not mean they live together."

"The little boy can't sleep, godmother."

Maria Eugenia listened to the silence. Paulina stood to leave. She didn't want to know where her grandmother lived, though Puerto Escondido was not so far. She wanted to go back to the hotel and have a nap and forget everything; her sick heart, her estranged grandparents and especially this woman who she wished was her mother. But she had come so far already and knew that she must continue. "Your grandson is calling you, god-mother," she said, handing back the photograph.

"*Abuelita?*" came the little boy's voice.

"*Ya vengo,*" answered Maria Eugenia. She also stood and took Paulina's elbow. "Look in my diary there," she said, motioning to her desk, "there you find Portensia Montelejos. She is your grandmother." Maria Eugenia kissed Paulina's cheek. "Go with God."

Paulina left Maria Eugenia's ranch house walking slowly, dragging her expensive new shoes in the sand. The mountains lengthened all around her in the dimming light of late afternoon. Two women carrying bundles of cloth passed her, their Indian shirts red and embroidered with small x's in pink, purple, and orange. One had a small child bound to her back in a brown *serape*.

"*Buenas,*" they called to her as she passed.

"*Buenas,*" she said in reply, strangely glad they had greeted her so informally, like a passing friend. She found the bus stop easily as she walked through the small town square; the ruined cathedral and shops full of clothes, sandals, chocolate and jewelry. Did she want to meet her grandparents? What would they say about her mother, her father? Had they opposed the marriage as strongly as her Aunt Gloria? Would they want to see her? Would they make her remember the man, her father, when she had already bid him goodbye?

"*Dos pesos,*" the bus driver's son told her. He was the color of mud when it rains and she liked the swirl in his hair. She handed him the two pesos and chose a seat near the back. The bus bumped along the highway towards Oaxaca City, past plateaus and huts made of tin and wood, farmers walking home with their feet in the ruts the donkey carts had made, and stray dogs who knew not to come too close to the highway. What if they didn't want to see her? She wondered.

Puerto Escondido, Mexico

    Paulina leaned her head against the seat ahead of her. The bus rocked to the left as it took another nauseous turn around the mountain. The first time it had done so she had looked out the window, down to the depths of the ravine below. She had only done that once: it had terrified her too much to try again. The jungle began a few hours into the trip — leafy branches bigger than the length of her arm scraping the windows of the bus. She had taken a third class bus because of the time she wanted to arrive in Puerto and so she made herself watch guiltily as more and more people took seats in the aisle or stood. Many carried cages of chickens or nearly empty baskets of fruit in one arm and small weary children in the other. Men and women used their shawls as pillows to cushion against the bumpy ride and appeared to sleep. She wished she had thought to bring something to cushion her own head against the window.

    As the bus wound its way up the mountains it grew steadily colder — broken windows in the back sending gusts of chilling air down her neck. She looked at her reflection in the darkened window. Her cheeks were very pink and she so looked the picture of health that she struggled to believe the doctor's words. How soon until the stress on her heart would show on the lineless skin of her face?

    Green flashed before her eyes and then there was the sea — grey in the light of dawn, it was dotted with fishing boats of all sizes. And then they were off the mountain and she shook herself to attention.

    She pulled her backpack off the bus, breathing in the damp clear air of early morning. Only the birds made noise, the sea silent — obscured by a ring of scrubby sand trees. Paulina lifted a hand without looking and a taxi appeared next to her. "*Hostal Playa*," she said as she climbed into the rickety vehicle.

The taxi driver bumped and rattled over sandy roads and brush until he finally slowed and they got out of the misshapen vehicle. Paulina counted out the fare as the driver grabbed her pack. She looked around the scrubby bare trees and the dusty street. There were no other structures nearby.

The hostel's owner came out to welcome her: there were not many tourists that month. "Hello friend!" he called out. He was youthful, tanned and well over six feet tall. He introduced himself as Jimmy, reaching out to shake Paulina's hand. "*Bien venidos* to my humble hostel. Please, let me to help you." Jimmy took her pack and said, "Here, feel in your home, friend. I will show you the arraignments."

Paulina followed Jimmy into the open patio, her flip-flops sinking into night-cooled sand. Jimmy took two steps and stopped short, causing Paulina to bump into him.

"This—this is our Cantina." Jimmy stretched out his hands to encompass the plastic patio furniture and wood-planked bar. "We sell at reasonable price the beer, the..." he made a drinking motion, thumb and pinky finger outstretched and bobbing toward his mouth. Then he abruptly turned and continued toward a door at the back of the bar. "Rooms here. I give you the Master's Suite — big room — deluxe." Jimmy opened the room's door with a flourish and stood aside. There was a double bed with mosquito netting, a night table and a metal rack that held four hangers.

She looked back at Jimmy who laughed loudly. "Ah, ah, ah! Yes, but look out the window, friend." Paulina stepped fully into the room and went to the large far window. The sea glittered blue and silver, like a giant fish in the morning sun. "Open the door," Jimmy said from behind her.

Paulina did and stepped onto the beach. She again turned to look back at Jimmy who raised his extra-long arms into the air and said, "Welcome to Puerto, friend." He paused for dramatic effect, coughed into his fist and shut the door behind him.

Nine streets away, at nine fifty-five that morning, Señora Portensia Montelejos had chosen a coral colored linen suit, the Christian Dior suit-pin sent especially from Paris and a light, tan, meshed hat that fell over the left side of her face. She had dusted herself with *Polvo Angel* and though it was ninety degrees in the shade, wore nude stockings. Her shoes — also tan — were a modest height (the Señora considered heels over two inches indecent) that matched her handbag and hat perfectly. From the Señora's punctual bath at nine o'clock to that moment she had been meticulously methodical in her preparation and the completion of that preparation. Nothing distracted the octogenarian's gaze from the task at hand. From the steadiness needed to apply her makeup to the careful fastening of the buttons on her suit — no stray thought entered her mind.

At ten fifty-five her regular taxi driver rang the bell and she took stock of that hour's work. Not bad for eighty-nine, she thought, standing before the round mirror of her dressing table.

"*Hola*, Señora," the driver greeted her. "*La Café Parisian?*"

"Yes, please Octavio." The lady answered as she got into the taxi and sat upright to straighten her veil.

"Strange weather we are having, no?" the driver adjusted his mirror so as to not stare directly at her: to do so would have been extremely rude.

"Yes," Señora Montelejos replied absently. "It seems something has blown its way in — for now it is quite calm." Her mind would not focus now — as if it were being called away, her attention obeyed another force.

They were silent after the exchange of pleasantries: the Señora did not like to be too familiar with those outside her class. The taxi approached Paz Street and stopped in front of the most exclusive café in that small seaside town. Unknown to the tourists its only patrons were old and methodical like the Señora: the Spanish who had come to Puerto would not leave their snobbery behind. Here, they founded new Orders of their established class. *The Café Parisian* was the Señora's favorite but certainly there were others she did not frequent that were just as fine.

The café was on a paved street. Its large glass doors mirrored what the Mexicans thought Paris should be: ostentatious, expensive, and exclusive. The café floors were marble, its potted palms well watered and dusted. The waiters wore white waistcoats and gloves and all drinks and platters were served on fine china lettered with a cursive P. The café awnings were striped white and pink and inside it seated only eight tables of four — complimented by white wrought-iron chairs cushioned with the same stripes as the awning. The patrons of café Parisian signed their bills with silver fountain pens and were billed at their homes at the end of each month.

That day the Señora was meeting an old friend — the Señora Flores. The Señora Flores — always forty-five minutes late, thus exactly on time — met her friend with a double kiss and a pressing of the hands. Señora Montelejos did not approve of Señora Flores' habit of practically bathing in Chanel but as usual said nothing about it. A woman is nothing but the sum of her manners, after all.

"What a pleasant day, no, Señora?" Señora Flores asked, her voice wavering.

"Yes, Señora, it is very pleasant. How are your children and household?"

"Yes, Señora, well thank you."

"Very good."

The ladies ordered their drinks and discretely arranged their hair-dos, each pretending the other did not notice.

"What have you heard from your daughter, Señora Flores?"

"She is well, Señora. In fact she was recently in Oaxaca City from the Capital."

"To what purpose, Señora?"

Señora Flores — though mindful of her friend's hatred of gossip — could not keep still. "She was there for her sister-in-law's wedding." Señora Flores fidgeted, clearly waiting for the correct question to be asked.

"And so, how was the wedding, Señora?"

"Oh excellent, thank you. Of course, very beautiful." The mint sprigs on Señora Flores' finely made straw hat trembled as the Señora struggled to contain herself.

"Has your daughter sent photographs?"

"They have not arrived yet, Señora."

Señora Montelejos watched her friend's wrinkled face tremble as she struggled to maintain her silence. She was well aware that Señora Flores had news of some importance but was watching the woman wrestle with the dictations of her class — the Señora Flores usually had news of some importance and this scene was one of Señora Montelejos' favorite pastimes. "Well, you might as well tell me whatever it is, my friend," she said when her conscience could not take any more enjoyment at the expense of her friend.

The other woman sat forward, finally allowed to divulge her gossip. "My daughter saw Maria Eugenia."

"Such is news, that the old nag is still alive?" Señora Montelejos had never approved of her daughter's friendship — especially because Maria Eugenia was the Señora's own age. What kind of woman befriends young girls, after all?

"And I swear it to you," Señora Flores continued, "she said she received a visit from Teresa's daughter."

"You lie," the Señora said coldly.

"I swear it to you. Her daughter, a girl named Paulina."

Señora Montelejos was quiet, trying to regain her composure. She had not meant to be so cruel but she was very angry — how could her granddaughter go to that old bat instead of her own flesh and blood? What could anyone say of such a girl? "So, what else did the old lady say?"

Señora Flores knew she had touched a nerve. They had never in twenty years spoken of Señora Montelejos' only granddaughter, born very late in the Señora's life, though everyone knew Teresa had been disowned. The lady had been resolute that it wouldn't cause scandal and thereby avoided it. "That the girl is fine and has good manners. As fine as Teresa's were."

"Fine manners indeed," commented the Señora. "Orphaned by a rebellious mother and raised by an American pig, I'm sure her manners reflect their origin."

Señora Flores accepted the drink the waiter offered her. "Regardless of what has happened, Señora, she is still your granddaughter and perhaps she will come to Puerto."

"Perhaps," the Señora agreed. The weather had indeed changed — bringing with it old arguments and new blood.

The phone rang three times. Paulina twirled the metal cord around her wrist. She could see Jimmy sitting at the bar drinking a Sol. "Ah, ah, ah!" he laughed with a guest — his hands beat the air as he told a story.

"Hello?"

"Oh," Paulina was flustered and forgot her carefully prepared speech, all her florid language and pleasantries. "Is this Señora Montelejos?"

"No. The Señora is at lunch. Can I take a message?"

Paulina was silent. She couldn't decide if it would be better to surprise her grandmother and be guaranteed she would listen at least for a moment or if she should give her name and let Portensia consider seeing her.

"Name? Who is this please?"

"I'm very sorry. My name, my name is Paulina Ruiz."

"I give her the message, Miss."

When the Señora returned to her home to hear a Paulina Ruiz had telephoned she simply said, "and so," and began arranging her memories.

When Teresa died Portensia Montelejos had locked her husband out of her bedroom for five days — and never spoke to him again. She could not forgive Hernando his complacency: his failure to win back their daughter. If he had only pleaded with Teresa himself instead of leaving it to Gloria she would have listened. Teresa would not have dared defy her father.

Portensia changed out of her suit; again donning the housedress she wore each day between brunch and mass, except on Sundays when she received visitors in her home. Teresa had never returned to their house on *Independencia.* Portensia had grown used to her bitterness at losing her only daughter to that dandified louse, and had long ago forgotten the child Teresa bore. The heart defect that had killed her daughter resided in her own heart as well — but Portensia was too iron-willed to let anything as human as a heart get the best of her: and could not forgive Teresa for succumbing to such a ridiculous malady.

The Señora had survived to eighty-nine by adhering to a strict routine and light diet. Her entire life she had followed her own deceased mother's advice — who herself had died when Portensia was only nineteen years old. "Rise at a decent hour," her mother Mariabella had said, "Eat a soft boiled egg and one slice of dry toast and a very small dinner at early evening. Never make exercise or walk more than ten minutes each day. Never do your own cooking or cleaning. Do this and you will live a long life, Sita." Mariabella had not followed her own advice but Portensia had — to the last detail.

Each day was the same as the last but for Sundays. And now this child, this Paulina, had come to bring her to her death. The irony of it was something she couldn't stand. Very well, she would have to visit on Sunday afternoon as the others did.

"Telephone the girl who called this morning," she ordered the housekeeper. "And tell her to come on Sunday." And she shut the door of her bedroom for her four o'clock siesta.

"Well, little friend," Jimmy addressed Paulina as she sat alone at his Cantina. "I have heard my little birdies tell me you will go see *la Reina de Puerto*. The eh, Dragon Lady of our fair village."

Paulina did not answer immediately: she sipped her Corona and scratched a mosquito bite on her toe.

"Are my birdies wrong, little friend? No," he said, "this is a small place and we know when the big things happen here." Jimmy lowered his voice and his face became very serious. "I know your mother's history. It brought us the Old Reptile on the Hill, the one who makes things difficult for us with her demands and — what do you call it...protocol?"

"Are you asking me or telling me?"

"I'm telling you because of your mother that old woman came here to impose sanctions on the rest of us who only like to drink beer and surf the sea. We were happy before, sleeping on the beach and playing cards by the fire." He ripped the label from his beer and crumpled it up tightly. "And then she came out here and organized the other old ones to make rules, laws, restrictions on our good times." He tossed the small paper ball toward the fan. "And it's been nothing but work since that time."

Paulina finally understood his complaint and laughed loudly. "You're family," she accused. "I can see it in your mouth. You look like Grandfather's picture." She took a big swallow of beer and muttered, "family."

Jimmy bowed slightly and opened himself another bottle. "That may be so — pleased to meet you," he took her hand and shook it. "I can finally make confession. I am Jaime, your cousin."

"Why haven't you said so before?" Paulina asked.

"I have been a shy boy."

Paulina covered her mouth to hide her giggle.

"Yes, me, shy," he insisted. "It was the Old Reptile on the Hill bought me this *hostal*. Many thanks to you," he said dryly and drank half the bottle at once. "And," he said, wiping away the foam that lingered on his chin, "left me in chains to that lady, the stepmother of my own."

"What's that to do with me, then? I just met you!"

"Ah well, you see." Jimmy resumed his good mood and tossed his empty bottle into the bin. "When the Old Reptile couldn't bear to live in Oaxaca City anymore she moved herself out here. Out here where *I* was living and in this way finally learned of my favorite pastime — the same as my friends, unfortunately. She offered to pay my debts and to make an honest grandson out of me and bought me this establishment. And as I will rest my soul in the wide sea I will never pay her back, so great were my debts."

"You should be grateful, Jimmy."

"So our dear grandmother mentions each Sunday, little friend."

They drank from their bottles and faced the sea.

"What is the world like, cousin?" Jimmy finally asked.

"It's like a dead place full of things where they shouldn't be."

"Sounds like Mexico," he said.

"Then I am sorry for you, cousin," she said.

"Why did you come back?"

"To hear what happened to my mother."

"Yes, I am thinking this is a sad story, no?"

"I am thinking it will be, yes."

Jimmy contemplated his bottle for a moment. His voice softened and he said, "I tell you what I remember, cousin. It is not a very much information but you have come so far only to find the bad, so I tell you I loved your mother more than the Pope."

"Okay, Jimmy. Tell me what you remember."

He settled his elbows onto the bar and said, "When I was quite young my mother and yours were not exactly friends, but eh, in communications. Your mother would ask to my mother if you could come when we went around the city or to Mass. She herself did not attend because she was sick in the, eh, chest. She could not breathe well and such. At any rate, one day my mother she took me to your home to gather something, I don't remember what. And because I had a large family, many brothers, I did not have much time to my mother alone. And this was fine, because when we became alone she was angry with me — ragh, ragh, ragh Jaimito, and so forth. But on this occasion she was in happy feelings and we sat with your mother and you to have coffee — you and I had chocolate milk. And your mother said to my mother, "Jaimito — he is special, Gloria." And mine, it is obvious she did not agree. For her I was always the one who was to be late, or dirty my clothes and cry because the others hit me. But your mother, she say, "He will always be the one you can turn to in need, who will lift your spirit, Gloria." And your mother kissed my head. And for that, for those words when I was a boy, I will always love the memory of your mother."

Paulina sat and contemplated his story.

"She always say kind words," Jimmy continued. "And for me, that was more wonderful than candy." He snorted and ran his hand along the bar top. "She was the only one with kindness for me in those days. And I am still so much as grateful."

At six-fifteen, Portensia Montelejos walked the five-minute journey to the cathedral. It was part of her daily routine to go each night to pray for the repose of her soul, and though she would never have admitted it, that of her daughter's. She pulled her heavy shawl tightly over her housedress and knelt on the cold stone floor to pray in front of the cross.

"Mary, mother of Jesus, hear my prayer," she began but found her mind too full of anxiety to continue. For the first time since coming to Puerto, Portensia did not want to pray. In fact, so strong was the feeling that the thought of prayer was almost repulsive. She sat back and marveled at herself. She had prayed every day of her life — surely this was a test of her conviction.

It was very still in the small cathedral. The damp salty air was thick with incense and flower pollen and she took out a handkerchief to dab at some invisible nuisance which tickled her nose. No one else was in the cathedral. She knew the Padre was around — an intelligent little man even if he was a bit dark-skinned — who did not show himself until the Mass began at six-thirty, which was why it was her habit to come at six-fifteen.

Portensia rubbed her spine against the seat and tried to induce an attitude of prayer. "Mary, mother of Jesus, hear my prayer," she whispered to herself, but as soon as she said 'mother' in her mind's eye, she saw her daughter — plump from a diet of potatoes and sweets and pink from being kept indoors. What had hurt her most was that she had wanted Teresa to be better than herself, better than everyone else. But more to the point, Portensia had never thought anyone would ever love her daughter. "What man would want a sick wife?" Portensia had thought then. A bad man, an idle one — that Jorge; always smiling largely to show his American dental work.

Portensia had kept her daughter relatively free, so strong was her belief that Teresa would never attract any man's attention. It wasn't that she was plain looking — for though plump she held a sweetness and promise of warmth in her soft body. Portensia had known that well enough. But what overruled that sweetness were her daughter's eyes — dull and hard, with the unrelenting pressure of illness that scared suitors away. Who wanted a wife who could not bear children or keep her own house? A womanizer, a cheap lying scoundrel. The only prayer Portensia could pray was for that man's eternal damnation, but such a prayer would only stain her own soul. She squeezed her eyes shut, trying to purge the sight of Jorge Ruiz but he interfered and pushed his way into her memory. She imagined him at her daughter's funeral — laughing over the casket with a drink in one hand and a woman's bottom clutched in the other. What a picture to have in her mind before Mass!

The little girl she couldn't picture at all. Of course, she would not be a little girl anymore — she must be Jaime's age by now. Ah, Jaime: her other problem. His debts were easy to pay — it was his repentance that was difficult to obtain. Jaime didn't have a repentant thought in his mind. Would Teresa's little girl be as difficult? Teresa showed not an ounce of defiance until she met that accursed *gringo*. Portensia remembered her daughter as good-natured, intelligent, always there to help her button her suits and pin her hair. And then *he* came, and the stubbornness born of a donkey itself came out of her. Teresa would not be reasoned with; no amount of sense could reach her higher faculties. She was in love with the worthless man. The day Teresa married the overbearing monkey Portensia gave her daughter up for dead. She would not attend the wedding and dressed for a funeral instead.

"Please show yourself at this wedding," Hernando had pleaded. "She will be heartbroken if she looks down the aisle of the church, and you aren't there."

"If she cared so much to see me in the church she would be marrying a different man."

"She has chosen this one."

"Then she is a fool and was tricked by the devil in a silk suit."

The wedding proceeded as planned — she heard all the details from Gloria. Then Teresa became sicker, trying against hope and reason to bear a child. But Portensia clung to her oath. It was, after all, one taken before God. She would not come to the bedside of her sick daughter. Three times Teresa lost children, and three times Portensia locked her bedroom door to prevent herself from going to Teresa's aid — if only to lay a cooling hand on her daughter's brow – for to do so would kill her.

And then finally Gloria told her that Teresa had borne a child — a little girl. And still Portensia would not allow herself to go to her daughter's side. She dared not fly in the face of God and yet—Portensia was relieved. At last her daughter could rest from her efforts. She had a child to live for now; surely she would conserve her strength. Thus, greater was Portensia's shock when Teresa died and so much greater her grief that the hated *gringo* took the child away. Portensia swore she would hear no more of Teresa or her child, nor walk the streets that reminded her of her daughter's childhood. She moved to Puerto a few years later and banished the past from her mind.

"*Ade domine,*" intoned the fat little priest, and Portensia stood to hear the Mass.

"Okay, what's the game plan?" Paulina rubbed her eyes and sat down at the cantina.

"Game plan?" Jimmy handed her a Sol. "This phrase I like. Game plan," he repeated.

"I'll go see her on Sunday and ask her where to find my grandfather."

Jimmy clucked his tongue. "Is not so easy," he said.

"Why not?" Paulina asked.

"I tell you, grandmother is a Dragon. You must — how you say? Put sugar on top."

"I see. And how do I do that?"

"Are you married to a good Mexican?"

"Uh, no."

"Have children?"

"Nope."

"Education from far away school?"

"No."

"Ah." Jimmy slapped his hand down on the bar. "Still, you are not me, and this is how we put sugar on top."

"I don't understand."

Jimmy grinned and held out his huge hands. "I will go with you."

"Won't that make it worse?"

"No, no, much better."

"But you said you don't get along."

"Yes, we don't — however." Jimmy raised a long bony finger in the air. "In contrast, you look much better."

"I am an unmarried half-American orphan, I have no children or career, and she disowned my parents — and I'll still look better than you?"

Jimmy leveled his half-drunken gaze at her and said, "I am the gambling, womanizing, drunken son of this woman's step-child. Please believe me, cousin, when I tell you — you have the advantage! Ah, ah, ah!"

They arrived at the villa on the hill exactly on time. Paulina nervously plucked at her lavender dress. She had not expected to meet her grandmother in such a formal way. The walkway to the house was lined with lush jungle ferns, magnolia trees, and wild flowers. The air smelt of salt and for some reason, juniper.

Jimmy patted his head. There was no need to smooth down his hair: he had none. But he had dabbed on aftershave and with his white suit and Panama hat held in one hand, looked more like a casino boss than a man visiting his grandmother. He ran a hand over the front of his suit and held out his large hand.

As he lifted his hand to knock, a woman opened the front door. She was dressed in a severe black dress with buttons that ran down the front, a heavily starched apron and a tight braid coiled into a bun on the very top of her head.

"Hello, Lupe." Jimmy stepped forward to embrace the woman but she held up her hand. "None of your antics today, Jaime," she said in Spanish. "The *Señora* is in such a foul mood you cannot even imagine"

"Ah, ah, ah, I bet I can." he winked at the housekeeper.

"And this is the Miss, I see."

"Hello."

The housekeeper looked Paulina up and down and said, "Well, you'd better come in; she's expecting you in the music room."

Guadalupe ushered the cousins into a wide room which was curiously cramped. Paulina suddenly felt all her strength drained away; she felt trapped and nervous and her heart beat wildly. Along the perimeter of the stuffy closed room were salon chairs and in the middle of the room a grand piano — chestnut brown. With each step Paulina heard a distinct rattle from the piano — as if the floorboards had rotted to the point that even the slightest movement on the surface affected the other furniture. The planks groaned and creaked with the cousins' weight, the strings of the piano buzzed with the movement of the wood planks, and then Paulina saw the woman. She was standing in the far corner near the window with her back to her guests. She wore a lace-trimmed formal black dress with a short bolero jacket and as she wore formal sandals of black leather Paulina could see the woman had painted her toenails a modest shade of pink — her toes looked like ten little seashells.

The housekeeper closed the double doors behind them as they reached the middle of the room, and then the woman said, "Go wait outside, Jaime." Her voice was soft but bold — she gave the order and waited.

Jimmy shrugged at Paulina and left the room, his footsteps echoing his displeasure loudly. When the door had closed, Portensia Montelejos turned to look at her granddaughter. Paulina straightened her back against the scrutiny, feeling strangely indignant that this woman did not speak.

There was a small round table set with two places near Portensia. She sat, motioned for Paulina to join her, and began the ritual of serving coffee. First, she poured Paulina's cup from a height of six inches and did the same with her own. Then she motioned to the sugar with an open hand, and Paulina quietly answered the unspoken question, "Two please."

Portensia added two sugars to Paulina's cup and picked up the milk, pausing for Paulina to say, "Yes, thank you." She poured the milk in Paulina's cup and then her own. When she had finished, Paulina took her hands out of her lap and in the same movement as Portensia, picked up her spoon to slowly stir the coffee. They stirred quietly for some time as they listened to the sound of waves outside hitting the beach below them. An old cuckoo clock chimed quarter past, and finally Portensia lifted her spoon out of the coffee and set it back on her plate. She picked up the cup to sip and looked expectantly at her granddaughter. Paulina likewise lifted the spoon out of her coffee, resisted an insane urge to lick it, and set it down on her plate. She picked up her cup, blew away some steam and began to drink.

Unlike Maria Eugenia's coffee, Portensia's had no chocolate. Instead the coffee tasted of nuts and earth, and Paulina wished she had not agreed to have milk — she would've liked to get a stronger impression of this strange taste.

A bird called out and was answered by another. The sun streamed in from the window that Portensia had been standing before and bathed the piano.

"Do you remember your mother?" Portensia put down her cup.

"Not very well, no."

"Neither do I. I chose to forget her a long time ago."

Paulina did not put her cup down as Portensia had; she took a long sip and savoured the earthy taste despite the milk and sugar. "People don't just go away," she said after she had swallowed.

"They do if one is insistent."

Paulina smiled. "They have their own way of being insistent."

Portensia did not like the smugness of the girl. She had come to disturb an old woman and did not even have the good grace to let her finish a thought. Portensia glanced out the window and then said, "So it is not you doing the insisting? Why not let things rest in the past?"

"Because after she died, she was erased from my memory — taken from me."

"And it is then different who causes the forgetting?" Portensia finished Paulina's thought.

"I'm not asking you for anything, Señora." Paulina paused, considering the seeming insincerity of her words, "Or rather, I need one piece of information from you."

"And what is that?"

"Where is my grandfather?"

"That is all?" Portensia asked coldly.

"Yes."

Portensia rose out of her chair and opened the door. "Lupe," she called, "Bring me my diary book." She stood at the door until the housekeeper returned with the leather-bound date book. Portensia took it from her hands and shut the door. From a drawer, she took out a pad of paper and a pen. Standing at the window she copied Hernando Vasquez' address and gave it to Paulina. "Now go," she said, "and never let me hear of you again."

When the girl left, Portensia Montelejos sat down. She felt older than her years. She felt dead, empty and brittle. She had not expected the girl to look so much like

Teresa had as a child — had certainly not expected to hear the same voice as that *fulano*, Jorge. It was the voice more than the smugness of the girl that had made Portensia dismiss her. She realized it was more than disgust for Jorge: it was fear. When she heard the girl speak, it was as though Teresa had swallowed Jorge's voice — that's what she had thought. Teresa speaking with the mouth of her husband, and it terrified her — as if he had taken not only her daughter but Teresa's soul as well. And she knew then that her daughter was damned.

"What happened?" Jimmy asked when she returned. "What, what?"

"We're going to Puebla tomorrow." Paulina.

"So soon?"

"Yep." She said and went to pack her bag.

"I help you?" he called after her.

"No," she said and closed the door.

The taxi arrived early the next morning to take them to the airport. The air was unusually clear, and Jimmy took a long time breathing it in and bidding his *hostal* goodbye. He double-checked the outlets and main power generator. He made sure — three times — that all the windows and doors were locked, that the bedding had been rolled up and stored, that there was no fresh food in the kitchen, and generally made a fuss. At last, Paulina had gone to wait in the taxi and Jimmy emerged from the *hostal*, patted the front door frame and joined her — looking as if he had just left a sweetheart.

"You'll be back, Jimmy," Paulina said trying to reassure him. "In no time."

In Mexico City, they landed and went to rent a car. The process involved Jimmy alternatively yelling, cajoling, and laughing outright. Finally they had a suitable vehicle and started on their way to Puebla.

"What are you doing?" Paulina asked as Jimmy dug in his bag.

"Maps," was the muffled answer.

"You've never been to Puebla?"

"I have never been outside the state of Oaxaca." He laughed at her look of concern. "Don't worry, cousin. All roads of Mexico are alike — bad!"

With the music blasting loud enough to feel the vibrations on the dash, Paulina fell asleep. They entered the city of Puebla around six p.m. It was an old city, the second largest in Mexico. The French had made their mark on the architecture, which was now crumbling. The plaza squares were adorned with intricate stone fountains — dry for lack of interest in them. There were water sellers here as in Oaxaca, but their calls were not as shrill or long. They had regular customers and huge trucks which played a jingle. "Come buy my water," it sang in Spanish. "Refresh yourself with tasty water!" The other cars jostled theirs; no one seemed to follow the lines painted on the road. The houses had great wooden doors, tall shrubs and broken glass cemented to the tops of their fences.

Jimmy pulled up to their expensive hotel, courtesy of Jorge Ruiz's money. A man in a three-piece suit came out to greet them.

"Wake up," Jimmy called to her and got out of the car. "Jaime Vasquez Fuentes de Solis," he said to the man in the suit. "And my cousin."

"Yes, yes," the man said, instantly groveling as he heard Jimmy's name. "We are at your service, *Señor* Vasquez." Paulina got out of the car, groggy from her nap and the heat. Jimmy leaned over to whisper in her ear. "Much nicer than my humble *hostal* but undoubtfully not so much as fun."

Paulina's room had a window which opened onto the main plaza of Puebla. She watched as a man fed a huge flock of pigeons. The square was full of other interesting scenes but the man with his birds stuck out in her mind. Like Jimmy and his birdies, she thought. Birdies. He had said his birdies told him about her call to their Grandmother but now she realized — no one could have known about that. So who were these birdies? She wondered.

She found Jimmy sitting in the lobby, watching the tourists as she had once done. "Who are your birdies?"

He turned to look at her and smiled. "You ask me to tell you my secrets."

"Are the birdies your secret?"

He reached into his pocket to take out a battered pack of cigarettes. He lit one and handed it to her without question and lit one for himself. "When I was younger, I heard voices speaking to me. They tell me things then, things I should not know. When I tell your mother these things she say, did a little birdie tell you this? And I say, yes Tia Teresa, a little birdie."

"It is a phrase in English to indicate when someone we don't want to name tells us something."

"So this phrase means this here."

"So you hid your voices behind fictional people?"

"Of course, cousin. I do not want people to think me a crazy person — do I?" He laughed, "Ah, ah, ah!" and shook his head. "But I know I am not crazy. Your mother tell me when I was very young that I had the special gift."

"She did?"

"Yes. I was special but others...they think maybe I am a crazy boy. She say to keep saying they are birdies — that I did not sin by telling this lie."

"Did she have birdies too?"

"I do not know, cousin, but this would not surprise me. Yes, maybe she have birdies too." They smoked together in silence and continued to watch the tourists. "The foreigners are very different here," he commented. "They are not so...calm."

She smiled and suggested, "Perhaps they are not the type to sleep on beaches and gamble by the fire."

"Yes, I think not." Jimmy stood up and stretched. "The old man is probably at his dinner at the minute, but let us call on him anyway."

"Are you sure?"

"Yes, yes," Jimmy insisted. "It is more familiar in this way."

Paulina frowned. "But you aren't familiar with him at all!"

"Ah, ah, ah! He is our grandfather, no? We will be very familiar." Jimmy looked about him wildly, listening and looking. "I think we take a taxi. In this way it will be easier to find Grandfather's house."

She agreed with him and went outside to flag down a taxi. The hotel was on the main plaza of Puebla, a giant compared to that of Oaxaca City—but much more drab and business-like; even the colorful balloon and toy vendors seemed to fade into the dull grey square. A group of school children in navy blazers and pleated skirts passed by in front of them in a disorderly line. The children pushed and pinched each other as teachers called out, "*Ramon! No hagas eso!*" ineffectively.

"I remember my school days fondly," Jimmy commented when he saw the children. "Do you like my sarcasm, cousin?"

"Yes, Jimmy — well learned."

"Ah, ah, ah!" he flagged down a taxi. "Thirty-seven San Judas Tadeo."

The taxi driver snorted and began to argue. Jimmy poked his head into the open window and argued back and then told her, "He says it will cost extra because the street is difficult. He must go in circles for all the construction."

"So he goes in circles," Paulina said matter-of-factly. Jimmy shrugged and they got in.

The taxi rattled as they bumped along the cobblestones of the center of town. Buses blocked the taxi every so often so the people holding on to the sides of the buses could jump off and on. They passed through a busy market of household goods and piles of *chiles*, handmade dresses and vacuum cleaners. Bunches of people clogged the sidewalks bargaining and arguing between shop vendors, children, and themselves. The air smelt of boiling stew and butcher shops, piles of horse dung and the vials of perfume sellers. People shouted, children cried, cars backfired and then suddenly, as they passed a *piñata* maker and his huge tissue paper figures of Mickey Mouse and Rin-Tin-Tin, they were out of the market and in a quiet suburban neighborhood.

"Ah," Jimmy leaned a long arm out of his passenger side window. "That was very excited." He turned around in his seat to face Paulina. "Here we must now go in circles, the driver say, because the streets are bad and..." As he was speaking they stopped behind a police officer in his VW bug — florescent green — who was smoking and hassling a little man sweeping leaves from the street. "*Hola, amigo!*" Jimmy paused to yell at him. "That man gave me a rude sign," he said when they had passed the officer. "Anyway, and the driver was saying the place we find is very new and in gated land, so we must push the button and speak with someone there."

"But he doesn't even know we are coming." Paulina leaned forward and tried to control her nervousness and fear.

"Of no importance, cousin." Jimmy dismissed her concern. "He will be well pleased to see you, of this I am certain."

She leaned back and crossed her arms. "Sure."

The taxi driver stopped and leaned out to push the speaker button.

"Who?" a man's voice, gruff and unwelcoming, answered the buzzer.

Jimmy leaned over the driver to answer. "Paulina Ruiz and company. We are looking for Hernando Vasquez."

There was no reply. They passed two minutes quietly until the lock on the gate clicked, and it began to swing open. "Third house on the left," said the gruff voice.

"Thank you!" Jimmy called. "See, cousin? Easy like peasy."

The house was walled in with eight feet of bright white cement and at the top in place of broken bottles were pointed barbs. They got out of the taxi and rang the bell. There were quick, hollow footsteps, and then an old man in a wrinkled white shirt and black trousers opened the door.

"Who are you?" he asked.

"We have come to see our grandfather, Hernando."

The old man lifted an eyebrow but ushered them into the house. "He is in the bedroom," the man whispered. "Through there."

Through the dim house, the cousins made their way past an assortment of large rocks, scattered papers, antiquated survey equipment and several old, sleeping hound dogs. When Jimmy pushed open the door of Hernando's room, they beheld the old man watching a *telenovela*. He had cataracts in his murky eyes and only a few tufts of hair around the back of his head like a friar. But though his clothes were wrinkled and his hands trembled, his face was clean-shaven and his fingernails were manicured neatly.

Paulina stepped forward toward his kind face, soft outstretched hands, and cloudy eyes. "Grandfather?"

"*Dios Mio,*" his voice was scratchy and low — a baritone voice. "Paulina? Angel! So long, where have you been, *preciosa*? There, there." Hernando Vasquez held her close but then pulled away to wipe his eyes and look at her fully. "You look like your mother. Alberto!" he called faintly, still holding Paulina. "My granddaughter has come! Fix a big meal, use the fine china and call that wife of yours — only her *mole poblano* will do!"

Hernando let Paulina's hand go to find a handkerchief amid the disorder of his sickbed — only then did he notice the man with her. "And who is your consort, *mi reina*?"

Jimmy cleared his throat and shook Hernando's hand properly. "Jaime Vasquez Fuentes de Solis. Your grandson, *Señor.*"

Hernando gave a start and then slapped Jimmy on the back. "Jaime! My boy, it has been too long!" He struggled to look into Jimmy's face. "What has your mama been feeding you, son? You are so very big." Hernando frowned. "Your father was not so big, eh?"

"Ah, ah, ah! No, but his own father would dwarf me, *Señor* — so large was his size, the children played atop him like mountain goats."

Hernando nodded vigorously and mumbled, "I had forgotten, yes, of course. We used to call him Juan Hectares because he was like an acre of hillside. He was very hairy also," he joked to Paulina. "Are you shy, *mi reina*? Why do you not speak?"

Paulina felt her face begin to heat up, and her heart fluttered in her chest like a tree trembling in the wind. "I am ashamed of my accent, grandfather."

"Nonsense!" he said. "Your accent is nothing. It is what you say that is of importance. Now, now." He patted her head and leaned forward to look at her clothes. "I am nearly blind, you know," he explained. "I apologize but I have not seen you for so long. We must have a celebration!

A big *fiesta* for your homecoming." She smiled at him and nodded eagerly. He sat up, laboriously, and called out the door, "Camile!" A woman entered. "Tonight we feast," he told her. "Order a pig."

"A whole one?"

"Of course. Go, go, get started, woman!"

"Yes, *Señor*."

Late that night, his belly full of roasted pork, Jimmy sat in the hotel lobby and smoked an Alita. He had found a pack of the hand-rolled cigarettes in his cousin's pocket. He hadn't had one in years, since he was a poor gambling boy living on the beach. He savored the taste of the cigarette and listened to the dark lobby. He was listening for his birdies. Lately they hadn't so much as spoken as led him to believe they wanted him to act. Now he felt his birdies wanted him to wait for something. Why? He didn't know why the birdies cared so much. He wished they cared more for cards and the stones than for his American cousin — who could surely take care of herself. Before she had arrived, the birdies had been quiet for some time. He had always tried to trick them into giving away lottery numbers and his friends' poker hands, but they would never help him in that way. Then that morning the birdies had awoken him early saying, *Rise, Jaime! Rise, rise, clean this filthy hovel and show pride in yourself. Someone special is coming — rise, rise!* Jimmy, who wished the birdies wouldn't call him Jaime and who had not awoken earlier than ten a.m. for many years, was startled into action. And now he was here: a pawn of the birdies.

What do I tell her? Jimmy wondered. *The truth, Jaime*, said the birdies. And what is that, he wondered. He stubbed out the Alita and sent himself to bed.

Paulina's eyes opened early the next morning. The dull light of morning had barely reached her window when she sat up. She hugged her knees and looked out the window at the deserted plaza. Invisible paths crossed the square where later feet would tread and go about the business of the day. But now it was a huge area of possibility — unspoken paths where now not even the pigeons would go. A light breeze tickled the flags atop the governor's palace and with that sign of life the birds began to sing and one man and his broom crossed the plaza whistling a melancholy tune.

She had had a dream the night before of a bearded man who told her a story: Two brothers and two sisters walked through a field of corn. One brother, the smallest, stopped as they entered and said, "I cannot see over the tops of the corn. I will remain here and wait for you." The other three continued through the field until one sister said, "I wish to lie down on the luscious grass and play. I will wait for you here." The last brother and sister continued on. They had nearly reached the edge of the field when the boy said, "I can smell Mama's perfume; she is so close. But I must remain here and gather a bunch of corn so she can make tamales. You go ahead." And so the last sister went to the edge of the field to meet her Mama who smiled for her and sang a song in a deep voice.

"You are the last sister," the bearded man told her. "Your brothers and sister are still waiting for you to return."

The dream was obvious to Paulina — Maria Eugenia had told her of the three miscarriages — but what puzzled her was the promise of return. Must she die before she met these siblings? What was the song her Mama had whispered in her ear? Though she had found her family, Paulina still knew so little about her mother. She rocked back and forth, opened her mind and listened for the voices. But they would not come when she called them. They were devils, the voices - tricksters who only appeared to frighten or tease her with memories she did not want. And then clearly in her mind she saw her father.

"No more questions!" he had shouted when she was a child. "Stop your infernal questions! She is dead – gone forever! Think no more of her, ask me no more of her, or you will anger me." The plastered moldings of their home in Cairo trembled when he shouted. "I will lock you in the cellar again if you persist in these pointless questions."

The dank silence of that underground space loomed large in her mind – it was her father's favorite punishment when she would not bend to his will.

Paulina now knew – her father had feared the dead and the secrets they locked away in their coffins with a dread even larger than that which he had placed within his daughter. It was a fear that bordered on paranoia. When he locked her in the cellar for days on end, with only a small bottle of water at her side, she realized it was because her questions, once answered, would induce the dead to speak their secret words that would tell her what he had done.

The sun gathered strength and shone brightly, displacing specks of dust that danced into the room on beams of light. She got out of bed and put on her clothes. Taking her key with her she went downstairs and out to the plaza square.

Puerto Escondido

At eleven fifteen, forty-five minutes late and thus exactly on time, the *Señora* Flores stepped across the threshold of the *Café Parisian*. Usually, the *Señora* Montelejos de Vasquez awaited her; usually, she made a face. The *Señora* Flores was always forty-five minutes late because her mother had taught her this lesson: Women should never be on time, lest they appear eager, or worse - mannish. The *Señora* Montelejos was always on time and did not care whether she was mannish or not. She did not care for anything the *Señora* Flores might find, but only her daughter Teresa — and she died long ago.

That morning, before arriving in her son-in-law's car, the *Señora* Flores awoke with loose bowels. Her mother, a superstitious woman (God rest her soul), thought loose bowels were premonitions. Her mother-in-law, the Old *Señora*, believed they were only the result of eating Indian food or other such filth. The Old *Señora*, however, also believed that if one were wicked, she would be struck down when she least suspected it; and that if one were good, rewards would be heaped upon her both in this world and the next.

To the Old *Señora*, to be poor was to be wicked. The poor, she often told her daughter-in-law, blessed God with their lips but cursed him in their hearts. Obviously it was so, she reasoned, look how they live! They eat lies breathed by the Marxists while their insides burst in putrescence. *Señora* Flores never told her mother-in-law it was not putrescence that burst their insides, but bullets. The Marxists, the old woman would rant when she remembered her son through the fog of her mind, the Marxists did not trick the poor; they only gave them what they wanted – a Godless life.

The Old *Señora*, who was not in the least superstitious, ended her life drooling at the ceiling and died shortly after the Revolution.

Señora Flores did not like to think of those days when, newly widowed, she feared for an unborn baby and a senile in-law. How invincible we were, she thought that morning, staring into the toilet bowl, how much we cared for our lives. How little we cared for the lives of others, a voice whispered in her conscience. What we wanted, we received. What we feared, we destroyed. When they came at the point of a gun and said, *Vete*, leave — we did. And when we showed the men our mother's jewels and pointed to a house, they left as well. The Revolution was an exchange for us: their lives for ours; our lives for the People. We lost nothing. We lost everything.

Her loose bowels did not offend her nose for she no longer had use of that faculty. She looked at them a bit longer and pulled the chain.

The *Señora* Flores sat down beside the usual place of her old friend, the *Señora* Montelejos. She discretely arraigned her hairdo, pretending no one noticed. At eleven-fifteen, forty-five minutes late and exactly on time, the *Señora* Flores was not thinking any longer of the Revolution, her loose bowels, or her mother-in-law. She was thinking of *Señora* Montelejos, dying at her home on the edge of the sea.

"How strange that instead it would be you. How obligatory you fulfill your duty, Paulina," Portensia whispered. "Your mother had been obliging as well, but I mistook that trickery for concern. As a mother, even I was blind; even I was placated by that bestial gaze, the meaningless guile — the one that shines on your face now." The old woman lifted her head and listened to the sounds from the open window. "In the space of one meeting with a worthless social climber, she grew devious. It must have lain dormant for the short years of her life until the American let it loose. She became a person that day," Portensia breathed out regretfully. "And though it gave you life, it took hers."

"What bargain is there for my daughter?" Portensia asked the open window. "A daughter I could either love or treasure and forfeit my own life. A daughter who received no caresses from my fingers nor kisses from my lips. I could not give her my strength to endure, though the strength to disobey she stole in abundance. A disgraceful waste of my effort. To birth a child merely to see that lecherous man spend her life like change." Portensia clutched her withered bird-chest as it lurched painfully. "I too am mortal — talking of this will do the rest," and she turned to swallow juniper breeze and sea-salt dampness.

Puebla, Mexico

Paulina walked the crumbling sidewalks, mindful of dirty sun-bleached children and dog droppings. The market obstructed her path; loud colorful vendors in degrees of smell besieged her thoughts. A man strummed his guitar while sat on the side of the gutter, disregarding the broken strings hanging at his right hand. A young girl pursued Paulina for change.

"*Toma*," she said, "here," and gave a few coins to the girl. The little girl spit on them and rubbed the money on her dress, oddly practiced at appraising value.

Jaime says our grandmother is dying, Paulina thought, *and I give the beggar children coins for their father's beer.*

What Paulina did not know was that Portensia, like her daughter Teresa, had been dying since the day she first drew breath — as Paulina herself was slowly dying. At the end of each breath was a fight for the next. It began as acknowledgement: I am breathing again. Then it became a question: Will I breath this time as well? And finally a fight: Give me breath; I must have it! And a bargain struck: Who are you to deny me? If you are my Maker, only give me...and I will give you...And a price is paid. What Paulina did not know was that Portensia had been lingering in the final stages of haggling since laying eyes and ears upon her transnational granddaughter, that girl with the eyes of her daughter and the voice of a pedophile. The bargain was struck and she would pay the price of knowing her granddaughter.

Perhaps, Portensia wheedled when alone; perhaps if only God would strike her deaf she might live just a little longer. The greed of the old depends upon the ignorance of the young; for as much as Paulina was killing Portensia, so was true in the reverse.

And while Portensia in her grasping hands clutched at life yet, Paulina floated lightly and without consequence. She walked with the entirety of the present before her. She claimed her own soul where her grandmother counted heartbeats and the grains of time, where her mother had counted mistresses and late hours in an empty house among her chores. If Paulina is springing a light step across the cobblestones of the Plaza Mayor, breathing deeply of aromas once forgotten and now remembered, it is not because she mistakes herself for immortal. It is because Paulina, careening carelessly, knows now that fate has befallen her at last — and it is this knowledge, a fullness where once darkness obscured her mind and purpose, that gives Paulina the strength to endure an imminent death.

A breeze of grilled steak and cactus leaf wafted above her head, sending a tingle down goose-bumped arms, ruffling her shirtsleeve. The cathedral bell called out the hour, "four---four---four---four," as people of the City strolled back to work along invisible lines of destiny. Several streets away, Hernando contemplated the clouds of his eyes and tried yet again to either part them or find the past beyond their shade. Like Portensia, he too lay in bed. Like her, he thought of a long-dead daughter.

Air stilled to damp cool as Paulina entered the cathedral. The sun's gaze retreated, pausing to linger at crucifixes and gold-pressed panels, and having done so, waited outside. She entered and knelt at the nave, crossing herself. Her sandals shuffled along the ancient Italian marble floors as saints looked up at God in adulation, and downward at humanity, beseechingly. "Listen!" they said with saucer-like eyes stretched wide in glass and plaster. "Repent!"

Paulina no longer heard them speak, but she strained to listen anyway. Now it was their pasty faces that spoke to her. "I am in pain," a hand clutched in modesty. "I am forlorn," an eye turned inward. "I am damned," Paulina stopped before the Mocker, grimacing dramatically.

"This saint does not belong," she whispered.
"Excuse me?"
"It is a fraud."
"Oh?" the young priest, used to hitchhikers and their odious narcotics, humored her comment and bent forward to gaze upon the questionable statue. "It is Saint...eh." He paused in his own sins — vanity, pride, excessive flagellation. The name was trapped in his mind. *Saint?*

"That is not a saint."

"He is here, yes? He must be a saint then."

"He has slipped in unnoticed — he isn't right — no place here for him." Pain sunk its teeth into her chest.

"Please, Miss, speak gently — we are in God's house."

"God isn't here!" she yelled, "Look! He would know this is no saint!" Frantic, Pain shook her in steel jaws.

"Please, Miss, don't make trouble, if you could quiet down..."

But the cathedral had exploded into a blinding burst of light. Lifting her arms to shield herself Paulina cried out, and the light expanded upon its initial explosion, multiplied and burned the fingers she held in front of her face—it sizzled in the holy water the priest sprinkled on her cheeks.

"She is possessed," Paulina heard from afar. "Quickly, close the doors!" But she was falling through a cavernous hole - the scale of her personal universe - and did not respond. Somewhere a woman silenced a small yapping dog.

When next the light returned, it only blinded her for one moment and quickly softened through the thick rims of her lashes. Paulina opened her eyes to a blanket of whiteness: walls, a fan, and mosquito screens.

"You will recover," the nurse who bent over her said quietly. "But we fear for your heart, *Señorita*."

Puerto Escondido, Mexico

Paulina pulled the big brass bell of her grandmother's house two weeks later. At exactly ten-thirty that morning, she had been summoned to the house on the cliff facing the wide blue sea. As usual, Lupe opened the door, but instead of her customary disapproving face, her lips softened and her brows relaxed as she whispered, "We heard."

"Who told you?"

Lupe pursed her brows in disbelief, "Ay, *nina*—where do you think you are? What happens to you or me or anyone is held in common. It is the old way."

"She was upset?"

"She thought you were not like your Mama, and it hurt her very much to find you are weak." Lupe tisked and gave her keys a shake. "Go, you are expected."

The room at the edge of the sea, high enough to see the white-topped waves and azure depths smelt of medicine, juniper, and the rotting food, tokens, and bits of lace on Portensia's personal shrine. It was Saint Paul she had chosen to venerate, though she had never confessed her love of him to anyone. The old woman, small in her plain, white dress, awaiting death, did not speak.

"I am a product of so many Revolutions," Paulina murmured into Portensia's silence. "A fluke, an occurrence of necessity and accidental factors many times in the making."

Portensia's chest took flight and she wheezed and gagged. "Go," the old woman ordered, "Go, go," she told her granddaughter. "I cannot bear you; you should not have come."

Paulina backed out as Portensia choked on her own breath, her finger pointing to the window. "Look, there, you will see, look," she wheezed. "Ask that Maria Eugenia, ask her about your mother. I have nothing to tell you."

Guadalupe materialized as good servants tend to do, and held a satin handkerchief to her mistress' chin. She lifted her like a rag doll and thumped her back, while Paulina turned from her grandmother and ran, terrified of eyes that could burn with the intensity of fire.

In the café, the tiles at Paulina's feet clicked and clacked, echoed staccato taps of high-heeled shoes, swished whispers of waiters' slippers, grime pushed into corners and beneath solid oak tables, as Maria Eugenia accepted her chocolate coffee from the waiter's outstretched hand.

"My grandmother is dying," Paulina said. "Everyone is dying."

"Your grandmother has been dying for a very long time, *nina*. Don't worry about her – she made her choices many years ago."

"I never had the chance to love her."

"Love is like a song," Maria Eugenia mused, as her lipstick stained the white porcelain cup. "Which comes first — the notes or the words? One can hum along or recite the poetry of the lyrics, either can be beautiful alone." She looked out over the mountains. "What is death?" she mused. "It ends the mirage we tenaciously grasp like steam in the bath. Our lives are projections of our hopes and fears. Whether given us or learned through experience, they are only ideas in solid form. What is death but to release that wisp of the immortal? The ideas endure past us, *Nina*. We are only vessels of one template, a stamp of humanity."

Paulina put her head down on the table and allowed her legs to hang limply.

"We are worthy of the template," Maria Eugenia continued, "to be known as human — not animal or object? You are sick, *nina*, but you are not useless, a mistake. My friend Teresa fought for you so that you may live through her light. What is meant to move forward invariably does — with your life or from your death. Give or receive what was meant for you and you may both exist or expire in peace and confident you have not wasted what portion humanity has given uniquely to you alone."

"What do I have?"

"A faith to let love endure past death and fear—a goodness intact through tragic loss and pain. The ability to find beauty wherever you point your eye."

"But I am dying too."

"Do you have regrets of your life's choices?"

"I never loved anyone. I was too afraid."

"Is this too late for that?"

"Love will kill me."

"Why do you think this?"

"My heart is weak. Grandmother's heart is weak – it is killing her."

"Her heart might be killing her, *Nina*, but it was not love that killed her heart. It is not love that kills your women, but rejection. Our saviors are also our tormentors. Let go your anger, accusations, recriminations. Your grandmother's life will soon end, but yours is just beginning. Certainly you have more years left in your child's body than an old woman. Your grandmother rejected Teresa's love and it weakened her. I saw it with mine own eyes. Give and accept as true Christians do, *hija*, it is the only way to save your life."

"How can you love someone you don't know, godmother?"

"That I do not know, *hija*. I do not know."

Paulina went away, her mind buoyant above her. The red mountains in the distance vaguely stretched out their foothills. The air, clear but sprinkled with dust, was cool this far from the edge of the sea. A bath beckoned in her memory.

It was the next Saturday morning, when Spring had blushed its final hue, that Portensia awoke on a levitating bed. She went to grip the handrails, but when she saw Mariabella floating beside her, she did not bother to hold the headboard of her marriage seat. "Here you are, lazy woman," Portensia said to her mother. "You look much improved since last we spoke."

"Will you never seek my favor nor grant me forgiveness?"

"I see no need," Portensia answered with the haughtiness of her full eighty-nine years.

"You knew, *hija*, you knew how my heart yearned for you."

"I care not for your heart, Mama. I cared for your attentions and your teachings. But it was your cruelty that guided me in the end."

"How was I cruel to you, daughter? I gave you all I had."

"Such was the problem. You had nothing to give. Your cruelty was this: You were someone's property. You were not my Mama," she spat out. "You were always someone's whore, a plaything. No child clamors for garbage, for something that has been soiled by another."

Mariabella's eyes rolled into her head as she listened to the ticking of the clock of Santa Domingo. "I must go," she said, as though Portensia had not spoken. "You must come with me."

"I will do no such thing," Portensia huffed. "I am waiting for my daughter, Teresa."

"No, *hija*," Mariabella corrected. "She waits for you."

Higher the bed rose until it burst out the window above the azure sea and carried Portensia uncomplainingly on breezes of crystalline salt, red coral, and juniper.

There was no viewing. In the old days, the entire town would have gathered round the bed of the deceased to lay flowers beside her stiffened arms. The people would have come and lit a candle for her soul, baked bread for her family. They would have spoken in whispers. But in these times of sterility and lonely death, those surrounded by anyone at all were the exception. Portensia died alone and was hustled into her casket without the proper time to view her corpse at its deathbed, and at the funeral Mass, surrounded by throngs of strangers, she was framed for eternity only by that plain box.

Lupe waved flies off her face with her handkerchief and scowled at those she knew only wanted a look at the infamous Dragon of Puerto Escondido, to see if what was said was true: that the old lady would take to her grave all her fabulous jewels in a box lined in silk, satin and gold. Those who waited in line for such a look and sat through the Mass hoping for a spectacle were sorely disappointed.

But for *Señora* Flores' disconsolate sobbing, the service was uneventful. No long lost relative flung herself on the coffin in repentance, and the Old Dragon did not rise from the dead — indignant at such a bereft internment.

The mourners rose to their knees and partook of the rites and chanted, mumbling over words they did not understand. *Señora* Flores continued her drippy sobbing, mewling sounds, and dramatic displays of nose blowing. When the Mass ended the people followed the casket and the priest outside to the *Pantheon Frances*. It was oddly deserted: no men in ranchero hats strolled the avenue; no children played atop monuments of long-dead angels.

The men carried the coffin and set it beside Teresa Montelejos de Ruiz's grave and motioned for the crypt keeper to pry it open. A crack of a crowbar, a slow rent of marble against steel and then the sickening smell of decay, dust, mold, and the remnants of ashes.

The keeper stepped away as the priest chanted in Latin and threw holy water droplets onto the bones of Teresa Ruiz to cleanse and purify them in anticipation for her new companion. A wind rustled, disturbing the white gown Teresa wore, mottled with death fuzz and dirt, grey rot where the gown no longer concealed the decayed remains.

While the men lifted the body from the new casket – one man at the head, the other at his feet and neither man more than three feet from the other — other men took out a shovel and began scraping Teresa's bones into a black bag. The stale listless air imprisoned the bystanders within the smell of the dead; it hung between them like a promise, an insult, and inescapable dread. The people watched dispassionately as the men tied the sack closed and laid it at the foot of the old tomb. They murmured amongst themselves of other things: their children's lives, the dead woman's temper, the weather. All the while Paulina, transfixed and horrified, stared wide-eyed at the black sack which contained her mother's corpse.

The men placed the body carefully above that of Teresa, repositioning the arms to cross the bird-thin chest and covered the anxious face with the shroud Lupe had made. The frown, permanently etched for the ages upon the waxen face, was the last to linger in sight before the keeper replaced the marble lid with another crack. The men, the priest, and the keeper stepped away and melted into the cypress and magnolia trees, leaving the remaining few at the gravesite in a small knot.

"Will they leave me here?" Paulina wondered aloud. "Will they leave me here when I am gone?" She retched, the smell that had been pestering her all morning now combined with the thought of her mother's rotted, moldy body shoved aside for another. It was nearly too much. She turned toward the shrubbery beside her and heaved.

"Why to be sick?" a woman commented. "Have you never seen a funeral, child?" The woman, wearing a rabbit jacket and fox fur wrap (the little animal biting its own tail) and an alligator skinned bag in mint green, spoke heavily accented English with a sneer.

Paulina recovered herself and straightened up to assess the woman dusted in perfumed powder and a triple strand of pearls. "I have never seen that, no."

The woman briskly looked her up and down and turned to whisper to the woman beside her. They exchanged a grimace. "You are the daughter of Teresa?"

Paulina, immediately suspicious, guardedly nodded her head. "I am, and whom might you be?"

The woman smirked and adjusted her immaculate bouffant. "I am your aunt. My name is Gloria. I believe you have met my son, Jaime."

"You mean Jimmy. Yes, I quite like him."

"I'm sure. He is like you also." Gloria sighed dramatically and lifted her head. "Jaime has told me you stay with him to work at the bar and that you go to see your grandmother. I am sorry I missed the dinner my father gave to you," she told Paulina, "but I was shopping in Paris for the twice yearly voyage and it was not possible for me to be there and here at one time." She secretly studied her niece. "You understand?"

Paulina, not once fooled by pretension masked in bad English, tilted her own head. "Perfectly," she said. She also studied the woman. If she was indeed who she said she was, her face boldly belied her age – she looked no older than forty-five though she must have been at least seventy.

"I heard you were ill." Gloria, unaware of the sun beating down on Paulina's smooth dark hair, listened to the distant chatter of birds. "Are you recovered?"

"I am. If you'll excuse me?"

Gloria took Paulina's arm and leaned down to kiss the air beside her cheek. "Come see us in Puebla," she said. "I would love to remember your mother." The treacheries of the past glimmered within her eyes. "I have stories my step-mother did not know."

Puebla, Mexico

"The year your mother came to live with me was the best year of her life. You will hear you were the best year of her life, but this is not so." Gloria sipped club soda and watched her niece give no reaction. The sun streamed into her parlor, and as it settled onto Paulina, it was her aunt who reacted — there sat Teresa, as though time had not passed.

It was a nice day in Puebla, but this was not unusual. Every day in Puebla was a nice day. The morning had been crisp, the afternoon toasted the skin, and the early evening blew soft cool breezes to chill the shoulders. Every day was more or less the same, except when the rains came. On those days, the wind blustered, and the skies opened to pour down a month's supply in a single night. The cisterns would fill, and the streets would wash themselves, freeing the people to skip that particular morning's chore and leave buckets and water brushes forgotten on the stoops of their shops, homes and small factories.

"When did she come to live with you?" Paulina asked quietly, aware of the scrutiny. Her aunt leaned back against her salon chair and clacked her reading glasses against her teeth, contemplative.

"May I speak in Spanish?" she asked finally.

"I don't see why you haven't before."

"I want you to understand me fully," Gloria said in perfectly articulated, rounded colonial Spanish. "I did not want your mother with me. She was the daughter of that woman and my beloved Papa. She was not welcome. She had taken my Papa away from me, and between her and her mother my Papa was a hostage. I felt orphaned, and I was angry." Gloria set her glasses carefully upon the mahogany coffee table. "Your mother," she began again slowly, "was going to die."

Paulina grit her teeth. "You know, I am beginning to tire of this simple fact being repeated to me without end. She was dying; I understand that part."

Gloria drank some soda and deliberately paused to set the glass upon the table. "I realize that you may think you understand it, but until you have seen its face, no. You do not understand — you must know what it looked like." She leaned toward her niece. "Do you know Death — his smell, his visage, his weariness of life? Death stalks. Death looks upon the living with wistful longing and sometimes — sometimes with," Gloria gripped her glasses, "disdain." Gloria's eyes focused into the past, and her voice became husky. "When your mother came to me she could barely walk to the end of a room and back without wheezing. She was merry, she was a sweet thing, but her eyes did not lie. She knew she was dying and that each morning was an accomplishment."

Gloria saw her niece in front of her and shook herself. "When she left me it was to the state of holy matrimony and I am responsible for that happiness. Your grandmother vilified me for it — never forgave me for it." She lifted her head, "and I don't care. I don't care what she thought of me. Teresa was no more than a delicate doll and I gave her the chance to be a woman. That dried up crow should have been eternally grateful to me — but instead she turned her back on my father and he came also to live with me. So I suppose that all things considered, it turned out well for me." Gloria sniffed and touched her elaborate hairstyle. "I don't care what anyone says of me then or now. I did what was right by your mother."

Paulina drank her tea and waited for this woman to begin telling tales — but she did not. Instead, with sad eyes and an unmistakable air of truth, in a voice she had not used before, Gloria said, "Your grandfather has taken a turn for the worse. They say he will not last the weekend. It is my wish you go and see him."

Someone had opened the patio door of Hernando Vasquez's room. Sealed for fifteen years, the door allowed only stale air to pass from beneath its cracked frame. Paulina, a weight sitting between her ribs and pressing her from the inside, lifted a glass of water to her grandfather's flaky lips and said simply, "Drink this." He did, but only because she asked, and her eyes were like those of his daughter. The room smelt of crumpled bandages and vomit, of old blood caked around festering wounds. It smelt of an old man with bedsores on his thighs and pus in his milky, blind eyes.

"It was the summer of the rains when the fleas came," he began in a whisper, "Our lives were difficult then. All around us was prosperity, but we lived as proof that prosperity can kill, and so we were wary of it. And when the rains came the wallpaper melted. And with the fleas we grew sores, and with the prosperity we knew a greater shame – because we had lived when others had died. And then it was that your father arrived one day with hat in hand and asked for your mother. I could not refuse him for your mother was ill, and I wanted her to live. Evil omens were the only plenty we knew and still I argued — because I knew your mother would die without having known life and this I could not allow. Please forgive me, *mi'hija*. I know your life has been hard; that you know misery and evil — all for your mother before you to know life. Forgive me my selfishness: I only wanted her to live."

"Please Grandfather, save your strength. You can get better."

"Get better from what?" Hernando asked, "Old age? That is the one ailment from which a man can never recover." He bent his head to kiss his granddaughter's hand. "I rubbed my skin raw that summer with the bites. Look, you see these white spots? Even now, they are a reminder." Grandfather looked at the sky outside the patio door and laid his head against the white linens his wife had stitched fifty years earlier. "How could we let her die like that? A child only. Death is only tragic for the young." Paulina's chest fluttered uncertainly, and shooting sparks tingled in her veins. "The lemons were sour on the branches that year and a kitten was born blind from our family pet. Signs, signs," the old man muttered as the burning in Paulina's chest grew from spark to spark — looking for something to ignite. She rubbed a spot on her sternum, and the sparks began to burn away, leaving her numb.

"God will forgive me," she heard the old man say. "He will see I did only what I thought was good." He took her hand. "Tell me you forgive me before I die."

"You aren't dying, grandfather."

"This is my deathbed."

"You are being melodramatic." Paulina's arm, asleep from the effort of staying awake, twitched in time with the pulsing of her heart.

"Forgive me." Hernando demanded pulling Paulina's arm until her face was inches from him, insistently, until a very strange thing happened. A halo formed around his head, large and glowing, as the room burned away in a burst of white light. Paulina watched in amazement as her grandfather's eyes gathered all the light of the room — inches from her own. She gasped as the pain of his hold on her arm strengthened and became a living thing. "Yes! I forgive you!"

Exploding into a thousand pointed stars, the light broke away from his face and he fell back. The angel that came from the light lifted Hernando in its arms and looked down on Paulina fiercely. She trembled, unaware of her erratic breath, her heaving chest — and then the angel spoke. "Go from this place," and its voice was like thunderous wind, the rushing tide of the highest wave and it struck her down with its terrible weight. "Go," she heard it say before blackness wrapped her in its chilling embrace.

At the Convent of the Holy Order of Carmelite Sisters
Puebla, Mexico

"It was indeed a horrific summer." A thick curtain of cigarette smoke and French perfume hung heavily inside the small cell.

The voice was brittle and clipped — the voice of her aunt. Confusion. Images melded together and formed only more confusion. Paulina could not open her eyes. This place was cool; it was staccato steps and echoes, stone and mortar. It was old and dank in corners.

"It rained for five days of eight. We were batting at fleas with branches and rubbing our wounds with Indian's herbs. I have learned in this life, niece, that those who are wicked live long, unhappy lives." Gloria leaned forward to tuck a sachet beneath Paulina's pillow. She leaned her face into Paulina's line of sight; her eyes, immobile and unblinking, could not free themselves from her aunt's gaze. Gloria smiled with narrowed eyes and bright red lips.

"I have learned that those who cling to life the hardest are those who will never let go. But those like you, who are free and hold life loosely with a breeze in their flowing locks, crash down to the Earth in the end. Like you, fragile hearts burst like berries under the strain of life: poets, failures, infants, suicides, shut-ins, heart-sick lovers." She looked down her nose at the girl in the hospital bed. "You are with the nuns now, child. Here you will die."

Gloria stood to leave, brushed her skirt flat, and turned her back. Down the stone steps of the monastery she made her way elegantly past the plaza — past vegetable stalls and booksellers, their wares on display at their feet on carpets and hand-woven blankets. She turned up her nose at children's toys and fake designer handbags, cactus flowers and old camera parts. No vendor had what this woman wanted — her eternal youth in a bottle.

For Paulina, each day began the same, proceeded with slight variance, and ended exactly as predicted. The

Sisters rose at four thirty each morning, some going to the kitchens, others to the vats, and still others out to the gardens. The darkness of pre-dawn was like a whisper of compliance — the day allowed the sisters to make of it what they would.

Each morning for the first week of Paulina's convalescence, Sister Guadalupe brought chicken broth and mashed rice, neither of which Paulina could eat. The invalid had not spoken that week or the next, had not turned her face or made any expressions at all. She lay as a stone. The Sisters did not chatter as nursemaids did. They did not force amusement into their voices and animate their faces falsely. They accepted that the girl with the defective heart was fated to endure attacks until death took her and prayed silently that the end might be expedient and without pain.

When Paulina turned her face to Sister Guadalupe in the third week, the good Nun was so shocked she nearly dropped the cup of broth. When Paulina spoke and asked for Jimmy, the Sister (as calmly as possible) told her she would inquire as to his whereabouts. The Sister knew where he was but had been instructed to approach no one with the information but the Mother Superior should the girl gain the power of comprehension.

When Paulina opened her eyes next it was to see those of her cousin — mournful, cowed, often belligerent but strangely soulful, Jimmy. She reached for his hand and said, "Oh, Jimmy. I've been so lonely. I am so very glad to see you, cousin."

"I am glad to be of any help," he said, lame and helpless in his rumpled linen suit. "I am afraid for you, cousin. I feel the darkness that is eating at you, biting."

She smiled. Her face had fallen in the past weeks, had crumpled into that of an old woman's, but when she smiled, Paulina returned to the living. "You are a fool cousin, and blind besides," she whispered.

He looked up at her in amazement. Paulina wore his mother's face — malicious and wise, her voice cold and mechanical. Where did these words find strength to live on their own?

"I desire vengeance," the voice continued, Paulina's mouth bewitched. "And I fear I will die not knowing it."

Paulina struggled against invisible fetters to bring a hand to her lips and silence this mocking, hateful sound — these words that were not her own.

"Cousin, are you ill?" Jimmy asked, half rising out of his chair. The solid, heavy wood scraped loudly against the sun bleached tiles of the ancient stone floor. She nodded, her mouth still working to be heard but her hand clamped down firmly in horror.

"I will call the priest," he said calmly, backing out of her cell as Paulina's body rose from the bed through a veil of gnats that swarmed suddenly, appearing from nowhere, from nothing.

"Bring the Priest!" he shouted.

The Priest came as Paulina slunk into unconsciousness. "Has she had another episode?" the Priest asked her cousin as they whispered together in Spanish, unsure that Paulina could hear them.

"I am not certain," Jimmy answered. "I think she battled a demon." Both made the sign of the cross.

"Yes." The priest said, "Father Juan explained to me of her last attack — something about a false saint?"

Jimmy examined the knuckles of his hand. "Perhaps I am to blame?"

"No." The priest examined the young man as he continued to worry his hands. "*Hijo*, you know your cousin is dying?"

"Can't you just sprinkle her with some water, say some Latin, and make an intercession?"

The priest clasped his own hands behind him. "I am only a simple man of God, Jaime. I cannot perform miracles."

Jimmy squinted down at the smaller man. "Can we stop these episodes, these attacks?"

"If they are, in fact as you say, demonic battles it may be possible. However," the old man paused and drew a deep breath, "I knew both her mother and grandmother. This sickness is an affliction they have all shared." The old priest grasped Jimmy's shoulder. "I have been told she saw Dr. Sanchez some months ago. The girl knows her fate — help her accept it. Accept it yourself." The priest silently exited the small stone room, leaving Jimmy with his cousin's shell.

He fell down on his knees at her beside and began to voice the prayers the Birdies had been whispering in his ear since Paulina lost the ability to speak in her own voice. "Hail Mary, full of grace…"

Jaime Vasquez had grown as the object of a mother's scorn, a father's pity, and a grandmother's bitterness. And as he grew in stature and watched his brothers leave their mother's home to venture out into the world, the house in which he had been raised grew more and more silent with each passing day. Jaime dreamed of freedom. His father, mute and sorrowful, sat by the parlor window as his mother continued about her business in the center. Her advice was sought in all manners of public affairs, her opinions on the topics of the day by high-standing ladies in her circle, and her more notorious skills by anyone who could pay for them. Eventually Jaime outgrew the clothes of his eldest brother and asked to be taken to the tailor for his own set of suits; for the first time in his life he would not be shod in the cast-offs of his elder brothers.

"Ay, Jaime, you have always been such a nuisance to me," Gloria said when the request was made. "If I send you to the tailor will you take an apartment in town and leave me to myself?"

"I will, mother," Jaime replied, "if you promise you will not stuff father into the broom closet when I am gone."

"You know he is well looked after by the maids, Jaime. Do not go telling lies about me in the streets where you gamble."

Jaime put his hand to breast and swore he would not, and made plans to leave his maternal home. He began to drink heavily, gambled from night to morning with tourists and friends, stayed in the home of his girlfriend of many years, Lila Arce, and did not see his mother if he could help it. When Lila left him and his grandmother bought him the *Hostal* to manage and he met his cousin Paulina, it was as though he had finally seen a light in the darkness, as though his cousin was somehow both the key to and salvation from his lifelong misery. She was familiar to him of course, but more — he longed to be near her, to shelter and guide her, amuse her. He questioned his heart, this feeling of love towards his cousin.

Having only known love once in his life, with Lila, Jaime did not trust his instincts. As for Lila, she saw the destructive nature of Jaime's heart and the time and attention needed to clean up the filth others had already piled there and decided she was not the woman for Jaime. The day Lila married another man Jaime sat beside the sea to watch the colors change without her. His heart was too broken to miss her, but his mind lingered regardless for several years. Thus, he told himself his feelings for his cousin were the natural result of his life-long loneliness and left it at that. When his mother (for he was sure it was his mother) cursed her, he knew he was all Paulina had left and went to her, vowing that he would be the one to see she was well, or if God willed it, expired comfortably.

"Mother Mary, full of grace," Jaime whispered at her bedside, the sounds escaping into the vacuum of stone masonry which surrounded them. A shadow crossed him, and in the doorway stood his mother, her eyebrow raised in criticism, a smile on her expressive mouth.

"Has she died yet?" she asked in Spanish with another raised eyebrow and a flick of the wrist as she ashed her cigarette.

"Thou shalt not smoke at the convent," he answered and rose from his chair, taller than his mother though she stood on the stone steps. "And she isn't going to die."

"Yes she is," his mother responded.

"Did you want anything?"

"I want to look," she said and put out her cigarette on the floor, grinding the black ash beneath an Italian leather shoe. "*Ay, hijo.* Do not get your hopes high. Teresa lingered not much longer. I wanted to see what kind of progress the child has made."

Curiously rooted to the spot by his mother's words, he nonetheless shielded his cousin's body from her view. "Anything you do now will only make her worse," he said. "She suffered another attack."

Gloria traced patterns in the black ash at her feet. "I have been praying for her," she said.

"Oh? To the devil?"

"Don't be stupid, Jaime. No one really prays to the Devil." She turned to go, but turned as though she simply remembered a small nothing. "When she wakes, tell her that her father wishes to visit."

"Her father is dead."

Gloria glanced past her son at the small sleeping figure on the narrow convent cot. "No, *hijo* — your father is dead. Hers is an old man who lost his ability of speech many years ago, but he lives." Gloria's heels clicked on the stone floor, her face lit by glee.

"Remember that terrible stroke, my son?" she called behind her as she left the cell. "Remember?"

Jaime sat on the small cot and held his cousin's hand protectively — but much of her strength had been lost. Her color paled further with each attack, both from the heart and the demons which prayed upon her reserves. He would care for her, protect her as no one had before, but even he was powerless against the attacks and his mother's vicious words.

"Remember?" she had taunted.

He did remember. He leaned again close to his cousin and nuzzled his cheek to her as a small child might.

"Can she hear you, Jaime Vasquez?" The voice, old and weathered but touched with a simple familiarity, traveled across the small stone room as Paulina's eyes opened slightly.

"Maria Eugenia?" Paulina whispered.

"Yes, *nina*, I am here now." She placed a trembling hand shakily on Paulina's.

"I saw your mother in the courtyard of the Convent, Jaime Vasquez. But she has gone so let us sit awhile and talk," Maria Eugenia unwrapped her shawl and arraigned herself creakily beside Jimmy at Paulina's feet. "Do you mind if we speak in Spanish, *mi'ja*? My tongue is sore from so much of this foreign speech."

Paulina closed her eyes and nodded.

"Ah, much better," Maria Eugenia said.

"Will you cure her?" Jaime asked, when the old woman had finished accommodating herself on the hard chair beside the cot.

Maria Eugenia puckered her lips disapprovingly. "Why is it that you all think it is miracles and potions I provide?"

Jimmy smiled charmingly and extended his long arm and then brought his hand to his heart. "My mistake, dear lady. My mother told me you were a witch."

"It is your mother who is the witch," came the old woman's retort. "If I use Indian herbs to help digestion and small matters of health, a witch this does not make me, but a healer. It is your mother who seeks to destroy, Jaime Vasquez, who has already destroyed many lives and plans on more to come." Maria Eugenia reached into her bag for a flat-baked cake. "Fetch me that pitcher, boy." She soaked the cake in the water he gave her until the cake was like gruel. "Feed this to your cousin," she said, settling herself back into the hard convent chair. Maria Eugenia folded her veined hands upon her stomach and regarded the austere cell. "They put you in a nun's cell, *nina*." Nodding, watching Paulina eat, she grunted. "Put you in a nun's cell. You, unlike any nun I know."

Paulina's heart gave a flutter. "You are ill, also, *madrina*."

"I am an old woman, of course I am ill."

"But you cannot find an herb for what you have."

The old woman sighed and shrugged. "Will you, little nun, perform me a miracle?"

Paulina listened to the stony silence of the convent, its small whispers of the nuns who lived, those who died - unbelievers above and true believers below. "You have many to heal," she said, suddenly breaking her reverie to repeat the Voice's message.

"There are some," Maria Eugenia said, misunderstanding Paulina's words.

Jimmy scooted away from his cousin as Paulina stretched out her hand. As she did so, Jaime felt himself become as stone, the spoon held midair towards Paulina's mouth. Her hand stretched toward Maria Eugenia and it was as though a puppet master had cut the strings which held the old woman up, and Maria Eugenia collapsed upon herself, face in lap. The stone room echoed with running footsteps as the sisters, drawn by the cacophony of voices, multitudes, the din of shouting, came rushing in the direction of the invalid's room. Paulina's hand began to gather light. To Jaime's amazement, Maria Eugenia's back lifted toward the glowing hand, as though magnetized. The Sisters gasped as they filled the small opening of Paulina's cell. Maria Eugenia's spine arched and received the light Paulina's hand had gathered — seemed to take the light to the vertebra within and then, — a release. Paulina fainted; Maria Eugenia snapped back into place, upright and the spoon in Jaime's hand clattered to the floor.

"*Es un pecado*!" the Sisters began praising God. "*Un pecado* — a miracle, a miracle!" They ran from the stranger's cell. "Tell the Mother Superior!"

Maria Eugenia never knew what Paulina removed from her, but when she awoke from her state to face the Mother Superior, her back was blessedly relieved of an unexplainable pain she had endured for many years and yes, she assured the Mother Superior, it was her goddaughter's doing. When the Mother Superior herself came to Paulina she had to push through her own nuns gathered at the door.

"Is it true?" they asked her. "Can it be? Our own saint?"

"That girl is no saint!" Gloria scoffed when she heard her own foolish maids in the kitchen.

"But *Señora*, they say she healed Maria Eugenia."

"Suggestive speaking would have healed that old bat." She straightened the sleeves of her blouse. "Have you finished the *Señor's* soup, lazy gossip tongues for brains?"

The girls fell over themselves to hand Gloria her husband's carefully prepared soup of pureed broccoli and cauliflower. Gloria took the large bowl in both hands and went to serve her husband.

Word spread quickly in the town among those of their class (who heard it on good authority from their servants, who heard it from the nuns themselves). By midday next everyone who still knew the Montelejos family had heard. The devout claimed she was a saint; the rest had their doubts. The girl was half American, after all. Surely, God did not move through such an unworthy girl! Still, Maria Eugenia did seem younger, without pain or grumbles. In fact, she seemed to carry a glow within her. The maids whispered: could this American *pocha* cure illness?

Gloria's maids whispered the loudest. Not three days had passed since Paulina healed Maria Eugenia (for surely, there was now no argument of that) when they took Jaime into the kitchen.

"Jaime," one pleaded, "You must take your father to her — she can cure him."

"He is a dear old man, confined by that witch, your mother," said the other.

"Take her to him. The little saint can save him."

Jaime, bewildered by this new public adoration of his cousin, pulled at his hat. "She can?"

The girls nodded vigorously, in unison. "Take him to her, Jaime, so she may heal him." They pleaded until he could not but relent and wait for his mother to leave the house.

"Please, *Señor*," Jaime said. "Come to the convent with me."

Guiermo Fuentes de Solis arose from his chair, and it was thus that after eighty-five years of life, the *Señor* Fuentes de Solis and the boy who was actually his nephew made their way down cobblestone streets and colonial arches with silent trepidation, one in anxiety and the other in sadness. Jaime took the *Señor* to Paulina's bedside and bade him sit.

"Paulina," Jimmy said quietly, "I bring you your father."

He was sitting on his heels against the stone wall outside the cell and examining the tokens left in secret by the pious nuns, small notes, pink lilacs, ribbons, and candles, when a smell began to tingle his nose. It was a strange smell, damp and green. He stood as the smell grew stronger, nearly overpowering his senses, and then he knew what it was — moss. He smelled moss emanating from Paulina's room, pungent now, and as it began to be noticed by the nuns working, he heard a sound long denied him: his father's laughter.

"I am tired of this constant chatter!" Gloria screeched as she banged open the kitchen serving door. "I will hear no more of miracles, smells or signs!"

"They say she smells of lilac and moss," the farthest girl from Gloria spoke up.

"And?"

"And, well, *Señora*, the nuns, they say these are signs...of sainthood." The girl made ready to take flight out the door. "As are the healings."

"If someone leaves a bunch of flowers under some slut's bed to hide her stench, a saint this does not make."

The girls, afraid to tell her of her husband, merely looked down at their plastic shoes. They did not answer the *Señora* that the smells of lilac and moss had overpowered the entire convent and could now be smelt from the street beyond, nor that the entire town saw the *Señor* Fuentes de Solis stride out of Paulina's room confidently, proclaiming the miracle: he had regained his speech and all mental faculties — and told whoever would listen that Paulina Montelejos was actually his daughter, not Jorge Ruiz's.

"There have been many healings," the girl closest to the door muttered.

"You dare!" Gloria spluttered as she searched for an outlet for her rage. Her eyes flashed at the farthest girl who pushed open the door and ran as fast as her cheap shoes would take her.

"An outrage!" Gloria screamed again later when they told her the *Señor* Fuentes de Solis would not return to her house — he preferred to stay in a hotel closer to the Convent. Gloria, livid, red with rage, sat in the dark of the parlor and chain-smoked.

Those who remembered relayed the story to those born afterwards; the pure of heart in forgiveness, and the rest in skeptical disbelief. The midwife present at Paulina's birth broke her silence and held those who would listen spellbound. Even Guadalupe recounted the argument she had with the late Jorge Ruiz, and his insistence that the girl was his daughter, though Guadalupe had wondered for many years why a father with nothing to hide would escape in the dead of night. Gloria's servants did not illuminate their mistress to the turn events had taken.

When she emerged four days later, she was ready to go to the "little invalid" with pillow in hand to smother her, and prepared for battle. She would see this "little saint" in hell, put there with her own hands.

Paulina lay in her narrow convent cot. Her hair, brown flax tinted with premature flecks of white, lay plastered to her pale forehead – beaded with sweat and salt. She looked as Teresa had at her viewing — rigid, stiff, silent, though not yet dead. The smell of lilacs and moss which had first lit the nuns (and then, the people) ablaze with talk of sainthood mingled and overpowered the damp, closed smell of chalk – the arid, stifling smell of cloistered women.

Petitioners, placing photographs and pleading intercessions at her door, were shooed out regularly by the Mother Superior, who daily wrote to Rome of the "little Saint's" miracles. Each week one of the sisters would remove the mass of petitions, half-burnt candles, wilted flowers, photographs and childishly scrawled notes to be prayed over by the sisters in Paulina's stead.

The girl, gasping for breath and nearly blinded in her left eye, endured severe pain at each attack, had found her only consolation — the slow, methodical reading of English text by a foreigner's lilting tongue. The nuns read the lives of saints to her, of which she was ignorant. Others came and read English newspapers found in hotel trashcans. They came to Paulina after if there had been no attacks that morning, if she had the strength to nod her head in compliance, if she beckoned with a slightly raised finger. As the people continued to pray, her face became lined with a thousand new worries not of her own choosing. Inside her chest her exhausted heart pumped sluggish, thick blood through veins visible through white skin.

Thus, upon the convent bed she lay, the culmination of her mother's efforts. Her eyes, pin-pricked in pain from the merest soft light, stared at the vaulted stone ceiling. Her lips' movement was barely discernable. They prayed not for their own pain but for the pain of others, that God might show himself to be merciful and not the terrifying deity who had captured her, who held her now in immobile bondage. The people, she knew, had begun to revere her as a saint and this she mourned. What God could this be to make her his instrument?

Now mute, she lacked an explanation to give, to say, "I have done nothing. I am unworthy for such a calling as this. Why such light and healing pours out of me, as though I am but a conduit, I cannot understand. When people are healed, I am but a plaything of heaven." Surely, a saint (pious, good, noble, those told in the Sisters' stories) she was not. Yet still, the people came and laid hands on her and were healed – and did not know she felt unworthy. They came holding babies and bottles of water for her blessing. They came in faith while Paulina laid in doubt, fearful of this ability, this power she could neither understand nor control.

The nuns did not think to bring the girl a mirror, nor to cut her hair or nails. As the people came to whisper their ills and troubles, Paulina's wrinkles grew until she could not be recognized as a young woman. This the people also deemed miraculous. "A scapegoat!" they cried, "Praise God!"

When Gloria entered the convent cell that particular night she found it inexplicably empty, silent, freshly cleared of petitioners — as though in wait for her alone. The nuns, having tidied shelves, swept floors, refilled vats and left their work for the dawn, retired at their usual time of an hour after sunset, and left the door ajar. The convent walls, crumbling to the touch, echoed ancient mice and bedtime Hail Mary's. Footfalls ceased and the sounds of the street slowed.

Gloria entered on soft-soled feet and closed the heavy wooden door of Paulina's cell behind her. She stood tall and straightened her immaculate hair, noting the girl looked like an old Indian wash-woman, her hair in two braids and deeply folded wrinkles under her eyes. She placed her purse on the floor and crept to the girl's bedside. Exhaling in relief, Gloria realized the girl's condition had paralyzed her as it had her mother.

"I know you struggle for each breath but cannot find it," Gloria whispered to the inert form upon the bed of hard wood and hand-knotted coverlet. "Neither could Teresa at the end. We have no fancy breathing machines unless you go to hospital — and who could allow a saint to go to hospital?" Gloria lit a cigarette and leaned over Paulina to blow a light gray cloud into her face. "Wake up."

Paulina's eyes unfolded, and a slight dark line of pupil contracted. "I know you can hear me, *pocha* slut." Gloria rubbed her finger where sixteenth-century jewels met her moisturized knuckle and caused a rash, peeling layers of perfumed skin.

"You have convinced this town you are a saint." Gloria leaned close to the girl's misshapen face, hissing cigarette smoke and bile. "You have taken my husband as you once took my lover." She put her bejeweled hand against Paulina's mouth and nose and pressed down, leaning her weight upon the girl. Her face, still inches from Paulina's, contorted in hateful glee.

Paulina's eyes bulged as she stared into those of her aunt's and as Gloria watched, they began to gather light — light that expanded until it grew to the corners of her eyelashes and brows, light that seared into Gloria's gaze. She could not turn away; the light held her, forced her to look into its center circle. The light began to pull her gaze inside itself, from deep within, Gloria groaned, unable to either release her hand from Paulina's face or her eyes from Paulina's gaze. The illumination grew until the convent filled with the strange glow, and as it did, Gloria saw in Paulina's eyes a tiny beacon surrounded by pinpricked darkness. The fierce face of the arch-angel Gabriel appeared in the mist of the darkness; accusatory and wrathful. His voice echoed in her ears from the very walls of the convent, "Why persecute when judgment rests upon all? Why hatred when hell waits for those who knew no pity? Simplicity, forgiveness was the call to goodness you did not heed. No longer will you be called Gloria but *Waer Logga*, the betrayer of the faith, enemy of the One True."

His eyes glowered within hers, and as he retreated, Paulina's wrinkles melted away and became like baby's skin, and it was then that Gloria, now truly damned, was finally able to pull herself away. But when she reached up, she gave such a blood curdling scream that had the light not awakened all the sisters, surely the sound would have, for Paulina's wrinkles had become her own. Wildly, Gloria began tearing her hair and face, falling on the stone ground in garbled screeching.

"I am damned," she cried aloud, tearing skin with plastic nails, biting away flesh.

When the nuns could finally wrench her hands away, like the solid claws of a fresh water crab, she was carried out to an ambulance.

"A miracle, a miracle," the people cried. "She babbles ancient names — the little saint has converted Gloria Vasquez. A miracle!"

"Gloria praises God day and night," they told one another. "Her lips do not cease giving blessings and honor," they said of her.

"If you believe the people," Jimmy told Paulina as he peeled an orange, "you would think she had rent her clothing like Job." He tisked his tongue and bit the orange. "She has merely gone mad," he said. "They put her into the convent also — the lunatic asylum." Paulina, now able to speak again at will, either in English or Spanish said nothing. The stones echoed with the footsteps of the nuns, and somewhere a bird twittered.

"Jimmy," she said, "I want to tell you a secret."

"Yes, cousin, I am listening."

"The day my father died," Paulina whispered, "I climbed the steps to his hospital room." The once proud man, a tall Adonis unabashed in telling the world what was his, lay sleeping amid the blankets and wires, tape and gauze of a cripple. "I tiptoed around to the small Moroccan side table which held his medicines and needles, thermometers and bedpans." Unable to feel or move from the waist down, Ruiz did not know his daughter had filled half a syringe with air; did not see her inserting this needle into the plastic tube that fed his arm the nutrients that had kept him alive. "When his eyes did open, they saw me replacing the needle to the side drawer. He knew what I had done, cousin." She saw again the side table with the intricate inlay of semi-precious stones, herself wiping the glass clean with her t-shirt. "And he did nothing to prevent me. He closed his eyes and surrendered himself."

Paulina reached out her hand towards her cousin, her eyes searching his face. "What kind of a saint does that make me, Jimmy? What kind of a saint kills her father?"

Rome: The Vatican

The Roman sun lay at a slant across Father Peter Scettico's desk. Spread across by the father's hand, the intercessions of a new Latin American candidate for sainthood read of one Paulina Montelejos — photos, the Mother Superior's letters, testimonials of healings. They beckoned like whispers, but waited like pets. "Yes, yes," he murmured to them. He touched one lightly, reading only the words visible, the ones that did not require him to lift the page.

"They come from nearby pueblos, from Cholula, from the other cities," it read. "Puebla has not had its own living saint for over 200 years...the people come for healing." The Carmelite Nuns in Puebla had tried to keep quiet, the Mother Superior wrote, but when the smell became too pungent, the people hailed her as a living saint.

Is she still among the living? He wondered. Perhaps, for a brief time, for the letters were insistent that Paulina Montelejos was near death. Father Peter shook his head, an almost imperceptible motion. He was a man given to observation, not movement. *I want to meet her*, he thought. *Do I feel led by the Holy Ghost, or merely my own curiosity?* He shifted through the evidence to find the picture that caught his imagination the previous night, a snapshot of the riots in nearby Mexico City. Escaping the road blocks, several families had been taken in by the Carmelite Monastery in Puebla, and it was they who first began to venerate Paulina Montelejos when a number of them were healed of wounds.

Riots, roadblocks, semi-automatic machine guns; it was all familiar — though so distant from Rome. Father Peter had been courageous once in his life, helping Africans flee death squads and tribal warfare, but he was also a quiet man given to a few small but decisive moments; no history books would remember him.

I am not a priest for the fame, he often thought when he looked back on those days; newly out of the seminary, he blindly thought death an ideal — wilted bodies in flowing robes of oil paintings – not the collapsed faces rotten with maggots and children with bloated bellies face down in roadside massacres. Death quickly became a thing dealt with and blessed, and this manner propelled him into the ranks of priests the Vatican would call upon where no one else dared tread. He was never again faced with such personal peril, but death – with death he was intimate. They often sent him to investigate the lost cases, the third-world voodoo men, the villages where God was a dark and bloody master. They sent him because he was not afraid of tropical illness, open sewers, rough terrain, or hostile natives. He was an adventurer at heart — and had stood up to the worst of man to the delight of the Savior.

Miraculous signs in Latin America were not uncommon. Often, he believed that the people saw what they wanted to see: a physical manifestation of their most fervent beliefs. The father did not begrudge the people this, did not try to explain away their 'miracles' of weeping statues or magical animals. He merely noted the misrepresentation in his notes and went on his way. The Poblana saint, however, was not like the others. His closest friend from the University, those long ago days when as an undergraduate he learned of God's plan for his life, knew the girl, and had called the Father at the insistence of the Mother Superior.

"I hear she converted her Aunt Gloria," Gary's voice was small and tinny, barely audible above the static of the long distance connection. "I'll be honest with you, Pete, I'd have never pegged the kid for holy, but you know what they say..."

"Yes, mysterious ways. Do you believe she is what they say?"

"I saw Paulina a few days before *La Madastra*, that's what people are calling the Gloria thing," Gary's voice echoed. "And she looked like an old woman, wrinkled skin, the whole bit."

"And?"

"And now she's a young as ever and Gloria has got them now."

"Has got what?" Father Scettico raised his voice, unsure if he had correctly heard and understood.

"The wrinkles, grey hair, the signs of age that Paulina – for whatever reason – had slowly developed."

Gary paused, raising his voice as well above the bad connection, "Which, actually, is also a little strange, but not the point right now. As I was saying, before, Gloria Vasquez looked phenomenal. I don't know what hocus-pocus that woman had in keeping her looks, but she looked amazing. After that night with Paulina, she looks more like a crazy old woman."

"So you are saying Paulina, in some miraculous conversion, took Gloria's remaining vanity — her youth?"

"Exactly."

Father Peter Scettico contemplated telling Gary that rather than miraculous, the Holy See might think this vengeful. "I'm flying in next Tuesday," he said. "Can you meet me in Mexico City?"

Cholula, State of Puebla, Mexico

Along the streets of Cholula a man frying potatoes fell to his knees that Tuesday morning, spatula in one hand and a lime in the other. Before him stood a woman who he thought could only be the Virgin Mary.

"Follow me to my daughter," the woman beckoned.

Those who heard her voice left their occupations as easily as one lays down his burdens: the man frying potatoes, his customer seated on an upturned bucket, two women selling socks and roses, a small boy on his way home from school for lunch. They walked behind the woman whose feet did not seem to touch the earth, whose breath was mint and whose housedress was the color of the sky. She walked with assurance toward her goal and as she beckoned, more followed in her wake. They did not look behind them as they joined her. With full confidence in her purpose, they began to sing.

The crowd neared the main streets of Puebla, and those who saw joined the procession; sleepy with new devotion, they had not yet awakened to the fervor that would later come.

While the center of Puebla, busy and vibrant, bustled to the rhythm of the thousands of cars that bounced along the cobblestoned zocalo, down a small side street near the artist's Plaza Father Peter Scettio and an apprehensive Gary Lechney strolled beneath banana trees and tiled balconies, unaware of the growing tide. The side street, sound muffled by fifteenth century stone masonry and the million daily preoccupations of the citizens, gave leafy respite from the harsh Mexican sun.

Gary and the Father had made pleasant chit-chat along the lines of their former lives and now reached both an awkward silence and the door of the convent. Gary scratched his head nervously, and, as an animal smells commotion in the air, he lifted his nose.

The telling aroma of moss and lilac emanated from the convent, its door barred against the wave of novenas, prayers, intercessions and tokens which threatened to wash it away. A breeze blew the smell of homemade *tamales* and petrol, temporarily misplacing the miraculous aroma long enough to remind the father of the city's millions of other inhabitants — whose immortal souls he was responsible for.

"Let us go and meet this girl the people venerate," he told Gary as he straightened his collar and pulled the bell.

"Praise God," the Mother Superior said as she saw their faces through the door's small, iron-grated window. They entered the courtyard as the Mother lifted her face into the wind (as Gary had done before her) and then locked the gate behind her. A fountain's stream dripped a cooling flow of water, hedges of lilacs were lost to the saint's scent, and the collected murmur of the sister's noonday prayers filled the air from the small garden chapel.

The mist of the early morning, replaced by the bright noonday sun, gathered at the base of a narrow hallway.

"Yes," the Mother motioned, "Paulina Montelejos is down that way."

They left the Mother, not properly having made her acquaintance, and tremulously entered the small room at the end of the narrow hallway. Jimmy paused in mid-rosary when the two entered as quietly as one might a shrine, and then rose respectfully. Maria Eugenia took Jimmy's hand and stood to her feet nimbly.

"I thought perhaps you might miss it, but she knew someone was coming." Maria Eugenia motioned to the girl asleep on the convent cot. She lay beneath a bare wooden cross, both light and scent poured forth from her face — unlined, unmarked, sweet and at rest Paulina opened her eyes.

"Father," she whispered. Paulina struggled to touch Father Peter's arm. The girl's grip was weaker than a child's.

He shuffled closer as the girl dropped her arm back upon the thin cot. "Do you know the people believe you are a saint?"

"Yes," she whispered

"Do you believe you are a saint?"

Father Peter Scettio leaned close to the girl. Her chest heaved, and she garnered her remaining strength.

"It does not matter, truly, what I believe — only that this body, an imperfect vessel, allows His will to be done through me." Her melodious voice, serene and sincere barely broke above a whisper. "It has been difficult, but I have finally accepted this fate, Father – my own peculiar cross to bear. My heavy sins will be brought to account before the throne of Heaven."

The Father trembled as he looked upon her face. Something there was too large for his mind to grasp and he could only then define wonder. His understanding was not yet matured; he could not explain why her face held his fascination. Perhaps it was because the utter humility and acceptance it bore held his heart's yearnings. In truth, the father was simply drawn to the sacrificial acceptance of this girl's own mortal fate.

The mist at the base of the hallways stirred, and Paulina's eyes followed the sound of the crowd as it drew close. A haze within the mist formed at the door of the cell, and a shape emerged from it as the sounds of singing from outside the convent's main gate grew in volume and strength. A pain gripped her; a vice twisted her heart. Unafraid, her gaze returned to the mist as Teresa's form, now whole, stepped closer to her daughter. Father Scettio gasped and backed against the cold stone wall — this ethereal creature passed beside him with no hint of movement or sound to embrace the girl on the bed. Paulina's head nestled into the crook of her mother's arm as Teresa stroked her daughter's silken hair.

"I am here, *mi'ja*," the voice spoke from without - the form's lips did not move.

"Mama," Paulina whispered, "it hurts."

"It will pass." Paulina gasped and resisted the pain as her mother soothed her, lifting Paulina into the air slightly, and as she did, Teresa began to hum. The pain melted away in waves of heat, a soft light pulsing, until Teresa faded.

The body of Paulina Montelejos gently sunk back to the hard convent cot, and Father Peter's unwavering hand reached toward her neck. She was dead. A great sigh rose from the people, and the low voices of the seventy-three nuns of the convent began to sing prayers. The pilgrims who had gathered, attracted by the ethereal form of Teresa Montelejos, wiped wetness and dust from their eyes and joined the nun's prayers. Cracked lips opened, though amazed and saddened; they sang prayers that the saint reach heaven, find peace, and plead on their behalf.

Epilogue

The people came because a saint had lived among them. They came on their knees, lifted from their *petates* and wheelchairs, their crutches and bicycles to plead the saint's intercession. It was said she could cure sickness of the heart, rescue orphans, and find lost loved ones. The Holy Father came in a black Lincoln town car and cut off two of her fingers before blessing her with scented water. The fingers started new churches in the Northern desert. Novenas were said with the sighs of the faithful that blew around the undecaying body of Paulina Montelejos. The smell of lilacs and moss, perpetual, did not fade. The cell, once austere, now shone with unearthly light — ringed by peasants and tourists who heard it whispered in the cafes: there was once an American here who became a saint.

Acknowledgements

This book comes, largely, from the imaginative evolution of the stories my mother told me in my childhood of our family, Mexico, and the Revolution. Thus, this novel is fiction, but its genesis is very real. There are many Mexico's, goes the saying, and that of *la familia* Montes de Oca is only one of them. I owe them a debt of gratitude for inspiring this novel.

In the 10 years it took me to write this book, many people have contributed criticism, grammatical edits, and support. Robert Alan Jamieson at the University of Edinburgh encouraged my writing from the very beginning and helped this story climb out of a very deep rut. Claire Brown Kane voiced theological concerns which helped the story mature, and Lena Wanggren took care of what would have been painfully embarrassing mistakes. Kelly Johnston and Erica Canela skyped more than their fair share. Ryan Stanford made sure I was always working on it, even when I didn't really see the point.

There are, of course, many more who read the book at various stages, and gave their support and encouragement. Thanks, everyone. I love you guys.

About the Author

A M Montes de Oca was born in Guadalajara, Mexico, in 1980 and moved to the United States when she was two years old. She has taught English in the US, Mexico, Egypt, and Japan and has travelled to more than 30 countries. She earned both her Master's and Doctorate in Creative Writing from the University of Edinburgh.

A M Montes de Oca teaches Creative Writing both in and out of the classroom. Her series of 30 minute exercises to help combat writer's block are available on her blog at:

www.TheWritersBlockBuster.Wordpress.com

And if you liked this book, and have any comments or questions about it, please email the author at:

AmandaMoodyMontesdeOca@gmail.com

Made in the USA
Charleston, SC
26 March 2014